T0193250

Tears of a
Dragon

Tears of a
Dragon

AWAKENING

ANNA CLARK

TEARS OF A DRAGON
AWAKENING

iUniverse books may be ordered through booksellers or by contacting:

iUniverse
1663 Liberty Drive
Bloomington, IN 47403
www.iuniverse.com
1-800-Authors (1-800-288-4677)

ISBN: 978-1-5320-8853-7 (sc)
ISBN: 978-1-5320-8852-0 (e)

Print information available on the last page.

iUniverse rev. date: 02/11/2020

Acknowledgements

To my mother, who proof-read and offered advice till she was blue in the face. To my spleen-less cousin, who also proof-read and continued to love me despite my endless, infuriating rants while writing. To my dearest friends from church, who asked about and kept up to date with this book's progress, and encouraged me every step of the way. To my teachers, the ones who knew I was writing and pushed me to continue. To my uncle, who lent me amazing books from which I drew inspiration, and promised he would read this one. To my friends in school, who hugged me and screamed with me when I made the final decision to publish. To David Cole, from iUniverse, who contacted me and helped me make the terrifying choice to publish. To Michael Gagen, who offered great and hilarious insight, helped inspire me to work harder, and remained a positive, changing force at all times. Beautiful people like you have made all the difference, and have helped create a limitless world.

When Joy awoke, there was nothing,
And Joy saw nothing and was alone
So in its loneliness, Joy searched for its mother, the One
And the One had existed, even before time
When it met the One, Joy was overcome with delight,
Insomuch that it crowned the One to be queen over Joy
Indeed, over all the cosmos

Prologue

On this barren earth, this broken landscape, nothing remained. Not a tree, nor an animal, a single blade of grass, or even a single drop of water. Walls and columns of a once great and spacious building were strewn about, rubble filling the craters and empty spaces on the ground. The once azure sky was shrouded in grey, ash falling through the air, smoke rising from charred bodies and fires that ran across the ruins. On a fallen ceiling, a woman stood alone and silent, her hatred resonating off the air itself. It flooded through the flames, the earth, and the lightning bolts that decorated the sky.

"So — this is how corrupt you've become? You are truly an inhabitant of Sin," the woman said.

"This is your fault. My home was Freedom!" the blood covered man hissed.

"No," she retorted, "You did this to yourself, by yourself."

The man laughed, wheeling around like a drunk. "Tell me — do you think the dead will agree with you? They're probably all screaming about how you, their creator, did not save them! Their great Goddess of Origin, the maker of all things — they call you *mother*. You're nothing but a monster!"

"*Enough!*" Origin yelled. "If you want to speak for the dead, then die as they did. Either that or kill me, and I will tell you what they say."

"With pleasure," the man hissed.

He lifted up his left arm and rushed towards the armor clad woman, swinging his sword down heavily. Origin raised her right arm of glistening plates, stopping the blade in its tracks. Putting her right foot forward, she leaned towards him before pivoting in a circle and striking him with a back kick to the chest. He stumbled away a few steps and smiled.

"You always looked at me with such pity. You thought you were better than me, than everyone," the man said.

Origin straightened her back. "I never wanted this, Tora. You were my apprentice, a prodigy. You had such potential for good and greatness — but you left me no choice."

"No choice?" Tora shouted. "You had every choice! You, the creator of the universe, had every choice! And you chose to destroy my entire planet, my home, and my people."

"You *slaughtered* an entire civilization. Not just on one planet, but on *three*. You and your followers skinned and burned women, children, families, and for what? Because you were angry with me? Because I didn't give you what you thought you were entitled to? Destroying your world, your insane cult, was the only way to immediately quell the bloodshed."

"You made this bloodshed," Tora seethed. "You gave

me my power, and never helped me when it tried to kill me. You left me. I was the God of Rage. I was supposed to be favored, and instead I was feared, and hated."

Origin rushed up to him in an instant, her large, overpowering sword held firmly in her right hand. She swung it up at an angle. The man jumped away, narrowly missing the razor sharp edge.

"Is that the best you can do, little queen?" Tora mocked, watching her massive black sword slice eagerly through the air. Beneath the black mist that shrouded it, he could see a faint red glow, and could smell the blood that ran down it in torrents.

Origin lowered her body until she was crouching. Suddenly, she disappeared, almost as if her atoms had just ceased to exist. Tora began to look around frantically. Origin appeared behind him in an instant and attempted to stab through his throat. Tora caught her oversized sword using his thin, small one, and pushed himself away from her. He then lunged at her, faster than the eye could see, thrusting and swiping at her with his blade. She blocked and dodged at the same unbelievable speed. Tora brought his sword down on hers, trying to make her lose her balance. He looked at her face, but her features were hidden behind a mask of black scales.

All that could be seen was a metallic, fanged grin, blood smeared across the glimmering teeth. Her hair was hidden inside a large, metal, whip-like extension from the back of her helmet, razor sharp spikes decorating it all the way down; the spine of her armor was lined with similar protrusions. Three horns were positioned on top of the helmet, a separate head piece much like a crown, with a large, red diamond in the center of the forehead. Tora could see bits of flesh from when she had head-butted opponents clinging to its surface. The entirety of her armor, save the torso and inside of the legs, was covered in sharp, long spikes, fashioned to be lethal all on its own, with carefully placed plating, like dragon scales, to make sure she still had a great deal of flexibility. This was also made to ensure that no skin or cloth was visible no matter how she moved. She was reminiscent of an Iron Maiden.

Origin shoved Tora back, took a step forward, and swung her sword with great force at his left side. Tora used his sword to block, but his blade shattered into pieces, allowing Origin's sword to cut into his shoulder. Tora gritted his teeth and jumped away before she could slice him in half, the remains of his sword clattering to the ground.

"You ruined my good arm. Such a shame, considering that you already dismantled the other one," Tora hissed while smiling. He eyed the large wound that had rendered his right arm unusable.

"No, I haven't. Not yet." The fanged mouth of the dragon mask opened slightly, and a plume of flames rushed out, licking the air with malevolence. A sinister, curdling laugh lashed at the air. She drove her sword into the ground, rushed up towards Tora, took hold of his right arm and shoulder, and completely ripped through the flesh and bone, leaving nothing except a stub of the shoulder.

Anyone watching would have thought her savage and insane, thinking of doing something so gruesome, but this was war. To her, in such a situation, there was no clemency or tolerance. All those who dreaded would die in their fear, and those who fought would perish in their depravity or rectitude.

Blood spurted from where Tora's appendage should have been, muscles and tendons contracting in pain, the bone, sharp and white, protruding from his body, a sickening sucking sound accompanying the pulsing veins that flapped in the air. Scraps of flesh loosely clung onto his clothing. Tora wailed in agony, reeling and thrashing about. Origin brought the arm she had removed to the mouth of her mask, the jaws opening enough to get around the bone that was jutting out. The mask's fangs closed around the bone, and her head jerked back, ripping the bone out from within the limp appendage, more blood pooling onto the ground. A nauseating crunch was heard as the bone disappeared into the helmet, flames once again flowing out from within, illuminating the red stains of life that tarnished its lustrous, black surface.

Origin remained silent, dropping the limb and retrieving her weapon, a large crevice in the ground where it had been. All at once, she raised her weapon high above her head. The wind started to swirl and howl, ripping walls from where they stood, remains of walls being torn down and reduced to sand. It curled around her sword, shrouding it in a black mist. Origin held it in the air for a second more, and then brought the sword down upon the ground, sending a form of energy out at Tora. The energy was a black, shifting, thin mass with a razor edge, threatening to cut him into a thousand scraps. The black mass split into three separate pieces heading towards the man from different directions. He jumped at the last second, avoiding the attack as it crashed into the ground, sending dirt, smoke, and stone everywhere; it created a crater in the floor, drilling through the earth. Tora landed and laughed softly.

"Who would have thought you would have enough strength left to use that accursed power on me. Don't you run out of breath? Aren't you tired? When will you finally be done?"

She wasn't done — not even close. Origin rushed forward and swung her sword into the ground in a large arch. Lightning connected with her blade the instant it hit the soil and the ground exploded, stone, ash, and fire flying out in a wide circle. Tora rolled and skidded across the ground, coughing as he stood up from the wreckage. He could taste iron in his mouth. Tora stood and ran away from her, crouching behind a set of columns. He held his breath, trying to think of a way to escape her barrage.

"You can't hide." Origin whispered. "Fear chokes the air, like oil in water. It can be seen and felt." The sound of metal crashing through stone echoed in the air. "It smells, too."

Tora sucked in his breath, willing himself to remain still. He could hear her sword dragging across the ground, sending chills up and down his spine. Then it was silent. Nothing moved, nothing breathed, and Tora felt fear radiate through what was left of his being. Origin's voice, sharp and cold, danced across his neck.

"You can't escape this." A metal hand wrapped around Tora's throat. "Your bone was weak, and your marrow little more than sugar in my mouth."

Despite the pain, Tora twisted his head around and

bit down on the sharp plating that covered her neck, the edges biting into his palate. He rolled over, kicked her in the stomach, and lifted her off the floor. He sent her spiraling over him as he scrambled to his feet. His mouth burned horribly, the saliva like acid against the fair-sized holes he had bored into the top. Origin hit the ground and lashed out with her sword, slicing his abdomen.

"Fine," Tora said, stumbling away as she stood, his muscles clenching around the fresh wound in his stomach. "Let's take this to the next level!"

Red flames erupted from his body, and he soared upwards into the sky. His head grew larger and longer, his teeth turning into sharp fangs. His hand and feet grew and became rough and scaly, claws the size of a grown man emerging from the tips. A long red tail slithered out of him, whipping the air. Wings of red leather sprouted and beat at the atmosphere, carrying him higher. The red dragon, with flames engulfing his scale-armored body, roared down at the earth where Origin stood. Blood rained down from his massive body, the individual layers of muscles inside his shoulder clearly visible, squirming and flailing, with the ends drying out and turning an odd brown-ish color.

Anyone would have vomited and fainted at the sight. However, Origin was not just *anyone*, and she had fought far too much, slaughtered far too many, and not shown nearly enough mercy to be fazed by this. It was just another carcass refusing to be laid to rest. She would teach him to behave. The red dragon lashed out with his tail and sent the Origin's colossal sword flying through the air. She couldn't see or hear it, but she felt the sword skewer the earth. A new form of ire boiled inside of her.

Black flames and mist began to swirl around her. She started to change, growing larger and scaly, with teeth as silver as moonlight, her armor evaporating into dark mist. Her hands slammed into the earth, slicing the stones as claws that shone like diamonds emerged. Her breath became like poison, her saliva like scorching magma, dripping from her fangs and down the scaly cracks of her throat. Fire swirled around her mouth every time she opened her monstrous jaws. The tops of her wings were slightly visible. They sliced the crests of nearby pillars and churned the air like a twister ripping through open farmland. Next to this shadowed, black beast, the red dragon looked like a dog next to a cow.

Origin, now transformed, opened her jaws, a mouth that was more than big enough to completely crush her foe in one chomp. With fire billowing out of her mouth, black flames and mist surrounding her body and hiding her features, bolts of lightning cracking inside the mist, she let out a loud, petrifying, flesh-melting roar. It broke the earth open, shook the remaining walls till they fell down in ruins, and rent the air. Lightning flashed, followed by the deafening roar of thunder, and the clouds lit on fire.

One of her massive claws tore through the air as she endeavored to smash her meager adversary. The red dragon flapped away from the immense creature it had made its opponent.

"Come and get me!" Tora screeched, his mouth moving into a sharp smile as it spoke the words. Yet, soon after he had spoken, the dragon was filled with anger and fear.

He had realized that Origin was only half showing. The lower part of her body, starting right below her chest, was hidden inside a black, shadow-filled hole — a portal of sorts. The red dragon became fearful, finally knowing that she was still much more massive than she seemed. He thought for a moment that perhaps she was large enough to take up the entire world, maybe even swallow it. He imagined it for a split second, and his insides coiled with terror.

The new battle was fought in the skies, flames and lightning colliding as they struggled against one another. The eight elements of wind, earth, water, electricity, fire, ice, light, and shadow ripped through the sky. Tora reached his head into the air and summoned a thrall of magic. It was a shade of purple that glowed dimly. Origin summoned a shield — a spell circle — to protect her from the onslaught. The magic collided with her shield, and was sucked into the center. The spell circle's center made a full rotation, and Tora's magic was returned to him with immense force. It happened so quickly that he barely had time to move out of the way. He could hear the webbing between his wings hissing, proof that her wrath had reached him.

The black beast slammed a claw into the ground and pulled herself forward. She rammed her head into her small foe, horns and scales cleaving through layers of his body. The red dragon drove its bladed tail between the steel plates of her chest. Origin slammed her head into the other again, ripping greedily through him with an evil, fanged grin on her scaly face. Her horns dug through his open shoulder wound, breaking the bone inside him. Tora stabbed through her again and again, pain engulfing him with an untold ferocity; he thought he would be torn in two.

Origin roared in anger, fire spewing from her mouth. She grabbed Tora with her left hand and threw him with all her might, hurtling the red beast to the ground. The earth caved in underneath him, creating a large crater. He screeched in agony and cursed at her. Origin growled in hatred, clutching her chest with one of her claws.

Tora laughed inside his throat, pushing himself off the ground with his wings, seeing as how his arm was virtually useless. "Who would have thought someone so big would be so weak."

Yet he knew that he was far worse off than her. He could feel his lungs and spleen floating inside him in a mass of internal bleeding, and his stomach was swelling with the black dragon's acidic saliva.

Origin looked at the small dragon with flaming eyes. She slammed her massive clawed hand onto the red dragon's body, crushing him into the ground.

"Then let's end it." The black beast raised her head towards the sky, the clouds swirling in a circle.

"You wouldn't! It would completely rip your powers out of you! Something like that — you wouldn't survive!" the red dragon screeched.

"Then I suppose I'll have to cheat death. What was lost can easily be found or recreated."

A cylindrical thrall of magic, filled with all the elements, surged down and split through the red dragon, ripping its insides apart. The light from the magic separated in two directions, severing the land until it reached the ocean. The continent itself split and the two halves began to drift apart across the wide expanse of blue, leaving in its wake the exposed ocean floor that water surged in to cover. Tora fell into the new cavity, salt water sloshing inside his wounds, bringing with it a horrid sting. He let out one final roar of defiance before the seabed ripped open beneath him, swallowing him whole. Origin clawed at the ground, pulling herself away from the abyss. The ocean floor resealed itself, and the water flooded back in.

Light erupted until it covered the entire world and then faded. As it dimmed, the sky cleared itself of the ash and smoke; the red dragon lay deep within the center of the earth. Origin shrunk back to her human form, as the woman she had once been, clad in her armor. The shadows and mist dispersed. Lying on the ground, breathing heavily, she clutched her stomach. Her body jolted, and she was overcome by a wave of agony. She could feel something tear inside her, and she knew that she had paid the price for using such a powerful form of magic. She had lost her immortality. She could feel the entities of her power floating off across the world. Whatever form they decided to take, she would find them. Origin laughed quietly.

"So this is what it feels like to be human. Death really is cold when it's close."

She continued to breathe heavily in and out, in time with her heartbeat. She looked through the eye slits of the metal dragon mask, watching the stars fade away in the light of the rising sun. The bright rays warmed her body and soothed her worries, yet she knew that this comfort was false and too soon enjoyed.

"My, my," a chilly voice said. "Look at the state you're in."

Origin tried to twist her head, but lacked the strength to do so. She felt a jolt of pain slice through her spine.

"Even after all you've done, you haven't made a difference at all," another voice said. This one was more feminine.

Origin chuckled. "You would know all about making a difference, wouldn't you?" she said, spitting up blood. The iron was thick in her mouth, almost choking her. "My dear friends, Saate and Vashire."

"Now, are you really in such a position to talk to us like that? You're not so proper now, are you, little bear?" Vashire said, his voice dripping with sarcasm.

"Stop it. Now's not the time for your idiosyncrasies," Saate snapped.

Origin's stomach gave a violent jerk. Her insides resisted the urge to vomit.

"Right. Now is not the time," Vashire mused.

Origin listened with impatience and was taken over by a coughing fit, spewing blood from her mouth again.

"Dear me, we really don't have time to sit here talking, do we?" Saate declared.

"What do you two want?" Origin hissed, pain engulfing her. Her muscles contracted with pent up anger.

"You know full well that he isn't going to stay down there forever. In time he will come back," Vashire said.

"Yes, I am aware," Origin said, her strength waning.

"Then we will strike a deal with you. We will —
preserve you until you are fit to take your leave and
reclaim *All Things*," Saate proclaimed.

"And what do you want from me in return?" Origin
said weakly.

"Protection from Him," Vashire said.

Origin laughed. "You are such cowards," she hissed.

"Maybe so, but you don't have a lot of time right now,
do you?" Saate said.

Origin remained silent for a while, and then smiled.

"You fools. I do not need you to ensure my survival.
Yes, the body is weak, but souls are eternal. I will return
one way or another, even if this body rots. That is what
the laws of the universe dictate."

The two beings present shifted uncomfortably.

"Alright," Origin finally said, "we have an agreement.
Just do what you need to. Help the people rebuild."

"As you wish, **uor meratia**," Saate said, sadness seeping
through gritted teeth.

Another voice appeared, full of power and anger,
and split the air like a crack of lightning. "Making more
choices without consulting, are we?"

Every muscle in Origin's body tightened; she let out
a strangled cry. A hand rested on her head.

"Be still, my love. Be calm. It would do you no good
to lose your countenance now," the voice said.

Origin knew that voice. It was strong, yet surprisingly
still; it belonged to a man, who was much like her in many
ways.

"Be still," he repeated.

She could no longer stand it. She forced her body up

off the ground just long enough for her to turn her head towards his person. When she slammed back against the cracked pavement, her chest clenched and she thought for a moment that she was going to suffocate. The man, whose very being she loved, fell to his knees, laid her on her back, and soothed her with magic.

Saate and Vashire vanished from her presence, leaving her and the man alone. Origin looked at the sun as it shone down on her. Sadness engulfed her heart and soul. Her vision blurred, tears threatening to spill from her eyes. She held them back with all her remaining strength and began to surrender to the darkness that was slithering around her. She tried to look towards the man, but her head refused to turn towards the sky. Her torso was lifted from the ground and she was nestled in the man's lap. She felt a hand caress the sharp plating of her mask but they did not dare move her in any way that might strain her. His fingers shook uncontrollably.

"It's alright," the voice said, breaking slightly. "But why? What was this for, this price you decided to pay?" His heart clenched in pain, waiting for her response.

Origin rested a hand on his, the armor evaporating into mist, allowing their skin to touch. She felt him shake from the contact, from both relief and anguish.

"This is His last hope."

Her lungs gave way, empty and weak, and her hand slid down, falling on her abdomen. The man stared at her for a long time, his heart ripping apart at the seams. It broke wide open, like a crumbling dam. The ocean swept across the new shore, blackened by war and strife, guided by his tears.

WHAT BEAR?

– On and on I sonder, watching the world as it slides by on granite floors and stone walls, the history of fools and tyrants etched onto corroding surfaces. So many lives linked together, yet they have no knowledge of how important they are to one another, without meeting, without touching. One main character is just another extra in someone else's life, bumping past them in a crowded street. However, this means nothing to me. I am the weaver of tales, I am the teller of stories, and I determine who will die and who will survive.

It was Bercem, the last month of the year, and one of the coldest months for the plains people of the Shrine of Silice. Today was especially chilling, forcing everyone to wear three fur coats, something that was practically unheard of. Nevertheless, people didn't want to freeze to death, so parents forced whining children into thick clothes, and with much difficulty, fastened their own buttons. A blizzard was sweeping through the Shrine village, harsh and unforgiving.

Families and friends were huddled inside the largest slathe scale tent to be found in the village. Fires crackled and swayed from within the tent, smoke drifting up through a small, narrow hole at the top of the dome-shaped habitat. All of the villagers were hungry and thirsty. The men had gone off to hunt, but did not return due to the weather. Many began to believe that they had died and would not return at all. Murmured sorrows and complaints filled all the corners of the room. Mothers held their children, shielding them from the crazed, howling wind. Every child was held within warm arms, all except for one.

"I do feel sorry for the boy," someone said from beyond the blurry wall of tears that covered his eyes.

"You feel sorry for him? For heaven's sake, why?" another person said.

"No mother, and now his father may never return. Don't you have any pity?" the first voice snapped.

"I have pity for the pitiless. That child deserves nothing from me. You should forget he exists. God bless his mother — at least she was smart enough to leave him after his birth. It was giving birth to him that killed her. I bet she is much happier in heaven or hell than she would have been with that cursed boy," the second voice said.

Anger brewed up from deep within the boy's core. *"Contain it,"* he told himself.

"Quiet! He might hear you!" the first voice said.

"Let him hear. Better to hear the bitter truth than all

of those sweet lies you've all been telling him since day one," the second voice said.

"Mertha! I will not listen to you any longer!" the first voice said.

"Nor will I listen to you, Stana," Mertha declared.

His face started to turn red. Tears were brimming over his eye lids and his finger nails were digging into his palms. He stood up straight.

"Evil!" he shouted.

Mertha, Stana, and all others present turned to face him.

"Wicked and hateful beings are what you are! The only reason the slathes did not kill you three moons ago is my father was here to defend you all. Your husbands' were so overcome by fear they sat within the shadows of their families and waited for a painful death!" he screamed. Tears stained his cheeks and his lower lip quivered in rage.

"Silence, stupid boy!" Mertha yelled, "You are the very reason the Slathe came to us in the first place!"

He was stunned. His anger turned to sadness which slowly boiled into loathing for Mertha.

"I will not silence myself for you or for any other wicked being within this house, which is mine, not yours; if I say so, you will leave and not return no matter how long this storm may pass through our town!"

"Enough!" Stana said. "For just this one night, can't we forget our differences and depend on each other? We all have our disagreements, I know. But please, try to keep the peace with one another. Just for tonight, can't we sleep in the same room without holding a knife in our hands, or keeping a dagger concealed beneath our pillows?"

All were silent.

"Please, Oren. Try to get along,"

The boy sighed. "For the sake of us all, Stana, I will try. Forgive me for my outburst."

Oren sat down, and as he turned his back towards the others, shot a look at Mertha.

"You best keep your guard up tonight, Mertha, my dear, old friend," Oren whispered.

"And you, yours," Mertha hissed back.

Stana sighed and lay down next to her children. Her golden honey hair washed over her shoulders in thin lines, covering her blue eyes as she slept. Mertha leaned against a wall and concealed her brown eyes with her dark, curly hair.

Oren Raevin also lay on the cold, straw floor, his purple eyes watching Mertha as his black, soft, shiny, straight hair fluttered in front of him. He swept his bangs away and finally, with much effort, fell into a land of dreams. He dreamt of a place where his mother ran through beautiful pink and purple fields of flowers, her looks obscured by fuzzy shapes. His father joined her, his blonde hair lightly brushing the nape of his neck. Oren began to run towards them both. He was about to sling his arms around them and cover them in tender kisses. However, he suddenly awoke, interrupted by reality. Someone was screaming.

"Wake up!" The yelling voices burst through Oren's subconscious mind. He sat up and looked around the room. Stana was standing, and tears flooded her face.

"How could you?" she screamed.

"How could I what?" Oren asked, puzzled.

Stana pointed to a corner. There lay Mertha, throat slit, eyes glazed, blood over every inch of her.

"You believe I did that?" Oren said, startled.

"Who else could have?" Stana replied. "You hated her!"

"No!" Oren protested. "I did not hate her! I disagreed with her, but never would I kill her!"

"Liar!" Stana screeched. "You warned her last night to watch her back!"

"I did not kill this woman! I have the gods and goddesses to prove it!"

"The gods and goddesses don't exist!" someone shouted. "They left us!"

"Now, now, what is the ruckus about?" a deep voice said.

All the people turned. The village chieftain stood in the entrance of the hut.

"Chieftain, Oren killed Mertha!" Stana declared.

"Do you have proof?" he asked.

"N-no," Stana stammered, "But I am sure of it!"

The chieftain lifted a pale hand to silence her. "I believe she may have been killed by a wild animal. Look at the rip in the tent's side. Surely Oren would not ruin his own home. Leave, all of you. I will speak with Oren in private," the Chieftain said.

The people nodded and left.

"Stana," Oren said as she was leaving. She turned and faced him.

"I trusted you," she said through her tears.

Oren smiled. "You still can."

Without another word, Stana rushed to her home.

"Oren," the Chieftain said, a scowl on his face, "I cannot keep covering for you."

The Chieftain was a well-built man with long brown hair. He wore brown fur trimmed boots, pants, and shirt. He also wore a light blue, fur trimmed cloak that was tied underneath his chin. On his head, the Chieftain wore a silver crown-like object with oak branches and feathers attached to it. He carried a cane with him that had a decorated wolf's claw wrapped around the top. The Chieftain's clothes were a little loose, but that did not disguise his muscles. He also had a few scars on his face from previous battles. His eyes were hazel. Concealed beneath his cloak was a short sword made from very fine steel.

"Chieftain, please," Oren begged, kneeling on the floor, "I did not kill Mertha. You must believe me!"

"I do," the Chieftain replied. "But I do not believe that the others will agree with me. If you could prove that it was an animal that killed Mertha and not you, then perhaps the others would listen. Could you do that?"

"I could try," Oren said.

"Good. You can take as much time as you need."

"Thank you, Chieftain!" Oren said standing, then bowing low in respect. Grabbing a spear and a cloak, he ran from the tent and marched into the snow in search of the true murderer of Mertha.

"Listen, you foul beast!" he yelled, shaking the spear above his head in a fit of rage. "I will find you and take you back to the village as proof of my innocence! Do you hear me?"

Oren made his way down the Main Road of the

village. On this road, merchants pitched their tents. Oren did not understand what they were trying to sell. No one ever visited the Shrine Village. Who would want to? It was cold, storms hit without warning, and even during the day it was cloudy and fairly dark outside. All this, plus the monsters that roamed the woods at the village border, made it almost impossible to attract tourists. Also, because of the freezing climate, it was impossible to have warm gin at a bar. You'd have to wait quite some time for the drink to thaw. No one was patient enough for it.

Oren passed by the trinket shop, owned by Risc. Risc was a man that was not old, but certainly not young. He was just starting to mature into his "grandpa years". Risc loved gems, shiny items, and almost anything that sparkled. The one thing Risc couldn't stand was blood sucking monsters that glittered. Oren couldn't remember ever seeing someone wear something from the trinket shop. However, because none of the stores had any real business, they were allowed to continue living on the main road, keeping warm, provided with food, even if they didn't have any money.

The Main Road ran through the center of the village, from one end to the other. It was flanked on either side by the Secondary Roads, which curved slightly, and then behind the Secondary Roads were the Forgotten Roads, which marked the border of the village. A tall, stone wall ran along the perimeter of the Forgotten Roads. The insides of the walls were rough, and easy to climb over, but the outsides were slick, making it nearly impossible to scale without proper equipment. It was a reasonable defense.

More unfortunate people lived on the Secondary and Forgotten Roads. The Secondary Roads were reserved for people who lived alone. If they married, a place would be cleared for them on the Main Road so they could receive the village's family benefits. Normally, after Oren's mother died, his father should have been moved back to the Secondary Roads, but because Oren had been born, his father was allowed to maintain his place to better support his child as a single parent. However, Oren knew that many people felt that this was unfair. That much had been proven when his father had thrown him out of the house one night when a group of villagers lit their tent on fire. Those guilty of setting the tent ablaze were moved to the Forgotten Roads, and were forbidden to move to the Secondary or Main Roads until they died.

Then, there were the Forgotten Roads. No one went to the Forgotten Roads anymore. It was where Inns were built for travelers and wandering merchants. However, no one came to the village anymore, so the buildings were left to freeze and ruin. People who lived on the Forgotten Roads received no help or kindness from anyone. They were outcasts and people who had broken the laws of the village. If a child was born into the Forgotten Roads, the child was moved into a family on the Secondary or Main Road. After they reached a certain age, they were allowed to pay visits to their biological parents. Anyone with a family did their best to obey the laws. They did not want their family to live in such a place. However, some villagers, in the midst of their pride, condemned themselves and their children to the harsh living of the Forgotten Roads.

Oren watched the children run around, hurling small, clumsily crafted snowballs at each other. He watched people barter over prices of drink, food, and fire wood. Oren could hear the blacksmith's hammer pounding fresh heated steel as he walked past the last few tents. Oren looked around, snow flitting softly down from the cloudy sky. He marched up a hill that overlooked the village, keeping a sharp eye out for danger. Once reaching the top, Oren turned and looked over his home. He could see the rotting, ice covered wood that covered the Forgotten Roads, the smoke that billowed up from small tents on the Secondary Roads, and the Main Road, crowded with the villagers, all wanting a piece of the freshest wood they could get their hands on.

Trees covered the hill that overlooked the village, and while Oren was tempted to climb one for a better view, the limbs were too brittle to hold his weight. Instead, he sat upon the cold snow and waited. The air was freezing and nipped at his face. Oren pulled at his cloak, wrapping loose fabric around his nose. It warmed him but his eyes still stung from the chilly breeze. Oren waited for a few minutes. He was resolved to wait all day. Whatever this beast was, be it wolf, bear, or something else, if it was so hungry that it felt the need to hunt inside the village, it would come back for fresh meat. Oren was like a sitting duck, just asking to be taken for its next meal. He thought of what he would do when he found the beast. Oren thought about using its head as a decoration, its fur for a new coat, its meat for several days of food, and its claws for making new arrows, although he had no bow. His thoughts were cut short by a growl. Oren stood, spear in hand, ready to defend himself. The growl came again, directly below him, and Oren peered down at his feet. Again, the growl came and Oren realized, with much dismay, it was his stomach.

"Curse you mortal body, for not having the strength to wait!" he hissed, punching his gut to silence the grumbles.

Oren fixed his spear in the snow and trudged down the hill to his home. He began to notice cold, defiant stares as he passed. They dug into his back, the harsh accusations of people who sought to throw him to the wolves for what they believed he had done. He ignored most of the icy eyes, but one pair caught his attention. There he was, around the same age and height as Oren, but very curious as to why this boy was scorned so deeply. His hair was shoulder length and brown, and his eyes were an icy blue. He smiled at Oren, showing that the rumor had not yet reached his small, innocent ears. It made Oren somewhat happy to know that there were still people, no matter how small, that believed in him.

Oren was known to many as a devil boy. He was the only one with black hair and most certainly the only one with purple eyes, an eye color that was said to belong to the eyes of a great demon lord that lived long ago. Oren had heard the story many times from family and teachers. The tale was usually accompanied with singing or arguments on what was fact and fiction. Nevertheless, it was a story that fascinated everyone who heard it.

*"Now class, today we are going to discuss our own history,"
the teacher said.*

*Groans and murmurs filled the classroom. No one really
wanted to hear about the Shrine's history.*

*"Oh, come now, it's not that bad! Now, many thousands
of years ago, a Demon Lord and a Queen fought. During that
fight, it is said that the Demon Lord fled to our village. Here,
on this soil, is where the Queen drew the first drops of blood
from him. The blood soaked into the ground and froze this land
solid. The Demon Lord swore he would return, should he die,
and that he would rise from Ice and Rage."*

The students turned slightly to look at Oren.

*"They say the Demon Lord had black hair and brilliant
purple eyes."*

*The students began whispering, laughing, and glaring at
Oren. "Demon spawn, that's what he is," they said.*

"Demon spawn, indeed. How pathetic," Oren
sighed.

The shop keeper of the trinket store, who was usually
the friendliest person in the village when Oren came
near, looked at him in sorrow, and because of the other
customers' scorn for Oren, turned his back towards the
road. Other shop keepers closed their curtains to avoid
seeing him as he passed. Oren's home was on the south-
western side of the village, making the walk from the hill
to home and back a long one. A dog chased after a piece
of fabric into the street. It saw Oren and howled in fear,
backing away and running to its owner after scooping up
the fabric in its mouth.

"Even the animals fear me. Where does the influence of villagers end? Soon, even the sun will see me as a traitor, and the moon will be quick to follow," Oren muttered to himself.

He flitted past a few more shops and homes before reaching his tent. He drew back the fur curtain and stopped. The Chieftain and a man clad in leather stood, speaking in whispers. The man turned. It was a hunter, one of the men that had become lost in the blizzard. He bowed to the Chieftain, whispered something in his ear, and walked quickly from the tent. Oren watched him speed down the road. The man stopped abruptly and two arms wrapped around his neck. Stana's face pushed through the leather coat and rested on his shoulder. The man, Oren now realized, was Zem, Stana's husband. Stana opened her eyes and her breath caught when she saw Oren standing there. She freed herself from Zem's arms and spoke to him in a fierce tone. Zem turned to stare at Oren, and he could guess that Stana was feeding Zem the lies of Mertha's death. Zem patted her shoulders and laughed, as if he was casting her fear aside, saying she was just tired and confused. Stana became angry and walked away. Zem turned back to Oren with a frown, but smiled when the young boy shouted his innocence. Zem laughed some more and walked towards his home where hot soup waited for him.

Oren closed the curtain and turned towards the chieftain. "Why was he here? What did he want?"

The Chieftain looked up at Oren, his face deeply troubled, but the look on Chieftain's face passed and was instantly replaced with a grin.

"I'll explain later," he said.

The chieftain stood and left Oren to himself.

"More secrets," Oren said.

Oren hurried to grab some food. After he had gulped it down and pleased his stomach, he rose from the straw floor and walked from his home. As he lifted his head to the sun, a large hand met his face, and Oren fell to the ground in bewilderment.

"May the Gods curse your head, boy!" a man shouted.

Oren looked up at him, holding his throbbing cheek. His face was twisted in rage behind a thick brown beard. It was Tharace, Mertha's husband. Oren's fist clenched shut in anger and he stood tall and strong before Tharace.

"I did not kill her, Tharace. I do not know what lies have been drilled into your thick skull, but I did not do it! The sooner that gets to your fatter-than-pigs head, the better!"

Tharace backed away, shocked at Oren's tone and words.

"May Silice freeze your soul. May she freeze it and never allow it to thaw!" Tharace growled.

Oren stepped forward and let his hand fly. It missed Tharace's face as he backed away and left in fear. If Tharace thought that Oren had killed Mertha, then there was nothing to stop him from thinking that Oren would kill him as well. Even as a baby, Mertha never liked Oren. He could never understand why — Oren's father had told him it was because his mother was Mertha's best friend, and Mertha had never really gotten over her death. Tharace had always been the one to keep his wife at bay, to silence her insults or drag her away from a scene. Still, Oren didn't understand.

Oren ran down the road as fast as his feet could carry him. He bolted up the hill and sank into the snow, breathing deeply. He wanted to scream to the clouds and let his hate be known. Oren continued to wait endlessly for a sign of what could have killed Mertha. Finally, he gave up and decided to try again the next day. As he made his way back to the Shrine village he stopped at something in the snow. It was a deep imprint of a paw. It was fresh and left a trail up the snow to what appeared to be a large, furry, black bear. A piece of fabric dangled from its mouth.

"Yes," he thought.

"Villagers!" he shouted, the echo traveling through the air.

Heads turned to look at Oren, waving his arms around on top of the hill.

"Come look! The one who killed Mertha was a bear! He stands there upon the hollow rock!"

The people came running up. Oren pointed to where he had seen a black, fluffy bear after following the tracks up the snow. The bear was gone, as were the tracks. No sign of any creature remained.

"What bear?" a small girl asked.

"There is none, for Oren is Mertha's killer," Stana said. The people then left Oren standing there by himself.

The small girl watched Oren for a moment. "You didn't do it, did you?" After a pause, she added, "My name is Sara."

Sara had straight brown hair that was tied up in a

ponytail with a thick, pink ribbon. She had light brown eyes, and her hair swept off on either side of her face, however, the left side of her bangs was much longer than the right. Sara wore a fur trimmed, blue coat with two red lines all the way around. There was a red diamond shaped emblem in between them on the front, which had a small red circle in the middle. She wore blue pants that tucked inside of brown, fur trimmed boots. She also wore a short brown half skirt that covered the back of her legs with a small red piece of wool wrapping around her waist in the front.

"No, Sara, I did not kill Mertha. The black bear that I saw did."

"A black bear?" Sara said, delighted, "I saw one a fortnight ago. It told me it was here to guide the light of all to the darkness of many." Sara then turned and ran away. She suddenly stopped and flipped back around to face Oren.

"What do you think that means?" Sara asked. She then ran to her home and invited the other children to a snowball fight. Oren smiled, and then looked to the hollow rock.

"Here to guide the light of all to the darkness of many?" he repeated. "A bear that talks? And they call me weird. I'll meet you again, oh, foul beast!" he yelled. Oren then turned and marched home. From within the shadows of the trees, the black bear watched him.

I will meet you again also, the bear thought.

The bear twisted around and sped away into the forest that surrounded the Shrine of Silice. That night, Oren went to sleep with a heavy heart and a troubled mind.

If he could not prove his innocence, he would be exiled from the entire village. He would disgrace his father. How would he face his father when — if — he returned? It weighed greatly on Oren.

"I did not kill Mertha, did I?" Oren rolled onto his side. A small slice in the tent wall allowed moonlight to pass through. Oren saw a shadow pass in front of it, and his breathing hitched in his throat. Unbeknownst to Oren, on the other side of that slit was the bear.

"No," the bear said.

Oren couldn't see who was speaking. He covered his head with blankets in fear. The voice was deep, yet soft.

"No," the bear said again, "you did not kill her."

Oren tried to peek through his blankets by stretching the fabric. "Then who did?" he asked.

The bear sat down. "It doesn't matter. She needed to die."

"Why?" Oren said.

"Because," the bear sighed. "You need to be blamed. You need to be exiled. It's the only way to get you out of here. There's something very important you must do. Not now, but in a few years. For you to be ready, you must first be hated."

Oren closed his eyes, ready to cry. He couldn't understand what he was hearing.

The bear stood, and turned to leave. "You have done nothing wrong, but you will be the one to pay the price."

Oren heard the heavy feet walk away, and he curled into a ball and cried until he fell asleep.

DON'T PLAY WITH FIRE

– This is the first day of many days of which there will be strife. I seek to train him, to nurture him in the same ways as the others, but it is challenging. The essence within him is difficult to control, to override, and even more difficult to understand. He struggles greatly, mumbling about the voices he can hear. Alas, his power is derived from those voices, enraged and sorrowful. It will fill him up to the brim and there can only be two outcomes. He will subdue it, or it will tear him apart.

It was winter all over the world. But there was no place on all of First World as hot as the Shrine of Aros. Each Shrine Village was built around the area where a God or Goddess had supposedly built their temples. The Shrine of Aros, the God of Fire, was therefore hot and musky. It rested at the foot of a volcano, the only volcano that existed in First World, which made it a wonderful tourist spot. Hot springs were very common at this Shrine village, and it was at this village that a prized student of the ancients, who studied the Gods and Goddesses so much that he who had memorized 400 pages of ancient text, resided. His name was Syris — Syris Ulzary. He had red hair and green eyes to compliment it. He was the village's goody-goody boy, never doing anything wrong, never a mistake. All of the plains people were proud of him. He never fought with anyone, and seemed to befriend even the town bullies, but the black bear saw something within him that no one else did. It was a lust for power. Syris' heart was corrupted by greed. The bear decided to wait, and let time take its toll on him.

"Perhaps he will change," the bear thought. For the rest of the day, the bear watched him.

"This boy is the very opposite of the boy back at the Shrine of Silice. What do the Gods and Goddesses see in them?" the bear thought.

Syris started the day by eating. He cleaned his dishes, kissed his mother's cheek, and then ran outside to play. He shot past an old man on his street and bumped into him, apologizing over and over until the man smiled and waved him away, saying all was forgiven. The bear noticed that the boy had taken a small dagger from the old man's pocket.

"He's not as pure as they think," the bear thought.

Syris made his way down the street till he reached a large, rectangular courtyard lined by ferns and small fountains. To the left and right of the courtyard were cobbled streets leading off into small markets or housing areas. The front of the courtyard was walled in by blacksmiths, a tavern, an inn, barn, bakery, an old dance hall, and a small hut that led to an underground prison.

Syris breathed deep, taking in the smells of hot iron, fresh fruits and baked bread, washed clothes, wet dirt, and the barely detectable scent of lavender and spices that were spread on the ground.

Flowers and herbs were frequently crushed into fine powder, and then littered across the ground throughout the village. It was used in soaps, oils, cleaning solutions — truly a multi-purpose substance.

Syris turned in a circle, taking in the day's light, and the people walking by, and then ran off into the woods. He jumped over fallen logs and ran through ash covered bushes. The volcano loomed high above him. He ran until his legs became tired and then jogged for awhile. He then began to walk when his lungs started hurting. After he had regained his breath, he flipped his head up and smiled.

"Good morning, little rabbits!" Syris said. A small bunny hopped into view from behind a rock. It had gray fur but looked brown because of the volcanic dust that covered it.

"Come here, little friend," Syris said, smiling.

Don't go near him, the bear thought.

The rabbit inched closer and when he was at Syris' foot, Syris grabbed him by his neck and held him against the ground.

"Hello, little pest," Syris said, a wicked grin on his face. He raised the dagger he had stolen and held it to the bunny's gray throat.

"Say goodbye, little pest," Syris laughed.

"Goodbye," the bear thought.

The rabbit's scream filled the air and it became silent, cold, and motionless as Syris looked down on it. Syris then stuffed the dagger into the dirt and picked the rabbit up.

"I'm sorry, little pest," he giggled.

"I'm sorry, too," the bear thought.

Syris then ran back to the village and began to cry. All the plains people surrounded him as he began to tell his story of how he saw some birds and when he scared them away found the poor rabbit lying in the dirt. His mother ran to him and hugged him firmly.

"Can we help it, mom?" Syris said through his fake tears.

"I'm afraid not," his mother said.

An old man brought a small wooden box forward and Syris placed the bunny inside. Syris then dug a small hole and placed the box in the dirt. The villagers talked with his mother.

"He is such a sweet child. He felt so sorry for that bunny," an old woman said.

"I wanted to make rabbit soup tonight but I didn't have the heart to tell Syris that," the village butcher said.

"Yes, he is so caring. I wish my son was like him," another lady said.

"No you don't," the bear thought.

All the other children crowded around Syris asking him to come and play. After Syris swept away his tears, he stood and ran with the other children. As they decided on what game to play, Syris was filled with boredom. The children tried to dissuade Syris, but he turned and left the group of kids that were fighting over which game was better. He returned to the fresh grave and stared at it with a twisted smile on his face.

"Have fun, little pest," he said. Syris looked up towards the forest, and his insides froze. There in front of him was the bear, the box containing the rabbit's corpse held firmly in its jaws. The bear threw the box towards the boy and the lid toppled off. Syris looked inside and nearly screamed. There within the box was not the rabbit, but his own head. Syris looked back at the bear in horror.

"You will be sorry, Syris," the bear said coldly. His voice shook the earth as its anger boiled dangerously. Syris sank to the ground. "You will be sorry!"

Syris clamped his hands over his ears and shut his eyes tightly. The bear then trotted away. Syris opened his eyes and looked down. The box was gone and so was the bear. Syris stood and ran toward the forest. The children hadn't noticed his absence.

"Where are you?" Syris yelled into the darkening woods.

The bear watched him.

"You really want to know?" the bear thought.

"Come out, now!" Syris said.

"Suit yourself," the bear laughed.

The crunching started out low and then grew louder. Syris trembled as the black bear shoved his nose at Syris, sniffing him, his teeth protruding from within his mouth.

"You shed innocent blood," the bear said.

"I-it was just a rabbit," Syris stammered.

"No excuse. In the laws of nature it clearly states that even if the victim is an animal, one may not kill without a great or just, good cause, such as food, warmth, or for protection. You took a small, defenseless life for no reason whatsoever. However, this is not the first time you have been so selfish, is it?" the bear said.

"W-what makes you think that?" Syris asked.

The bear circled him, watching him closely. "If you're thinking of going for that dagger, give up."

Syris froze. How did the bear know his thoughts?

"You killed that rabbit with ease and you didn't hesitate. You didn't turn away at the sight of blood or gag at the horrid smell. You've killed before. I wonder what your mother would say?" the bear teased.

"I saw you steal the dagger from the old man you bumped earlier today. Everyone believes that you are perfect, but your soul and heart are flawed beyond repair. Only you can do the mending. So go home, and tell them all the truth of how that rabbit died. If they don't believe you, then I will come back and find you. Well?"

"I understand," Syris whimpered.

"Good. Now **go**!" the bear roared.

Syris screamed and fled.

"I impress myself. I truly am a marvel," the bear thought.

Syris ran, as fast as his young legs could carry him. When he got home, he prepared himself to tell them all the truth. He entered his house and opened his mouth to speak, but stopped. Was he really going to give himself away? The bear had told him to tell the truth, but what if this was all a trick?

"No," Syris thought. Syris went to his room and drifted into a deep sleep, but it was in his sleep that the bear found him.

"Syris!"

Syris screamed and flipped around.

"You didn't tell them the truth."

"Y–yes I did!" he stammered.

"Do you think I'm a fool? I can see you no matter where you hide. You said nothing to them!" the bear said.

Syris became angry. "Go away! This is my dream and I'm ordering you to leave!" he said.

The bear laughed loudly. His teeth shone and his wet snout shimmered.

"Your dream?" he laughed. "No, stupid boy, this is my dream! I found you. Not the other way around. You can't leave until I say so!"

"What do you mean?" Syris asked, shaking.

"You are trapped within a State. You can't escape until I open the door. As punishment for your lies, you will remain in this dead space until I decide to let you out, which could be—never. You will still age and grow, but you will never see your parents again."

"No! Please, don't do this!"

"Goodbye, little pest," the bear said.

Syris' eyes grew wide. He knew those words. They echoed like funeral drums in his head, pulsing behind his eyeballs, ripping away at his heart.

"Goodbye," Syris said.

The bear went away and Syris fell to his knees, crying, all alone, never to know the sweetness of life until he was allowed.

"Forgive me, mother," he wailed. Then, everything faded away.

The bear rose from the dirt with a pain in his shoulder. "Well," the bear said, "It seems I have a big job to do — so stay alive, Oren. Syris needs you. I need you, too."

The bear then went to Syris' house to see what was happening. It was difficult to reach the location while staying unnoticed by other villagers. The bear crept behind houses, squeezed through alleyways, and tried his best to appear stuffed when someone passed by too close. Upon reaching Syris' home — a simple, yet beautiful domain made of brick and mortar — with a sliding door, the bear peered through one of the windows. The mother was weeping and shaking Syris, trying to wake him from the nightmare he was imprisoned inside of. The bear quickly made his way to the door, nudged it open with his nose, and walked inside.

"Woman," the bear said, "silence your woes."

Syris' mother started to scream; dishes toppled as she scrambled to get away from the large beast in her home, but she eventually became still and quiet.

"What do you want?" she said. "My son will not wake. What do you want?"

"Your son was dishonest with you. I have locked his soul away. It will be returned. Until then, feed him, give him water, and lift his arms and legs daily, so that he will grow strong. His soul will also become strong, but you are in charge of his physical development. I must leave. Take care woman, and heed my words," the bear said.

"I will," Syris' mother replied, pausing in disbelief.

With that, the bear left, not saying a word, not thinking a thought. Just, silent.

"Is this truly what you wanted?" the bear asked,

looking towards the sky and the stars, and then turning to look at the volcano.

The bear heard nothing and he saw nothing, but something inside of him shook with reassurance and promise. He felt his heart jump to some foreign rhythm, and he understood.

"As you wish, **uor meratia**," the bear said. He then ran off into the forest, rushing past the trees, becoming nothing more than a dark blur in the night.

Chapter 3

WHEN TWO VILLAGES COLLIDE

– Souls are odd little things. They are visible yet translucent, and can only be manipulated through a means of touching but not feeling them. It's a strange thought, I grant you, but there it is. However, it is not impossible to fully touch a soul, but containing it is problematic. They writhe and squirm with much ferocity. If you don't take proper care of it, you'll destroy it and kill the host. Hence, the Void was created, the in-between, a place only accessible to those who have touched death but not fully embraced it, or are dead yet haven't lived. I wonder— which one am I?

"Get out! Get out! We don't want you here! Leave, demon!" the villagers screamed.

"That's fine with me. I hate you all as well," Oren said. Oren was now sixteen years of age. It had been some time since the incident with Mertha's death. Oren had not been able to find the animal responsible for her death and finally, after much pressure, the chieftain banished him from the village. Oren had become extremely skilled in the way of the sword, and had become one of the best warriors in their village. He now carried a 3 foot steel sword of master craftsmanship. It was true, his father had died in the blizzard at the same he was accused of killing Mertha, but he didn't mind. That was the message that Zem had brought, and the message the chieftain had said he would share with Oren later. He had grown strong and handsome, and *all* of the young unmarried women in the Shrine village were deeply saddened and disappointed to see him leave. The lady that was most saddened was sweet little Sara, who was the first to see the black bear. She ran from the crowd towards Oren's fleeing back.

"Oren wait!" she said, panting to catch her breath, "Must you really leave?"

Sara now wore a long brown dress with red circles on either side of her waist that reached down to her feet. She still wore brown, fur trimmed boots, and her hair now hung loose, flowing freely in the wind. She had grown considerably, but was still fairly small.

"Yes, Sara, I must. I'm afraid the chieftain has made his choice, and a wise one at that," Oren laughed.

Sara stamped her foot and pushed out her lower lip. "It was not wise! He's the chieftain! He should be able to overrule the villagers!"

"When a chieftain makes a decision, he makes it for the good of the entire village, not just for himself," Oren said.

"You are very smart as well. But I will miss you

terribly. I hope I will get to see you again someday," Sara said.

"You will, I promise."

Sara turned to leave.

"Sara!"

"Yes?"

"You are very pretty, you know that?"

"**Oren!**" Sara yelled, her cheeks turning scarlet.

Oren turned and walked away, laughing as he went. A woman caught his eye, and he turned to face her. Stana had aged considerably. Her honey hair was gaining streaks of grey, her blue eyes weary with exhaustion from taking care of her unruly children. Stana's eyes narrowed, but she allowed a smile of restrained hatred to grace her face. Oren smiled, turned away and whistled a tune as he ran through the forest, toward an unknown destination. Yet for some reason, he stopped short. Oren listened intently, his senses heightened, his hand on his sword hilt. He whipped around and froze. Anger poured through his veins. He straightened his back and narrowed his eyes in hatred.

"What are **you** doing here?" he hissed.

"I came to greet you on your way out," the black bear said, walking forward.

"You've done enough. You killed Mertha. I know you did!" Oren accused.

"You can believe what you want. I know you haven't matured at all," the bear retorted.

"Touché," Oren said. "What do you want?"

"I need you to come with me back to the Shrine of Aros," the bear said.

Oren eyed him suspiciously. "Why should I?" he asked.

"Cause I say so," the bear replied.

"And if I don't?" Oren said.

The bear thought for moment before answering. "Then your dear, precious Sara joins Mertha in heaven or hell, whichever one suits her best."

Oren's eyes widened. "You wouldn't dare!" he said.

"Maybe I would. After all, I am a bear. I can blame it on instinct," the bear smiled.

Oren ground his teeth together. What to do, what to do, what to do.

"No," Oren said.

The bear was stunned. "No?" he said.

"No," Oren repeated.

"But why?" the bear asked.

"Cause I said so," Oren replied.

"That's a level **one** response!" the bear yelled.

"Same answer you gave me. What were you hoping for, a level **three**?"

"Yes," the bear said.

Oren started walking away.

"Fine! Suit yourself. I'll give Sara your regards," the bear said.

Oren froze and flipped around. The bear was running towards the village.

"No!" Oren yelled.

He ran after the bear but was too late. The black bear was jumping from roof top to roof top, crashing through houses and breaking things apart. The villagers were running in all directions, screaming, shouting, and the men were grabbing their spears, swords, and chains.

"It won't do you any good," the bear thought.

Oren watched, his hopes lifting as the hunters advanced towards the bear. Yet, his hopes crumbled as the hunters halted, for the bear had Sara's arm in his mouth, threatening to crush it in his jaws if they came any closer. Oren's resolve shattered and he finally gave in.

"Okay!" he shouted. Some villagers stared at him in confusion. He was talking to the animal?

The bear released Sara, who ran behind the hunters, crying.

"Let's go," the bear growled at Oren.

Oren returned to the shadows of the trees. He stared at the bear's back, anger seeping through his veins. Behind him, the shouts of villagers echoed, saying 'demon', 'monster', and many other things.

"I know you're angry with me, but you left me no choice," the bear said.

You left me no choice. Oren knew those words. It was the same excuse the chieftain had given him when he was banished from the Shrine of Silice.

"One day, they'll learn to appreciate you. I promise," the bear said.

"I beg to differ," Oren mused.

"You doubt me?" the bear asked.

"More than I doubt my own ability to hold my drink."

The bear chuckled. "The sentiment is mutual!"

As the bear turned to walk towards their destination, he stopped and looked back at Oren with wide eyed curiosity.

"You drink?" he asked.

Oren blew out of his lips in exasperation. "No!"

The bear grunted in satisfaction and lopped across the snowy ground. Oren remained silent for a great distance. He had never been to the Shrine of Aros. That was when a question popped into his head.

"Why are all the villages considered Shrines?" Oren asked. It had occurred to Oren that if the bear could speak, he would have to be incredibly smart, so Oren wanted to see how much he knew.

"Each village was made as a Shrine to a different God or Goddess. Your village is the Shrine of Silice," the bear said.

"Who is Silice?" Oren asked.

"Silice is the Goddess of Ice. Honestly, you don't even know about your own home?" the bear replied.

"Then who is Aros?"

"Aros is the God of Fire, and is also Silice's opposite element. In that village, you might just meet your match," the bear said.

"Yeah, and he'll be a good little boy who murders innocent animals," Oren joked.

The bear smiled. "Close enough," he said. "Close enough."

Oren walked silently, thinking about many things, never focusing on one subject. He stared down at the snow, his thoughts swimming. After a while, Oren's vision started to get blurry. This confused him. As he wiped his eyes, Oren realized he was crying. Why, he didn't really know. He hadn't really thought about anything sad, just his parents, or rather, the lack of them, the hate people felt towards him, being shunned from his birthplace for all time and eternity.

"It seems I did have something to cry about, after all," he thought.

"Is something wrong?" the bear asked, interrupting Oren's thoughts.

Oren looked up with his cheeks wet and salty. The bear's eyes went from serious and stony to compassionate and soft. He understood the pain of being pushed away from everyone or thing that you held dear.

"Don't worry," the bear said, "Soon, all will be better. You'll see. Soon, you will do something so miraculous they'll be begging to have you back."

Oren dried his face.

"What kind of 'miraculous' thing?" Oren asked, his eyes starting to turn red.

The bear stopped walking and thought for a moment. "Well," the bear began, "You will become the hero of a mass adventure. You are going to do something that no one else can, because no one else is worthy of the honor. You are the only one worthy of such a thing as this. You will receive the chance to travel anywhere in the world, or everywhere, all in the name of a very, *very* special someone. That person is counting on you. We all are."

Oren looked at the bear in wonder.

"Why am I worthy, of all people?"

"Because," the bear said," you have suffered and therefore know the value of strength. Your pain will be your strength, your agony will be your joy, and your desire to give up is what will force you to push onward."

"What if I don't want to travel in the name of someone special?" Oren said, narrowing his eyes.

The bear looked Oren dead in the eye.

"If you don't," the bear began, "we will all *die.* Every one of us. Me, you, Sara, the whole world, no, the whole universe! It will all come crashing down around you, and you will be responsible for its destruction."

Oren stared wide eyed at the bear, swallowing what little words he had left and ceased talking. The bear sighed, seeing that he had just worsened Oren's depression.

"It's not all bad," the bear said.

Oren didn't answer him.

"What are you thinking?" the bear asked.

Oren looked at him, and then returned his gaze to the ground.

"I was thinking about my dad— and my mom," Oren said weakly.

"What were they like?" the bear asked.

Oren hesitated before answering. "My mom— I didn't know her. They say she died while giving birth to me. I've only seen paintings of her. My dad said she was very kind and loving, that everyone liked her and no one has ever said a bad thing about her. She was completely opposite from me. My dad— my dad died during a blizzard and I have been alone ever since. Everyone says it's my fault they died, that I'm cursed. I think— they might be right. Everything good in my life— it just gets ripped away."

The bear watched Oren and started to walk again.

"I know someone like you. She is resentful with the world. She loves everyone yet feels great hate for them at the same time. Everything she ever cared about was taken away by a very bad person. She's all alone, with no one to care for her."

Oren followed the bear, twirling his long black fur.

"Do you think she wants to kill that person?"

"Oh, no," the bear said, laughing, "I don't **think** she wants to. I **know** she does. She wants to rip him into bite-sized pieces, roast him over a well stoked fire, and eat him for breakfast, lunch, dinner, and then some."

Oren looked at the bear in horror.

"Like I said," the bear sighed, "she is filled with much hate. However, that doesn't mean she is completely and utterly filled with vengeance. There is some kindness in there. It's just that no one is brave enough to dig deep and find it."

Oren thought about this, trying to loosely wrap his head around it. He felt sorry for whomever the bear spoke of.

"What about this boy at the Shrine of Aros? Is he hurt, too?" Oren asked.

The bear snarled angrily at the thought of that putrid, red headed, selfish boy. "He is hurt only by his own greed, arrogance, and pride. The sooner he gets over himself, the better."

"Is that why you're taking me to see him — to knock some sense into him?" Oren asked. The thought of being able to hit a complete stranger over the head delighted him.

"Not — exactly," the bear said, concerned about Oren's obvious glee.

"Then why?" Oren asked.

"To be plainly honest with you, he is in need of a babysitter," the bear said.

Oren's glee vanished.

"**What?** What do you mean 'babysitter'? I'm not going to watch over some stupid kid with self-esteem and mental issues! Why must I? It makes no sense! Why can't you do it?" Oren yelled uncontrollably.

"**Because no one else is worthy!**" the bear roared, snow falling off of nearby trees.

Oren backed slowly away, making little squeaking noises as he did. The bear was frightfully angry. Anyone could see that.

"O-okay. I get it," Oren said, his voice cracking.

"We should go. It's dark out," the bear said, his throat hurting from the sudden outburst.

The sun set on the west, and the moon rose from the depths of the earth on the east, gracing the soil and trees with its faint, white glow.

"Oren, would you stop wandering off?" the bear said, growing more irritated by the second.

Oren had been running to and fro, getting himself lost, steering the duo wildly off course. The bear had more than once picked him up by the collar of his shirt and dragged him along. Oren had never been outside his own village, so the bear understood his curiosity, but even the bear's patience had limits. After about the fifteenth time Oren got himself lost in another part of the snowy forest, the bear decided to knock him unconscious.

"You can only blame yourself," the black furry beast mused, grabbing Oren's shirt in his mouth and pulling him along the snow covered ground. The bear was dreadfully behind schedule because of Oren's sudden need for adventure. The walk to the Shrine of Aros was only supposed to take a day and a half. Due to Oren's roaming, it would probably take them two or three days. The bear growled angrily and glared down at the incoherent boy. Oren twisted slightly, but then remained still. The bear looked at the sky after hours of walking and squinted into the new sunlight. The snow seemed to glow underneath its rays. Oren squirmed and his eyes slowly pried open. He looked up at the frustrated bear and decided to remain silent and still. The bear however could smell the fear on Oren's skin and turned swiftly, ramming Oren's side into a nearby tree. Oren cried out in pain and sunk to the cold ground in agony. After what seemed like years, Oren pushed himself into a sitting position. He groaned and looked at the black ball of fur with utter loathing.

"What was that for?" Oren hissed, clutching his side.

"For causing me trouble and costing me time, time that I don't have at the moment!" the bear seethed.

Oren used the tree to steady himself as he stood up, stretching his back, making sure it still worked properly. He wouldn't be surprised if he fractured a rib from the pounding he had just been given. Oren felt his ribs, pressing here and there trying to root out any sources of pain. Finding nothing wrong, he carefully made his way over to the bear's side.

"Let's go," the bear said.

The two of them continued to walk. Oren continued to admire the world around him, but did so without wandering off. The bear was pleased with this and decided to leave him alone, focusing solely on taking the correct route to the Shrine of Aros. They had already made one day's journey. The hours of walking seemed to fly by, in seconds. Oren ran ahead when he saw a pond boasting fresh, pure water to drink. He stopped and stared at the pond curiously. Half of the pond was frozen over and half of it was thawed. Oren would have asked the bear why, but he was too thirsty to care. He circled to the thawed side of the pond and drank from it deeply. As he stood, something else caught his attention. Oren looked at the side of the forest that he had just come from; it was buried in snow and ice. He then turned and looked at the woods ahead of him; those woods were covered in black and grey ash. It also appeared to be warmer on the thawed side of the pond. The bear walked up beside Oren.

"We should rest here," the bear said, staring up at the darkening sky.

Oren nodded in agreement, and sat down on the new ashy ground. The bear decided to sit on the snowy side of the forest. Oren watched the water in the pond as it remained stock still. He put his fingers in it and waved them around. The water didn't move even a little bit. Oren took his hand out of the water, and to his surprise, his fingers were completely dry. No water was dripping off his fingertips. It was as if he had never put them in the pond at all.

"Stop playing around," a deep, musky voice warned.

Oren flinched and looked at the black ball of fluff, curled in a circle. The bear's eyes were closed. It was obvious that he was tired from walking and dragging Oren.

"If you're hungry, you have permission to go hunting," the bear said, changing the subject.

"My father told me about that place, the forest covered

in ash and fire. He said that the hunters never ventured in there, for those that did never returned. Is this where we're going?"

"Yes," the bear growled. "We'll be safe. The Gods and Goddesses are watching us, or at least some of them are. Now go get food."

Oren smiled at this, for he was indeed hungry. He stood with sword in hand and marched off into the snowy side of the woods. Oren could hear the hooting of owls as he walked silently through the white powder. He picked up some snow and shaped it into a finely packed ball. He then threw it at a tree. Birds swarmed out and flew off. As they did, another predator slinked out from behind the tree, eager to catch the new prey that had taken flight. Oren ran swiftly up behind the creature, wrapped his arm around its torso, and drove his sword into the underside of its throat. The beast, known as a Slathe, writhed in pain.

Slathe were reptilian at best, but also looked like wolves. Their skin was like armor on top but underneath, it was soft and easy to cut. At birth, they were as small as newborn infants and grew until they became as large as an adult man. Between being a newborn and full grown, Slathe were the same height as the average teenager. Unfortunately for these nocturnal hunters, their sense of smell was horrible, rendering their scaly nose useless. However, what they lacked in smell, they made up for in sight. Their hearing was average. A face to face encounter was sure to be dangerous. Slathe had razor sharp claws. Their backs, tails, and hind legs usually had up to three spikes on them. They also ate just about anything, including metal and their own kind.

The Slathe squirmed on the ground, its slit tongue flicking out, before becoming still and silent.

Slathe made a kind of screech that was like a high pitched buzzing noise. It was loud and could scare anyone. When by themselves, the monsters were a good fight, although they didn't put much effort into their battles if confronted directly. When in groups, it was best to avoid fighting them. Slathe were swift, cunning, stealthy creatures. If you lost track of one, your death would most likely follow.

Oren picked up the scaly beast by its hind legs and dragged it back to the pond. Along the way, he cut at some low branches on trees, grabbing the fallen twigs for fire wood. As Oren dragged the monster across the icy ground, the bear raised his head and peered at Oren.

"I see you found food," the bear said matter-of-factly.

"Yes, I did," Oren said.

Oren gutted the beast, stripped it of its scales, and roasted its legs separately using the fire he had made with the tree branches. Oren stayed on the frozen side of the forest. It was more familiar to him. The smell of fresh cooked meat flowed through the air. Oren plucked a leg from off the fire and took a small bite. It tasted wonderful. He savored the flavor and continued to eat away. It didn't take long for him to get the bone. Oren had taken the other leg off the fire previously and offered it to the bear. When the bear declined the food, Oren set it on the cold ground, covered it with snow, and left it there so the meat wouldn't go bad. After filling his stomach, Oren lay back on the snow and stared up at the starry sky, pulling his warm clothes tightly around himself. He tried counting the stars, but he would always lose his place and have to start over. Eventually, Oren's eyelids grew heavy and he drifted off into a deep slumber.

"Hello?"

Oren flipped around, searching for the owner of the voice.

"Is someone there?" the voice asked.

"Who are you?" Oren said.

A laugh resonated from within the blackness of this world that Oren found himself in.

*"In the end, you'll know. I'm right here. Too bad you can't see me. Not just yet. You're still too blind. It's all **her** fault!" the voice seethed.*

"Whose fault? What did she do?" Oren asked.

The voice laughed again.

"She stuck me in this hell. Do you know what it's like? To be trapped in such a fragile existence?"

"No," Oren said, searching the never ending darkness for the voice.

"Who are you?" Oren asked.

The voice didn't speak.

"Where are you?" Oren asked.

A short gasp made it to Oren's ear.

"Where am I?" the voice cackled, "Well, I'll show you. I'll show you the pit of hell she put me in, the gift from our creator!"

With that, flames erupted from the earth, the ground underneath Oren began to shake and fall away, revealing large, endless pits filled with fire and shrieking entities; humans. Oren backed away from the edge only to find that he was now standing on a small, circular platform. A hand reached up and grabbed at his ankle, a melting human face opening its wax-like mouth, attempting to scream for help. As the mouth opened, the bottom jaw fell off along with the rest of the melting skin, showing a skeleton with bones burned black, stained with blood. Oren screamed and kicked the dead thing away.

"W-what is this?" Oren yelled, panic flooding his mind.

"I told you. This is the hell she put me in," the voice said.

"W-what are these things?" Oren said, fear gripping his soul.

*"Them?" the voice said, laughing, "Those are all the people I killed, all the people that she **loved**!"*

Oren wanted to run away, but to where? Another hand reached up and grabbed his ankle. Oren screamed, slipping on the skin that was melting onto the floor. He then fell over the side of platform, down into the raging flames and the screaming victims of this horrid nightmare.

Oren's eyes shot open to a twilight sky. He was in a cold sweat, but calmed down, realizing that his horrible fate was nothing more than a dream. Oren groaned in annoyance at the sky, thinking the sun was just starting to rise. The bear kicked his head and Oren swore at him.

"Get up. It is nearly nightfall," the bear said.

Oren blinked a couple of times, trying to register what he had just heard.

"How long have I been asleep?" Oren said, rubbing his head where the bear had kicked him.

"All last night and all today," the bear replied.

Oren's eyes went wide. How could he have slept so long?

"Come on," the bear said.

Oren rose to his feet, wiping the sleep from his eyes, forgetting about the Slathe meat beneath the snow. The bear began walking forward into the ash covered woods, Oren at his heels. As usual, the hours seemed to melt away as he took in everything around him. What impressed Oren the most as they walked was the looming volcano spewing smoke into the air every now and again. The bear smiled slightly at his sudden childish behavior, but then again, Oren was only sixteen. In a sense, he was a child.

The bear stopped short and ordered Oren to be silent.

"What's wrong?" Oren whispered, only to receive a growl in response.

The bear could hear it, the scraping of claws against rock, the malice filled snarls, and the crunching of dried wood underneath padded feet. The bear knew, without a doubt, they had stumbled into Slathe territory.

"Oren, draw your sword," the bear whispered.

Oren did as he was told. A fierce screech came from behind them. The bear twisted around and slammed the reptilian creature into the ground before it could clamp its powerful jaws around Oren's throat.

"Defend yourself!" the bear said, slicing through the monsters throat, watching it writhe around in pain as death consumed it.

Oren looked in front of him, a monster quickly approaching. It snapped its jaws angrily, foaming at the mouth. As the reptilian beast pounced, Oren fell onto his knees and drove his blade up into the air, stabbing the creature's throat.

Blood ran down Oren's sword, onto his arms, and dripped onto his head. Oren threw the Slathe to the side and sliced at another one that was headed for a preoccupied, furry, black beast.

The bear crushed his current opponent into the ground, using his sharp teeth to sever its head. Just as Oren was about to cut through another one, the bear scooped him up, throwing Oren on his back, and ran away.

"What are you doing?" Oren yelled.

"We don't have time for this!" the bear said through clenched teeth.

As the bear ran, a reptile wolf pounced, knocking Oren off from the bear's back. Oren rolled on the ground, the scaly foe landing a few feet from him.

"Oren!" the bear yelled, stopping as quickly as he could.

Oren lifted his head, trying to find his sword that had been knocked out of his grasp. He saw it, just a few inches from him, but the monster was on all fours, ready to attack once again. Oren lifted himself off the ground and threw himself as far as he could. He landed in a puff of ash, sending gray and black wisps into the air. Oren grabbed his sword and rolled onto his back just in time to use the blade to keep the Slathe's jaws from reaching him. The beast tried to get around the blade that was being pushed into the folds of its mouth. Finally, the beast resorted to a more effective tactic. The Slathe began to close its mouth, fighting against the strong steel until the sword that Oren held broke into pieces, the Slathe eating a few shards inside of its mouth.

"That," Oren said in disbelief, "is beyond unfair!"

Oren grabbed the monster's head in an attempt to

keep it from crushing his. The bear grabbed the beast from Oren and threw it against a tree. Oren could hear bone and bark being crushed, and he winced, thinking how much that must have hurt. The Slathe fell to the ground, the splintered tree falling on top of it. Oren watched as the beast twitched, blood bubbling from its mouth. Finally, the reptilian wolf stopped moving, its eyes dimming as life finally disappeared from it. The bear growled, with fury evident in his eyes.

Oren grabbed what remained of his shattered blade, examining it with disappointment. The bear grabbed a water gourd from Oren's waist, bit holes into it, and dumped it onto the teenager. Oren shouted in surprise at the cold liquid that was suddenly running down his back.

"What was that for?" he said.

"To get the blood off," the bear replied, unfazed.

Oren looked down at the ground and watched as red liquid seeped off of him, running across the ashen land.

"Thanks," Oren muttered.

The bear began walking away, listening intently for sounds of approaching monsters, but as far as he could tell, there was nothing. Oren ran to catch up with the fast moving black bear, keeping a distance, fearing a sudden outburst of rage.

The night fell on the forest, and as it did the gates to the Shrine of Aros came into view. Oren marveled at the fine craftsmanship on the large, double door gate. Swirls, circles, and all kinds of elaborate patterns decorated the surface with mixtures of red, orange, yellow, and a dark shade of pink. Oren grimaced as he looked at the gate. He hated the color pink, no matter what shade it was.

"It's red, actually," the bear said, having followed Oren's deadly glare.

"It's pink," Oren said, examining the dreaded color.

"It's red. It only looks pink because it is dark out," the bear said.

"About time we got here!" Oren said, changing the subject.

"You're the one who kept detouring! Now be quiet!" the bear snapped.

Oren lifted his hands, palms forward, motioning the bear to calm down. The bear studied the gate and began walking to the side of it.

"Follow me," he said.

"Sure."

The bear slinked through the trees as he had done so many years ago. He stopped at the edge of the town, his eyes set on the home where a boy slept, waiting for the bear to let him live once again.

"Are you ready, Syris?" the bear thought.

The bear started forward and carefully made his way toward the house. He stopped short and listened.

"Please, Sylvia, bury him already! He's dead! Can't you see that?"

"He is not dead! The bear said so."

"The bear, the bear, that's all I ever hear from you! Let go of those foolish fairytales! Bears can't talk and you know it!"

"They can too, and I know that they can because a bear talked to **me**!"

Oren listened intently. Were they talking about the same annoying, patronizing, furry, unsophisticated, bossy, smelly, fat, demanding, killer, and seemingly self-centered bear that Oren had to put up with on the way here? To be honest, Oren didn't know of any other bear that could talk.

"Fine. You keep dreaming, but tomorrow I'm burning this hut and Syris, even if you're still in it!"

"Go ahead!" Sylvia screamed. "The bear will come back before you have a chance!"

"Yeah, whatever," the man said.

The black bear then trotted towards Sylvia's home. "Bears don't talk, huh? Then please tell me, if bears in fact don't talk, what am I?"

The man stood rigid, unable to form words. Sylvia smiled and covered her face as tears threatened to spill over her cheeks. The man grabbed a short sword and prepared to advance towards the bear, but Oren stepped in and drew what remained of his poor sword.

"Can't we all just get along?" Oren said.

"Apparently not," the bear said.

"You see, you old fool? The bear **does** exist!" Sylvia said.

"And I've come to give you your son," the bear said.

"Really? Oh, thank you! Thank you so very much!" Sylvia said, bursting into tears.

She fell to the floor and clung to the fur around the bear's ankles.

"Set his body on my back," the bear said. "Oren, climb on."

"What? Why?" Oren asked.

"So he doesn't slip off," the bear said as Sylvia heaved his body up with much effort. She situated his arms and legs around the bear's rib cage and held him still while Oren climbed up behind him. Sylvia looked at Oren suspiciously, and then her eyes turned sorrowful.

"Please," Sylvia implored, "please take care of him."

"I will," Oren said, steadying himself as the bear began to walk.

The bear lopped from side to side, Oren tightening his legs around the bear's ribcage. The bear exited Sylvia's tent and climbed back into the forest. The furry beast walked and walked, jumping over a log. Oren hit his head on a branch above him, crying out in pain.

"That had to hurt," the bear thought.

"You bet it did!" Oren said. "Also, put some meat on your bones, sheesh. I thought you were fat, but is this plushiness just fur?"

"What?" the bear said, obviously alarmed. "You heard me?"

"Yes, I heard you. That's what happens when you speak, moron."

The bear jumped another log and Oren covered his head with his hands, slamming them against another branch above him.

"This is going to leave some bruises," Oren said, rubbing his hands furiously.

The bear said and thought nothing but merely waited.

"Not as big as the bruise it's going to leave on Mr. Ginger in front of you," he finally mused, testing a theory.

"Mr. Ginger? Ow. I feel kind of sorry for him now."

"You heard that?" the bear said.

"Yes, I did. You were speaking, weren't you? That's

what happens when someone who has ears is near someone with a mouth," Oren said, his tone blunt.

The bear eyed him warily. "Interesting," he said.

"What's interesting?" Oren asked.

"Nothing."

The bear walked for a bit more and came to a halt at a small pond. Weeds grew up from around it and ivy vines lined the edges. Its crystal waters reflected the black blur that moved into view and stop silently. The bear sat down and Oren and the other man slid off his back. Oren landed on the ground hard and cursed at the bear when the other man landed on top of him. The bear kicked backwards and landed his paw firmly. Oren fell backwards and slammed his head against a rock.

"Darn you, stupid bag of fluff!" he groaned.

The bear did not pay attention but instead began to draw a circle in the ground by dragging his back left foot. The bear then picked up the man and dropped him into the pond's center, where he sank silently.

I don't get it. I just don't get it! " Oren muttered, "We came all this way to get a hairy guy just so we could drown him? Does that make any sense to you? Why, why do you keep hitting me, on a side note? What have I done? I thought I was worthy! Do **worthy** people always get smacked around where you're from? Hello? Are you deaf? **I demand justice!**"

Oren got up and waddled over to the water beside the bear, hunched over, protecting himself from the bear's feet, which were twitching, wanting to kick him again. They did, and Oren fell over again in agony.

"Why? What did I ever do to you?" Oren yelled,

raising his head, staring pleadingly at the bear for it to stop.

The bear did not stop and let loose another kick, connecting with Oren's jaw and sent him rolling in the dust. The bear then fell to the ground in a deep sleep. The circle he had made lit up with orange and white lights. Small orbs of blue flitted out from the trees and rested on the water's surface. The lights then drained away. Oren dragged himself back towards the pond using his hands and fell at the water's edge. The water shook and the man resurfaced directly underneath Oren's nose. Oren opened his eyes and stared into the wide green eyes that were filled with shock and dismay. The bear awoke when both Oren and the other man screamed in alarm and ducked behind something. The red haired man splashed underwater and then shot to the surface, dragging himself out of the pond, hitting his foot against the hard stone underneath. Unluckily, Oren ducked behind the bear and once again was sent face first into the dust.

"**Bastard**!" Oren said, raising a finger to point at the black bear.

The man watched the bear closely. "You actually came back," he said.

"I told you I would," the bear said.

"And you two know each other, how?" Oren said, head down trying not to cry from the abuse.

"Oren," the bear said, "meet Syris. He will be your companion from today forward."

Both men froze, and Syris flipped around and sped away, screaming.

"You're landing me with **that** crazy?" Oren said, struggling to his feet.

"Yes," the bear replied.

"I don't know anything about him!" Oren shouted angrily.

"All you need to know is that you both need to follow me and not ask stupid questions. Don't ask me where we are going and why. It's a need to know basis, and you don't. Is that understood?" the bear snarled.

Oren didn't answer, his lip curling slightly. The bear could be scary when he wanted.

"Let's go get Syris," the bear muttered.

Oren nodded and trailed after the bear.

Syris was a long way away from home and the pond. He had been running blindly and refused to stop. His muscles pumped and his breath rose in thick white puffs, while sweat poured down his back and across his hands. Even though he had lived here for some time and slept for the rest of it, he never could get used to running in this dreaded heat. He didn't know anyone who could.

Syris' feet hit the ground in loud thumps, kicking dust and dirt up his sweat dampened pants. Dirt clung to his wet legs and got caught in his teeth when he drew in a breath. When Syris could run no farther, his lungs feeling like they were going to explode, he stopped and looked around. There were trees and ash covered ferns. Syris turned around and there, poised high above him was the tall, looming, mountain that spewed fire once every two years. The last one had been six days before his birthday. Syris looked around and saw a red bird with a hooked beak and long, sharp talons.

Its plumage was thick, and in some places it looked more like fur. On its head was a crown of feathers, a small red gem directly in the center, however, the gem was only half there. It was an adolescent phoenix, which only came to this region when the volcano was supposed to erupt. The gem grew on their head as they aged, and when they died, it fell off. From the gem hatched a new phoenix.

Syris knew the hell fire was quickly approaching. He looked up at the sky and saw the clouds were forming a strange pattern, almost like a flower, and Syris knew that the hell fire would come in just two days. There were always signs. The clouds and the birds were two of them. The bird would tell people which year the fire would come and the flower in the clouds always appeared two days before the event.

"No!" Syris gasped, fear radiating through him like static through wires.

The bear wanted to leave, but Syris couldn't, not when the village needed everyone they could get to help build the Metalwalls. It was the only thing that kept the lava flow from incinerating them all. But would the bear listen? It seemed highly unlikely. The bear was stubborn and didn't seem to care for the welfare of others. A loud snapping ruined Syris' concentration. There was a flash of silver, a whip of fangs, and then a strong musky smell mixed with damp and decay. The bear kept one paw on Syris' chest while Oren fixed what was left of his sword at Syris' shoulder. Panic caused his chest to constrict and he felt like there was an iron weight on top of him.

"M-my people need me," he choked out, his tongue falling over itself. It was almost as if he had forgotten how to speak after being in the void for so long. His muscles and limbs seemed unfamiliar and making them move was strange and new to him.

The bear gazed at him, unfazed, not caring for his excuses. Syris looked at the strong black haired boy with a clean shaven face staring down at him, purple eyes flickering silently, as if deciding whether or not he should plunge the long steel into him.

"The day of fire will be here in two days. They will not survive it if I don't help them build the Metalwalls," Syris said, trembling.

The pressure on Syris' chest relaxed a bit, but not enough for him to slide out from underneath the great moist snout that sniffed him. Syris lifted a hand and pointed towards the Mountain of Iscara.

"In two days' time, Iscara will rain red and if the Metalwall is not built, then the village will cease to exist," he said, his voice wavering.

The bear removed his eyes from Syris and raised them to the mountain. Just barely, he could see a faint red shimmer. The bear snorted and backed away from Syris, allowing him to stand. Oren sheathed his weapon and waited for action.

"Two days?" the bear said, narrowing his eyes slightly.

"Yes," Syris replied, "In two days the walls must be built."

Oren shifted his feet and picked at a strand of hair, twirling it around his fingers lazily, yawning in boredom.

"Very well. You may return *only* to assist them. Anything else and I'll return you to the void and keep you there until we have strayed far, far away from the Shrine of Aros," the bear said.

Oren muttered something under his breath.

"Oh, yes," the bear said, his eyes widening. "Syris, this is Oren. He is from the Shrine of Silice."

Syris flicked his childish green eyes up to catch a glimpse of Oren.

Oren's hair was sleek and shiny and his bangs flipped around his face in straight strands. It grew out like little spikes, touching his shoulders, and the tips were red. His eyes were a light purple that shone in the moonlight. Oren was becoming agitated, and Syris noticed that the more upset he became, the deeper the shade of purple they grew.

Oren's eyes didn't always turn darker when he became agitated. It was after his father had died, after Oren had realized he was all alone, that his eyes showed the emotions that his face and his voice couldn't. He wore faded red clothes with a white dragon hide belt tied around his waist tightly. Connected to the silver steel armor that covered his shoulders was a long billowing blue cape with gold trimmings. On the back of the cape, colored ice blue on the inside was the Tiara of Silice. It was one of the more elaborate crests, unlike some of the simple ones that Syris had seen in ancient textbooks. It was a series of sharp triangles and odd, jagged shapes pointing up, left, and right, and joined at the bottom by a small rectangle, much like a crown, hence the name. Each crest was a one of a kind.

The Flare of Aros was also somewhat elaborate. It was a sun, nothing more, nothing less, with hollow areas in its center, and oddly shaped "rays". Outlined in burgundy, it had an orange hue inside. Just as the Tiara of Silice, it was unique in its own special way.

The sword at Oren's side had a very remarkable sheath. It was gold and had several white swirled and leaf like designs on it. The sword handle showed sharply, being colored a deep, dark blue, much darker than his cape, with a green emerald fitted on the top, and a green hilt outlined in red steel. Syris had nothing that looked so beautiful. Yet, he had noticed that it was 'damaged' when Oren had thrust it in his face.

"Um," Syris said, not sure if he should say anything at all, "why is your sword broken?"

Oren's eye twitched in annoyance, and he glared at the boy called Syris. "It had an unfair advantage!" he hissed childishly.

"What is 'it'?" Syris asked, perplexed.

Oren again glared at him harshly, as if to say with his eyes, "Shut up!"

Syris scratched his face and screamed out in alarm. He jumped to his feet and dashed towards the pond. When he reached it, he fell to his knees and peered into the water, panting and huffing like a tornado had spun through his lungs. His face was covered by a thick mustache and beard of crimson. It looked as though he had killed some random creature and glued it to his face.

"Do any of you have a filed claw?" Syris asked, holding out his hands in desperation.

"I do," Oren said, reaching inside his pockets to retrieve it.

The bear kicked Oren softly. "You'll need to keep the

scruff until the Fire Day is over. No one must know who you are," the bear said.

"But why?" Syris asked, almost pouting.

The bear glared at him fiercely.

"Rule number one," Oren began, "don't ask questions."

"But why not?" Syris asked, frowning deeply.

The bear growled and Oren slapped a hand to his forehead. "Stupid, stupid boy."

Syris turned back to the pond to look at his ugly reflection. He traced the beard and moustache and grimaced in disgust.

Chapter 4

THE OLD MAN

*– Today, he asked me something that I thought he'd never realize till his Awakening Ceremony. Apparently, someone in the city had been telling a story that conflicted with our own historical records. Seeing as how I was present for **all** the past events, and I will be for all future ones, I know that the error is not with us. I told him that people base truth off their memories of what they've seen or heard, and that the more you replay that data in your head, the more skewed it becomes. His mouth made some weird twitch; I believe this is a muscle response for the emotion of anger. He asked me, "If they perceive life in such a way, what is the absolute truth?" I stared at him a moment, and then said, "Death, what ends life."*

So it was that when the sun rose after a long and much needed sleep for some of them, Oren, Syris, and the black bear marched back into town. Oren tied a rope to the bear to make it seem as if he were a pet. People stared at them with wide eyes, and mothers hurried their children along when the trio passed by. Young women gawked and squealed when Oren came into view and followed for a bit until he turned round and shooed them away with a wave of his hand. Several hunters watched the bear closely, many wanting to spear it and use it for food, but Oren kept a firm grip on the rope and a sharp eye on the bear. Two small boys were playing in the street and looked up in awe when the bear's shadow cascaded over them. Shop tenders dropped merchandise they had been holding in pure amazement. A thought struck Oren. He bent low to reach the bear's ear.

"Do we have any Talents?" Oren asked, still watching the people around them.

"I'm sure you have a few hidden in your shirt somewhere," the bear snorted.

Talents were a type of payment that everyone used. Bronze Talents, also called Reip, were the cheapest form of payment and fairly easy to come by. If you had 500 Reip, that was equal to one silver Talent. Silver Talents, also called Zeron, were a more desirable form of payment, and it took 1,000 Zeron to equal a gold Talent. Gold Talents, also known as Xzixzeria, were the highest and most desirable form of payment. The average person usually only got one or two Xzixzeria in seven months. The silver used to make Zerons was found in the Shrine of Aros, and therefore, it tended to be the only kind of payment they used there.

"I mean do we have any Zerons?" Oren said, pulling out an empty hand, for he brought no money.

"Ask Syris. His mother probably stuck a few in his

pockets just in case," the bear said, his nose twitching slightly before he gave a great sneeze.

Oren sped up and leaned over Syris' shoulder. "Do you have any Zerons?"

"I should," Syris said.

He reached inside his shirt pockets and rifled around for a bit. Syris withdrew his hand and produced some Zerons and Reip. Oren slowed, counted them, and was back at the bear's side.

"Sixteen Zeron and thirty-three Reip," Oren said. "Is that enough?"

"We'll see," the bear said.

An old drunk in a bar saw the bear and threw a glass pitcher in his direction, shattering it all over the ground. The bear stopped, stared at the glass briefly, and then turned on his heel and let out a long, bellowing roar in the drunk's direction. The old man squealed and tripped on a foot stool behind him, sprawling on the ground. The bear began to slowly advance.

"Whoa! Down boy! Down! Stop it-," Oren paused. He realized that he didn't know the bear's name, if he even had one. Now what?

The bear continued to pull, dragging Oren's shoes across the cobblestones. Syris ran forward and grabbed the rope as well, tugging as much as possible. The bear took one giant step forward and then he had his snout in the drunk's face, sniffing him, his big brown bear eyes cutting into his soul. The old man whimpered and shook. The bear lifted his head a few notches and growled, his fangs showing. The old man put a hand on a small glass bottle, gripping it tightly. The bear saw this, opened his mouth wide and plunged forward.

"No!" the old man screamed.

Splintering wood shot into the air and a great snarl could be heard over the many shouts of villagers. The bear, instead of decapitating the old man, had rammed his head into the wooden wall behind the drunk and created a gigantic hole in it, as a warning. The bear lifted his head, shaking the splinters out of his fur, and walked back to the road, where Oren and Syris flicked his nose several times. The bartender picked up the old drunk and shoved him into the street. Oren, Syris, and the bear walked past him silently and continued down the road.

"Pathetic human," the bear hissed through his teeth.

"Go easy, please," Oren sighed.

Syris walked silently and then turned around. "What is your name, bear?" he asked.

The bear's head lifted slowly and he smiled.

"At last you ask," the bear said.

"Well?" Oren said impatiently.

"My name is Ral," the bear said.

"Ral?" Oren parroted.

"Yes," the bear said.

"I like it!" Oren said, a wide grin spreading over his face.

The bear chuckled and lifted his eyes to the road ahead of him.

Oren had never really paid much attention to the bear, what he liked, disliked, or dreamed about. Somehow, knowing his name made Oren feel a tad bit closer to the ferocious beast. Ral was strong, brave, and spoke his mind, never fearing what others thought of him. Truly, Ral was a lion in a bear's body.

Ral continued to stare ahead of him. He saw Syris, and then saw his mother.

"Not good," Ral thought. *"Not good at all."*

Sylvia knew what Syris looked like, and if she spotted him his cover was blown.

Ral sped up and grabbed Syris' shirt with his teeth. He then pulled Oren and Syris into a shop that had cloaks, hats, shirts, pants, and trinkets of all sorts.

"Perfect," Ral thought.

Ral pulled Syris close to him.

"Syris, buy yourself some new clothes."

Syris lifted an eyebrow in question. Ral strode forward and picked up a shirt, pants, shoes, and a red cloak. He then dropped them in front of Syris.

"Buy them," Ral whispered.

The shop keeper was stunned when Ral had picked out clothes and given them to Syris. Syris still doubted the bear, but he paid the man two Zeron and quickly changed in a separate room. The shirt was loose fitting and brown, the same color as the well-fit pants with a red belt tied around the waist. The cloak Ral had given him was violet with the Flare of Aros on the back, just like Oren's cape.

"A wise choice," the shop keeper said. "You look like a prince in those clothes!"

The two boys smiled.

"How old are you?" the man asked.

Syris' smile weakened. He had been asleep for a long time and couldn't remember. He looked over to the bear for help. Ral mouthed some words.

"I'm nineteen," Syris said.

He looked at the bear questionably. Oren was fuming.

"You're older than me?" Oren raged.

"I don't know. How old are you?" Syris asked.

"I'm sixteen!" Oren said.

Syris was really beginning to doubt Ral now. Oren and him were about the same height and seemed to be the same age. Nineteen? Was Ral stretching it? Ral pulled Syris out of the shop, shoved him behind a pole so he wouldn't be seen, and loped down the road. The bear, big as he was, somehow managed to sneak into the Civil Hall and into the records room unnoticed. He blended in almost perfectly with its deep brown walls. A few minutes passed and Ral appeared again, small papers carefully held in his large mouth. Once again, he passed unnoticed, despite being so large.

"If you don't believe me, then look at this," Ral said, laying the papers down at Syris' feet.

Syris picked them up and examined them quickly. His eyes widened and his face paled considerably. He stared at Ral, dumbfounded, his mouth opening and closing like a fish. He forced his tongue to corporate, struggling to get the words out, partially because his body was still numb from sleep and partially because shock still had an iron grip on him.

"How — how did you —" Syris stuttered, "How did you get these? These are birth records, **my** birth records and the Alotom that goes with them!"

Ral said nothing but waited patiently for Syris to read aloud the information he had received.

"What's an Alotom?" Oren asked curiously.

"It's a psychic paper that follows a designated person's life. When they age, it records that change in age. If you grow, it records your new height. It keeps track on everything about you, your personality, habits, likes and dislikes, virtually everything except secrets, without actually having to be near you." Ral said, yawning.

"According to this, I'm nineteen years old and I have —" Syris stopped short, clutching the paper viciously. "I have a "nasty case of narcissism". Not only am I a narcissist, but I'm "second-rate; he's not even professional at being selfish"? I am highly offended! You are a nasty, cruel paper!"

Ral sighed, restraining a laugh that was welling up within him. That paper was very mystic indeed. Oren smiled and pinched the bridge of his nose, watching Syris fume and then sink into some sort of despair that was not fully understood.

"I can't believe it," Syris said. "I'm so old!" Syris whined for a bit, and the shop keeper watched him with confusion. He had been so regal in his outfit earlier, but now he seemed like a child, sniveling on the ground.

"And you didn't believe me," Ral said, a smug grin crossing his face.

"Why should I?" Syris hissed, contempt making him crinkle the paper without realizing it. One of the delicate corners frayed slightly; however, when Syris loosened his grip, the paper quickly mended itself and smoothed out the creases in its surface.

The bear growled, annoyed at Syris and annoyed with the paper. It had drawn a poor, scribbled, childish picture of the bear on its surface and had written a title above his name.

"Ral: The Fishy One," it said, its blue ink smudging

under Syris' fingers. "His Breath Doth Smell of Deceit. Brush His Teeth Before They Fall Out, Lest He Should No Longer Eat Deer."

Another line of text slowly appeared, obviously mocking Ral.

"Let There Be Deer! Let There Be Deer!"

Oren and Syris laughed heartily, repeating the line in deep, gruff voices. The next line caused Ral to shudder, worry rising in him.

"Son of Lightning, Son of War, We See You. Son of Lightning, Son of War, We See You. You Cannot Hide, You Cannot Run. You are the Spade and Shall Be Thrown to the Earth. Son Lightning, Son of War, Face Your Fear, Your Father."

Ral turned away from the paper, but he felt the words writhe under his skin, singing with mock triumph. Oren cleared his throat and turned to lecture Syris.

"Rule number one," he began.

"Yes, I know. Don't ask questions!" Syris finished, folding the paper up and sticking it in his pocket.

Oren grumbled angrily. Why was Syris older? That meant that Syris might be bossy and would try to tell Oren what to do. Oren would not allow that. He'd show Syris who was boss!

"Oren, would you buy some water?" Syris said.

Oren's eyes widened. "I knew it!" he screeched.

Syris was surprised by the younger boy's reaction. Oren could see it. Syris would try to take control. Next the red haired grizzly would ask him to sweep the floors, and handle the delicates.

"No," Oren said, crossing his arms tightly.

"Why not?" Syris asked, confused.

Oren said nothing, but shot Syris a deadly look. Syris didn't see it, and shrugged his shoulders. Ral smiled at the petty, one-sided feud.

"This will be fun," Ral thought.

"The hell it will be fun!" Oren fumed.

Ral sighed and shook his head. There was no helping any of it. A low rumble broke the silence. All heads turned to Syris.

"Heh. Guess I'm hungry," Syris said, a little flushed.

Ral's smile broadened. They were all hungry, even though Oren kept saying he was fine above the roar of his belly.

"Let's get some food," Ral said.

As they walked, Ral stared at the shops and stopped suddenly when something caught his eye. That item – Ral knew it all too well – what was something as powerful as **that** doing here, in **this** village, in **that** dusty little shop? Ral pulled Oren and Syris towards it. Ral had to get his hands – paws – on it.

"Oren, buy that now!" Ral hissed.

"Buy what?" Oren asked.

Ral motioned towards a sword. It wasn't like any that Oren had seen. The sheath was large and white with a series of red designs on it. A long, winding chain was hooked to the top of the handle, and at its end was a small, spade-shaped blade.

"Ah, I see you have taken an interest in that item," the shop keeper said.

The shop keeper was an old hag. She looked like she could be a witch. Ral glared at her, but not in a hostile way. It seemed like he knew her, or at least had suspicions about her. The old hag picked the sword up and partially unsheathed it. When Oren and the others saw the hag pull on the sword more, sweating and mumbling about the "stupid blade", they realized that she had a problem. It wasn't that she didn't want to fully unsheathe it; she couldn't. The sword wouldn't budge more than half-way. It absolutely refused to be taken out of its current domain.

The blade shone as if it was made from diamonds. The sword was a flamberge, a beautiful specimen with its curving blade, but a slightly shorter version. However, even being shorter, it was still longer than Oren's sword had been. It had a black handle with an extremely large, crimson hilt. Oren looked at it in awe.

"Buy it," Ral whispered again.

Oren nodded and offered to take the sword off the woman's thin, bony hands.

"How much?" Syris asked.

"Fourteen Zeron!" the old hag laughed.

"W-what? That's almost all we have!" Oren said.

Ral glared at the hag again, clearly sending a message. The woman saw Ral's fierce eyes and nodded.

"Alright," she said, "Just this once, I'll make an exception and give it to you for — seven Zeron and thirteen Reip."

Oren nodded and Syris handed the money over.

"Be careful with this," the hag said. "Many a strong man have died trying to use this blade."

"Why did they die?" Syris asked, no longer wanting the sword.

The old hag laughed. "Because," she said, "only the

sword's true owner can wield it. They call that sword the 'Destroyer Blade, Blitzkrieg!"

"Blitzkrieg?" Oren parroted, the sword's title making him feel uneasy.

"What is a Destroyer Blade, exactly?" Syris asked.

"A Destroyer Blade is a sword said to be made from the blood and fangs of over a thousand immortal beings, carried through a hundred years of war and crafted by a Spirit Blacksmith. It is a sword made by the dead and can only be used by the person it was intended for. Notably, this is just speculation. Destroyer Blades are all different unless made by the same Spirit Blacksmith. Each blacksmith marks the sword as their own by the way they craft it, be it through the shape of the blade, the colors of the hilt, or the sword's sheath. Destroyer Blades are feared for their massive power when in their true form," Ral said, no longer caring if the woman knew that he talked.

Oren and Syris looked at the bear, shocked that he would speak in front of people.

"What do you mean their 'true form'?" Syris asked, eyeing the new sword cautiously.

"Destroyer Blades aren't just swords. They can be any weapon of any kind – a gauntlet, a gourd, or even a skillet. One quirk that some Destroyer Blades have is that their power is restrained in a smaller form. When the owner of the blade becomes strong enough to wield it, they can unleash the Destroyer Blade from its restraints. This causes the weapon's form to change into how it was before part of its power was sealed away. The Destroyer Blade becomes only as strong as its wielder. The stronger the owner, the stronger the weapon. You can practically tell how much power a Destroyer Blade has through its name," Ral said.

Oren took in what Ral said, and his insides felt frozen. The access to possibly limitless power was contained in a hollowed-out shell for piece of warped metal.

"How do you know who it belongs to?" Syris asked, his curiosity growing.

"Some Destroyer Blades have their owner's initials carved onto them," the old hag said.

Oren searched the weapon for a name. His eyes traveled down the length of the white sheath, he examined the welting on the chain, and the curves of the blade at the end. Oren looked at the hilt and then the handle of the sword. He narrowed his eyes. There was nothing on the sword that gave any clue as to who owned it.

"There's nothing on it. It's blank except for the designs on the sheath." Oren said.

Ral's muscles tensed. Of all the Destroyer Blades to come across, why did it have to be this particular one? He had never seen it in person before, but he had heard about its fearsome capabilities, and about its remarkable death toll.

Syris peered at the sword with frustration. "Do you know anyone who doesn't have any initials or insignias on their weapon?" he asked, staring at the old shop keeper.

The old hag looked close to having a heart attack. She was sweating horribly and her eyes were rigid on the sword.

Ral took notice of her behavior. "It could be anyone," he said, his tone deep and slow.

The woman snapped back into focus, wiping the sweat from her brow hastily. "Yes," she said. "Yes, it could be anyone! No need to assume anything!"

Oren glanced at the hag. What did she mean, "No need to assume anything"? What was she assuming? Did she know who the sword belonged to? Oren was suspicious, but shoved the thoughts away.

"How do you know that the sword is actually called Blitzkrieg?" Syris asked.

The hag smiled. "My, my, where have you been living all these years? Under a rock titled Stupidity?"

Syris glared at the hag, his nostrils flaring.

Ral cleared his throat. "Syris, Oren, please pay attention. Destroyer Blades all have a title that they are given by their owners. The title serves no real purpose other than to identify the weapon. However, sometimes, the name of a weapon is also a Summoning Phrase."

"What's a Summoning Phrase?" Oren asked.

The hag laughed. "A Summoning Phrase is a word, sentence, or paragraph that is said by an individual to command something. Its most commonly used to summon beings from other plains of existence, such as spirits or guardians. For a Destroyer Blade, a Summoning Phrase is used to activate the weapon's most powerful attack. The title, Blitzkrieg, is also the Summoning Phrase for this sword. Now, this is not always true. Sometimes the title of a weapon and the Summoning Phrase of its attack are completely different. It just depends on the taste of the owner."

"That still doesn't tell us how you know the sword's title!" Oren said, squinting at the hag suspiciously.

The bear cleared his throat again. "Well, why don't you ask it? Ask the sword, "Who are you?"

Oren and Syris looked at Ral with confusion. They peered down at the sword. "Who are you?"

The red designs on the sheath began moving, swirling around each other until a word on the length of the sheath became very distinct.

Blitzkrieg.

"Well, that's not strange at all," Syris said, inching away from the sword.

Oren was speechless. He stared at the weapon in his hands. Just carrying this sword made his stomach feel queasy. He no longer wanted it. Why had Ral wanted them to buy something that apparently couldn't be used and killed anyone who tried?

"Are you serious?" Oren breathed, staring up at Ral.

Ral smiled. "All Destroyer Blades, no matter their form or age, are sentient beings. They are alive, like you or me. They have desires, and thoughts, and sometimes emotions."

"Ask it something else," the hag said, delight shining in her eyes.

Syris jumped forwards. "What are you made from?"

Blood of God. Bone of God. Soul of God.

Oren stared at the sword, shivers running down his spine. "How many people or monsters have you killed?"

An ∞ Amount.

"What is that supposed to mean?" Syris said, scowling.

"Isn't that the sign for infinity?" Oren said.

Silence loomed between everyone as they took that shred of information in, and it made everyone feel slightly sick to their stomachs. Oren looked at the sword. Somehow, he felt sympathy for the weapon. How was that possible, feeling anything for an inanimate object?

"Where is your owner?" he asked.

The War Came. All Fought.

Some Died. Some Forgot.

None Prevailed. None Lost.

Price Paid. Terrible Cost.

Each line of text appeared separately, one after the other. Ral's eyes narrowed at the sword.

"What cost? What happened?" Syris asked, curious.

Throne Lost. Power Torn.

Time Sealed. Crystal Formed.

Life Gone. She Was Warned.

They Will Return. Vengeance Born.

"Who is She? Your owner? What's her name?" Oren asked, desperately wanting an answer.

She is Not What They Once Were.

She is Fallen.

She is Unknown.

Ral snatched the sword from Oren, holding it in his mouth. "Let's get some food," he said, forcing the words to form around the white sheath.

"I still have questions!" Oren yelled.

"Questions are over! I'm hungry, this weapon is old, and some things-," Ral paused, sorrow flitting through his eyes, "some things shouldn't be known. Not yet, anyway. Syris, please navigate us towards a place we can eat."

Syris and Oren were angry that Ral had ended the interesting yet odd "conversation" they were having with the Destroyer Blade, yet Syris led them to the best tavern in the village. It wasn't very large and it didn't even have a name, unlike most other taverns. Oren remembered how the Shrine of Silice used to have a tavern. It was called the Nomad's Retreat. It was a decent place, but in a village that was cold as the new moon, it didn't stay in business. After all, no one wanted to have frozen ale.

Walking in, the smell of alcohol and food assaulted them. The scent of food was making Oren's stomach rumble in want, but the pungent scent of alcohol made him want to retch in the nearest waste bin. Near the back of the tavern men and women were dancing, drunk as Oren's father after he was done celebrating a good hunt.

Oren remembered it like yesterday, the smell of ale and rum on his father's coats, staying up until the sun rose trying to scrub the smell out, and dragging his father to wash in freshly heated water. Oren remembered all the huntsmen celebrating in his home, the sound of metal mugs smashing against each other, spilling sticky, bitter drink onto the floor. He remembered how the men would taunt Oren to come and drink with them but his father, smashed as he was, would always rebuke them and remind Oren for the fifth time that night to make sure he grew up well.

"My boy," his father would say, "drink is a man's best friend, but I want you to do right by me! Marry a sweet gal, give me lots of grandkids, stay away from the booze, and die a happy hermit! Grow up good, little ducklin'!"

The other men would laugh at that.

"Have you ever heard in your whole bloomin' life of a happy hermit? He'll be just like his old man, he will, enjoying the drink with the rest of us sod!" someone would shout.

The whole room would break in a chorus of laughs and roars, and Oren – young as he was – would always respond the same way.

"I'm going to be just like dad, strong n' brave, just like 'im! Ain't anybody goin' to stop me!"

His father would laugh more and pat his back. The men would take turns telling Oren about the hunt, leaving out all the gruesome details.

Looking back, Oren grimaced at how horrible his speech used to be. He missed those times.

Oren followed Syris as they seated themselves, the bear sitting at the end of the table on the floor, the new sword next to him, keeping close watch on the women and men around them. A dirty woman shuffled over to Oren.

"Wow! You must be pretty brave to 'ave a bear with ya!" she said.

Oren ignored her. Her breath smelled horribly of ale, wine, and rotted teeth. He was amazed what rum could do to your health, as well as your speech. She had messy blonde hair and a torn blouse.

"C'mon now, don't be shy!" she said. Her laugh was like a cackling witch.

Ral stood and trotted over. The woman saw the bear heading in her direction and raced away.

"Thanks," Oren said, wiping some food off his clothes that the women had spit on him upon laughing.

"You're a real ladies man, aren't you?" Syris joked.

Oren didn't appreciate this. That hag was the last thing he would ever consider as a lady. The tavern woman sidled over.

"What can I get you?" she asked.

She looked round the table and caught sight of Ral. A thin smile spread over her lips. Oren and Syris gave her their orders. Oren was about to speak for Ral, but she cut him off.

"I think I know what the big guy wants. It's not the first time that he's been in here. The usual?" she said.

Ral nodded.

"What's the usual?" Oren asked when the lady had walked away.

"An entire smoked deer to myself," Ral said, smiling so wide it looked as if it hurt.

"And how does she know this?" Syris asked.

"I came here once with an older gentleman a few years back. He requested a deer for me and that was what I received. After that I returned with several different travelers and also ate a deer then. It has become natural for me to get a deer when I come here," Ral explained.

Oren eyed Ral, as if he would get some information that the bear wasn't sharing.

"How old are you?" Oren said.

"No questions, remember?" Ral said.

"You said no questions on where we were going, why, and when. Your age is still on the 'Okay List'," Oren said, refusing to give up.

"Well, now it is not," Ral said.

Oren's head sank into his arms and he closed his eyes. He thought of better times. Times when he had his father and when he and Stana argued. Then an image of Mertha, stone cold and bloody, flashed into his head. His heart pumped at the thought and Oren forced it to the back of his mind. He then thought about eating food. Feeling the meat slide down his throat, the water wash over his tongue, and the sweet smell of food inflating his nostrils as he savored it in every way possible. Well, almost every way. He could almost smell it now. Wait a second. He *could* smell it! The lady had brought it to their table and laid it in front of his nose. Oren lifted his head and stared. Beautiful food had been set before him. Oren grabbed the meat with his hands, took a big bite, and ripped the meat from the bone, chewing it until it was soft enough to swallow. It tasted heavenly.

"My, aren't we hungry!" the lady laughed. "Since the big guy is here, this meal is on the house!"

Oren smiled widely, looking at the tavern lady with sparkling eyes, and then looked at Ral. He too, was nose deep in his food, gnawing on a freshly cooked deer leg. Syris ate his food slowly. He wasn't as desperate as the others. Syris thought it was bad manners to eat like a hog. Still, he couldn't help but laugh at the way Oren and the bear seemed to gorge down their food in almost the same way. It was bite, rip, chew, and swallow for both of them. Oren might as well have been a bear himself.

The tavern lady brought out some mugs filled with water.

"You look a little too young to be drinking. This ought to do just fine!"

"Thank you!" Oren said, quickly grabbing a mug and gulping down its contents. Oren thought back to the mornings after his father's hunts.

The smell of ale covered the floor and Oren was on his knees all night trying to scrub it out. His knees hurt and his arms were tired from the repeated circular motion. He was fascinated by the fact that men could drink so much! Where did all that liquid go, anyway?

Oren wiped the sweat from his brow, sitting up and stretching his back. He was about to continue scrubbing when a firm pair of hands rested on his shoulders.

"That's enough, my boy," a deep voice said. It was soft yet demanding.

Oren looked up into his father's burly face and smiled weakly, sleep tugging at his eyes. His father smiled and chuckled, picking him up and carrying him over to the large bed. It smelled of Oren's dad with a hint of booze. It was a comforting smell, one of home and safety.

"Rest up, young lad. You've done enough," his father said softly.

Oren drifted off to sleep, his mind flitting lazily from dream to dream, never settling on one thing. He would rest like that for hours until the sound of water being dumped into the kitchen sink would wake him up.

Oren opened his eyes slowly, allowing them to adjust to the light. His father was at the sink, scrubbing the many mugs from the night before. Oren dragged himself from the warmth of the bed and slowly made his way over to the sink. He picked up a dry rag and grabbed a mug. The furious sound of scrubbing stopped momentarily. Oren could feel eyes on him, his father's. It made him shy, knowing he was being watched.

Oren began drying the mugs that had been cleaned and setting them aside. As he worked, a large hand ruffled his hair. Oren looked up at his father's face.

"Aye, young lad, what would I do without you?"

Oren grinned. "Drink until you were in your very grave!"

Oren's father's eyes widened greatly at that statement. The older man stuttered in disbelief at what had been said. The older man then laughed, a hearty one, full of love and pride.

"Yes indeed, my son! I probably would! A good answer, to be sure! Ah, my boy, never end up like me, drinking my spoils away."

Oren smiled at his father's words. "Just wait, dad," Oren began, "I'm sure the Ice Queen has a whole room full of rum, just for you! An' you can drink all ya want when you're there!"

A hand patted Oren's head. "Aye, little one, I'll drink it all!"

A moment of silence passed between them as they washed and dried the mugs.

"You are so much like your mum," Oren's father said.

"Daddy, what was she like? People say all sorts of things, but what was she like to you?" Oren asked.

The man looked down at his curious son, still so innocent and bright. The man smiled and handed his young boy another clean mug to dry.

"Well," he began, "She was a pretty little thing, that's for sure. I was in love first time I set my eyes on 'er! Now, boy, it's not every day you meet a gal like that! She didn't stand for anybody! Yet, she was the kindest woman you'd ever meet. All sweet and thoughtful, she was like fire in this cold place. Believe me, boy, she loved you very much. She didn't know you long, for sure, but even before you were crying — when you were still growing inside 'er — she loved you very much."

Oren's eyes were wide and his face was pale as snow. His father took notice and panicked slightly, kneeling and grasping Oren's shoulders firmly.

"Aye, boy, what's wrong?" the man said.

"What do you mean I was growing inside 'er?" Oren said.

His father flinched slightly and stood quickly, raking his hand through his thick hair. "Nothing, my boy! Nothing at all! You must 'ave been hearing things! I didn't say any such thing, to be sure!"

Oren watched his father. He didn't believe what he had

*been told — Oren's hearing was perfectly fine — but he let it
go and returned to drying the mugs. His father sighed in relief.
Oren was still too young to know about such things.*

*Oren put the last mug with the others and examined them.
Dents were all over the surfaces, remnants of the many hunting
celebration parties that had passed. Oren ran his hand over
the mugs, imagining the day when he would be able to put his
own dent into the mug.*

Oren looked at the mug as he set it down. It had no
dents or scratches. Somehow, it made him sad. Did no one
have a reason to celebrate in this village?

A deep voice boomed from the back of the room.
An old man was sitting within a circle of children and
villagers eager to hear the traveler's stories.

He was old, with a long white beard and a snowy
moustache. He had bright blue eyes that, despite his
obvious age, were still alive and shining. He wore a long,
pale blue cloak and had a large book attached to his side.
In his right hand was a tall oak wood staff with a large
green orb fixed at the top. His smile was warm, like a fire.

"Now, what should I tell you today?" he asked.

A small boy lifted his hand.

"Tell us about the Gods and Goddesses!"

A few murmurs went about the tavern but the old
man just laughed.

"Of course," he said.

"Now, there are nine celestial beings in all, the not-
so- important eight and the main ninth. Rumor has it
that the first eight were all originally human, but a great
being made them apprentices. Now, long ago, a war swept

79

throughout the land. Nowhere was safe anymore. Anyone who resisted the Dark Lord was killed or made a servant. The Dark Lord laid waste to everything, killing all living entities in sight. But as the Dark Lord ravaged the land, a champion arose. He and the Dark Lord battled for many days and nights, striking each other with steel and fire and all manner of weapons.

The champion could not kill the Dark Lord, he knew. In a desperate attempt to win the long fought war, the champion called for the great being, the **Goddess of Origin**. She is the strongest force, and is our beloved creator. But the Dark Lord also had aid. He called forth the God of Rage. The Goddess killed the Dark Lord, destroying all remnants of him, and the God of Rage retreated into hiding. The champion died from exhaustion, but because of his valiant acts, was made a God. He became Aros, the God of Fire, and the first apprentice. The Goddess of Origin was pleased with him and blessed him with immortality, but at a price. Aros was to forget the life he had once known, for all those he had loved would die while he remained. Aros found this hard, but he accepted the terms."

The old man went on to tell the tales of the Gods and Goddess. There was Aros, God of Fire. Silice, Goddess of Ice. Vashire, God of Electricity. Osaea, Goddess of Water. Usher, God of Earth. Saate, Goddess of Wind. Kryptos, God of Shadow. Finally, there was Lunatra, Goddess of Light. All were apprentice Gods and Goddesses.

"I thought you said there were only nine beings," a girl piped.

"I did," the man replied.

"But the God of Rage makes ten! Why isn't he counted?" she asked.

"He defiled Origin and many, many years after the fight with the Dark Lord, he destroyed her followers, and started a war with the Goddess herself. He was an abomination in her eyes and in the eyes of many others. So the God of Rage was stripped from ancient history so no one else would fall prey to him."

"Some people say that he'll come back. But Origin will protect us! She'll protect us, right?" a tall man said.

The old man gazed towards the children, a sadness portrayed within his old blue eyes, a frown barely visible beneath his flowing white beard and moustache.

"But there is troubling history. It was said that a second great war ensued and Origin lost all of her powers, which took the form of eight orbs, each containing a single element. They are said to be somewhere on this planet. How she lost them, no one knows. But during that awful time, it was said that the God of Rage could not die, so Origin preformed a magic spell that only she could conjure. This magic struck a devastating seal upon the God, which in turn, shattered her powers. It is said she wanders the world, looking for the orbs, searching endlessly, and that she has sworn an oath to destroy the God of Rage and all other evil beings like him. That was over ten thousand years ago," the old man said, finishing his story.

All were silent. The strongest being in the universe, and she might not even have her powers? What good was a goddess turned mortal?

"How do you know these things, old one?" a girl asked.

The old man laughed. He moved his beard and pointed to his neck, just above his collar bone. Two red circles were branded onto his skin.

"I am still one of Origin's most faithful followers."

Oren's eyes grew wide.

"I am an Excelsias."

THE STRANGER IN THE NIGHT

– I saw someone I did not recognize today, which is saying something, because I know everyone and thing. She stared back at me in the mirror with a mocking air, and even though the room was silent, I could hear laughter, cruel and unfeeling. I stared at myself and saw the remnants of war on my hands, hands that are not smooth, but are not rough either, blood soaked into the pores. They are burdened with much strife, but have no scars to show. My thoughts were interrupted by my dearest companion. He smoothed my hair and said, "You are filled with love." I did not understand what he meant, but his next words were a comfort. "I will always love you."

The moon had appeared. The lodge Oren, Syris, and Ral had decided to rest at was cold, dark, damp, and smelled of spilled ale and rum. Outside, the rain hit the streets and rooftops heavily. Every now and then, it would drip through small holes in the ceiling. Moonlight flooded into the room when the clouds opened up a small hole in the sky. Oren gazed up at the moon through the window, not really looking at it, but not looking past it either. His mind swam with thoughts. What was he doing here? He was crazy according to anyone with a right mind. He was traveling around with a talking bear and a complete stranger who, from what he had seen and heard, had done something sinful and had been punished by Ral. What was going on? What was an Excelsias? Oren's head hurt from all of this confusion.

Oren rolled onto his stomach and reached underneath his bed. His hand closed around cold metal. Oren lifted the object and rolled onto his back again. The white sheath shone in the moonlight and the red designs seemed to glow.

"Was the story true, the one the old man told the children? Were there really three wars between Origin and the God of Rage?"

The designs swirled across the metal, forming words, riddles for Oren to solve.

Time is Lost. History Undone.

Only One War is True.

The Dark Lord is False.

The Demon Lord is False.

The First War is False.

Oren's eyes widened. If the Demon Lord is false, then that would mean that the history of the Shrine of Silice was false, also. The Dark Lord is false, which means that there was never a Queen, and that Aros never fought in a war before he became a God. The sword also said the First War is false, which means that Origin and the God of Rage fought only once, not twice, and definitely not thrice. Oren couldn't understand how history could become so muddled, so wrong. He couldn't understand how people could add stories to reality. People knew nothing of the truth.

"But the man said he was an Excelsias. Why did he not know the truth?"

There are no Excelsias Here.

All Excelsias Lay Beneath the Earth.

The Man Speaks No Truth.

Oren allowed this information to wash over him. If there were no Excelsias, then why did that man claim to be one?

"What is the truth?"

Truth is an Illusion.

A Belief is Made by the Mind.

Reality is Built by Memories.

You Are All Wrong.

You Are an Illusion.

Oren looked at the sheath in wonder. He didn't understand any of what it just "said".

"Is your owner angry?"

She is Sad. Sorrow Prevailed.

She is Lonely. Our Goddess Failed.

She Had Hope.

She Had Faith.

Oren smiled weakly. "She" had faith and hope. Was that faith in Origin? Oren supposed if you thought about it, Origin did in fact fail her people.

Are You Sad?

Are You Lost?

Have You Sacrificed Much?

Have You Paid a Terrible Cost?

Oren was speechless. He thought that the sword could only answer questions, not ask them.

"I have lost a lot, but it's nothing compared to what

Origin gave up. She wasn't able to help her people. They were destroyed." Oren set the sword on the floor, watching the words meld back into designs. Suddenly, the sword made a last set of words appear.

Everything is Alright.

Everything is as It Should be.

What Was Lost Can be Found.

The Earth Will Tear as She Walks.

Oren didn't understand what the sword was saying. "What do you mean?"

Rage Rises. The Mother Confronts.

Skies Shake. The Demon Hunts.

The Earth Rips. Time is Torn.

Another War Comes. Another War Comes.

Oren sat still, fear tracing his being. When the sword said, "Another War Comes," was it being literal or speaking metaphorically?

"What do you mean "Another War Comes"? Are you saying that in the future, we'll fight?" Oren whispered.

The War Comes. All Will Fight.

Some Will Fall. Some Will Survive.

One Will Prevail. One Will Die.

No Price Paid is Considered Too High.

Oren threw the sword under his bed. He didn't want to hear anymore. He didn't want to read about the sword's version of the future. However, what if the sword was right? What if a war came? Who would fight it? Oren reached under the bed and retrieved the weapon.

"Tell me straight up. I want a clear answer! Who is going to fight? What will happen to the people they fight against?"

Origin and Rage.

They Will Slaughter All Who Oppose.

Nothing You do Can Stop Them.

Their War is The Will of Gods.

They That Win Will Rejoice.

They That Lose Will Burn.

The Gates of Perdiasic are Opening.

Perdiasic? What on earth was that?

"What is Perdiasic? I've never heard that name," Oren said.

It Is the Language of the Ancients.

It Is Long Forgotten.

Perdiasic.

In Your Language, It Means "Hell".

Oren felt a chill run through him. Hell – was such a place real? He finally set the sword down, watching the words meld back into designs, trying to calm the tremors that had come over him. For someone, or something, to slaughter all who went against it – what kind of being was that? What kind of god or goddess would do that?

Oren sat up, his limbs trembling, and examined his living space. It was a relatively small room. A small fireplace on one wall with a few shelves on another, and a desk with a chair near the door. Oren was to sleep on the bed next to the window while Syris curled up on another bed nearby. Ral slept on the floor, close enough to the billowing fire to stay warm, but not close enough to singe his fur. Both of them slept soundly, not twitching or moving at all, their chests rising and falling evenly.

Oren got to his feet, remaining as silent as possible. He tested the floor and gingerly walked across it. Oren reached for the door handle and twisted it. He heard the soft click of it opening and proceeded to exit the room. As

Oren pulled the door shut, it groaned and creaked loudly, like nails scratching down a chalkboard. Oren froze, his breath held, trying not to move in case someone had heard. After a while, he clicked the door shut and tiptoed down the hallway. Oren then walked down a flight of stairs, testing each step just in case it might make noise. After reaching the first floor, Oren shuffled to the inn entrance. He looked behind him one last time.

It was a quaint inn. A few dozen tables, some lamps hanging from the ceilings, a bar that led to a small kitchen, and storage closet where rum, ale, and every other form of alcohol was kept. Here and there were tapestries with the Flare of Aros sewn on them.

Oren sighed and peeled open the inn door. It was cold out, but Oren didn't mind at all. After living in the Shrine of Silice for sixteen years, the nightly weather at this shrine was a warm vacation. Oren glanced around quickly, and then started down the road. He needed a break. Looking behind him, he took note of the inn's name: The Perched Bluebird. Oren trudged through the rain and mud, looking back now and then to see if Ral or Syris had awakened and noticed he was gone. So far, it seemed they hadn't. Oren reached the forest and closed his eyes. He thought back to when the trio had first arrived, to when they had gone from Syris' house to the small pond. Oren's eyes slowly opened. He moved his right foot forward and plunged into the darkness before him.

The woods were much trickier at night, even though the moon's light beamed downward and the volcano's fire roared overhead, lighting Oren's way. He made several twists and turns, and sometimes had to retrace his steps, due to becoming horribly lost. Oren eventually found his way, jumping over a familiar log, pressing onward. It suddenly became very cold. Oren glanced around, rubbing the goose bumps off his arms. He turned to walk, but whirled back again. Just there, not too far away, very close actually, and very loud, was crunching. The crunching of leaves, twigs, and tree branches. Oren put his hand at his side. Sudden fear gripped him like a plague.

He shoved his cape out of the way and looked down. His sword was gone! Where was it? Did he loose it along the way? Did someone at the tavern take it? Suddenly, Oren remembered where it was: leaning against his bedpost. Oren began to panic. He couldn't defend himself. He didn't know what to do. Out of fear, Oren ran towards the pond, hoping the creature wouldn't follow. Oren thought the creature would find him. His breathing was so loud and his heart was pumping so fast, he was sure that whatever it was, it could hear him. Oren looked in front of him and saw the pond. Relief washed over him. As Oren reached the water's edge, he sank down onto his knees. Oren bent down and pressed his lips to the slick surface, drinking deeply. It was like drinking a mirror. The water didn't shake or ripple. It remained still, still as the moon, still as the silence all around. Oren lifted his head, gasping for breath. Now, he could think in peace. He closed his eyes and retreated to a happy place.

"No manners. Typical!"

Oren's eyes burst open and he shifted on the dirt to see who was there. The figure was female. She was tall and had a mature air about her. Oren couldn't make out any facial features. She wore a black, clean cloak with the hood pulled over her head, and a piece of black cloth covered where he imagined he would have seen her mouth and chin poking out. Even her neck was covered. Something about this girl seemed off, though. Oren looked her up and down. He could have sworn she was transparent. She seemed misty and dream-like. The ash falling through the air looked like it blew right through her at times.

"Well? Introduce yourself," she said.

Her figure may have suggested an adult age, but her voice was still quite young.

Oren stayed quiet.

"Fine. I'll tell you my name if you tell me yours," she said.

Oren thought about this.

"My name is Oren," he said.

"That's a nice name. I'll be sure to remember that," she sang.

She threw something at him. He caught it easily.

"You'll need that where you're going," she said.

"What?" Oren asked, looking up at her, but she had disappeared, vanished into nothingness.

He had never gotten her name, either. Oren looked at what she had given him. It was a rusty key, about the size of his forearm, yet not very heavy. What would he need **this** huge thing for? It was just more baggage. Nevertheless, he tied it securely onto his belt. Oren looked where she had once stood and saw his sword laying there. He rushed over and picked it up. Somehow, it felt heavier. Oren unsheathed it and gasped, having no words in his mouth. There was his full sword, fixed, in one piece, with not a scratch on it.

"When did she —?" Oren said, bewildered.

Where had she gone, and who was she? Oren didn't have a clue. Yet something inside of Oren, maybe his gut, told him that he would see her again. Where, he didn't know. When, he didn't know that either. It didn't matter right now, though. Oren had grown tired. He decided it was time he got back to the inn.

As Oren left the pond area, he looked back one more time, hoping maybe she'd be there, waving goodbye. She wasn't there. Perhaps she never had been.

As Oren made his way back through the forest, he had this distinct impression that he was being watched. He ignored it and continued on. When Oren finally reached the inn, he was exhausted. He began to wonder why he had ever even bothered getting out of bed in the first place. It was highly illogical. He needed sleep, not another adventure. This journey with Ral and Syris was taxing enough all on its own. Extra pressure and stress was not needed.

Oren lazily climbed the stairs up to the room he shared with his two other companions. He inched quietly across the floor and planted himself into his pillow. Oren gathered his bed covers around him, and sank into the dark, warm embrace of sleep.

Chapter 6

THE HELL FIRE

– I witnessed today something I had feared for many decades. He lost control in an instant, malice seeping through his bones. The voices were too much, and he broke in seconds. Luckily, it was contained swiftly, so not much damage was done and no one was injured, save me. A mere cut is all it was, but my dearest love is powerful and loyal to a fault. He rushed over, enraged at the failure of my student, and kept brooding over that simple cut. However, my student left without a word, and I can feel the aura that seeps off him. He has tasted power and the adrenaline that rage gives him. He will not submit easily.

There was a shrill scream seeping through the air, followed by a earth-shattering, sonic explosion that awakened Oren the next morning. It shook the walls, broke anything glass, and Oren crashed to the floor, his bed having capsized. What in the world was going on? Oren stumbled out of the room, down the stairs, and into the street. The sky was an angry, blood red. Everyone was screaming and shouting. Men were digging trenches and women helped them. Oren caught site of Syris and Ral, and ran up to them.

"What's going on?" he yelled above the commotion.

"The Fire Day is here and they're all getting ready!" Syris yelled back.

A man dashed up to them.

"You two, please, head over there and finish digging the circle!"

Syris nodded and dragged Oren over to the area and began to shovel out soil. Another deafening explosion ripped through the air. Oren and Syris fell on their backs. The earth was shaking and rumbling. Oren pointed up.

"Look!" he said.

The volcano was erupting, red liquid spilling over its sides. Ash and smoke shot into the air, red rocks flashing out in all directions.

"It's early!" Syris said. "No one was prepared because it came too soon!"

Syris' voice was lost in the screams echoing around him. A strong hand gripped his arm.

"As long as we're still here, we have a chance. Keep digging!" Oren said.

Syris nodded. Oren was right. As long as they remained, this Shrine village had a chance. Syris looked up every now and then to see the lava. It was eating through the forest, fire consuming everything in its path. It was like a glutton at an All-You-Can-Eat Buffet.

Oren and Syris finished digging their part of the trench. Men began to fill large basins with water. The weight was too much to carry, so they dragged the basins over to the trench and dumped the water. It was poured in again and again until the circular trench around the entire village was filled. Then it began. Another explosion rang out, and a volcanic rock pelted into a hut.

"Now!" a man said.

The entire village stood at the edge of the circle and began to recite a small hymn as flaming rocks fell all around, pounding craters into the earth. They pressed their hands together, and then extended them outward. Small red sparks flicked out and the water at their feet began to bubble. When the last volcanic boom sounded, the water climbed speedily upwards, creating a magnificent, clear dome. All seemed well. Oren could see the muscles in the villagers necks relax slightly. Just before the dome closed, a volcanic rock crashed through the shield and struck a man. He collapsed, his neck twisted halfway around, blood bubbling over his lips. He had been ripped clean in half. A doctor ran over.

"He-he's dead!" It seemed obvious; Oren was confused as to why he bothered saying it out loud.

Part of the dome was left wide open, but there was no one who could replace the man. Everyone started screaming. The magma was only a few feet away now and it would flood the village through the open space. Syris dashed forward. He didn't know if he had the strength or the experience, but he had to try. He extended his palms and repeated the hymn. The water didn't budge. Syris started to sweat. He tried again, but still nothing. What was wrong? That's when he understood. The one thing everyone did before the Fire Day was drink the water from the pond in the forest, the same pond that Oren had slurped up the night before. Oren was the only one who could make this work. However, Syris didn't know this. He sank to his knees in despair. Oren wasn't ready to give up just yet. He ran forward and took Syris' place.

"What's the hymn?" Oren asked.

"What?" Syris said.

"What is the hymn?" Oren yelled, grabbing Syris by his shirt.

Syris recited the hymn to Oren. Oren then turned and extended his hands outward. The mystical words rolled right off his tongue with ease. Red sparks flew and the water bubbled. It surged upward, but the lava had reached them and both forces were racing for the gap, trying to beat each other to victory. Oren pressed his hands to the water and his knees buckled. His energy was being sucked out of him as it strengthened the spell. The water sped up and towards the dome. The lava already had an advantage and it began to spill in, melting the ground. People began to scream and shout, running away to avoid being burned alive. Oren stood fast, refusing to give up. Finally, the water circled around the lava, connecting like a puzzle piece. Oren held his hands there in the water, his head spinning. The lava poured around them, hoping to find a gap in the shield, a break, but failed to do so. It curled and flowed around them, and after what seemed like days to Oren, hardened. Ral nodded, impressed at the magical attributes in the water that caused the lava to harden almost instantly upon contact. Oren's hands fell to his sides. How did these people do this every two years? He didn't understand why anyone would willingly live next to such a danger. Oren looked up.

"Why are they called the Metalwalls when they're made from water?" Oren asked.

"Because," a woman said, "when the lava hardens, it produces metal which we take and use for our own purposes."

Oren only half heard her. His head hit the dirt and darkness surrounded him.

Oren's eyes shot open. He saw a familiar blackness.

"No, not this again!" he said, stumbling to his feet.

A malicious laugh flooded the air. Oren searched the black world frantically.

"Where are you?" he screeched.

"So, you came to pay me another visit?" the voice said.

"Like hell!" Oren said.

"Yes, Hell is currently where you are, though, it's not the same as before," the voice said.

"W-what do you mean 'not the same as before'?" Oren asked, afraid of the answer.

"Well, in her vision of Hell, it always changes, but no matter what it becomes, it will always make you suffer," the voice hissed angrily.

"So, now, your Hell is —?"

"Yes, it's different. Although, I do believe that I have been through all the stages of Hell at least once. Oh, wait, I lied! This one is new," the voice said, chuckling.

Water surged up from the unseen floor, crashing around in waves. A giant beast writhed in the depths. It wrapped a spiked appendage around Oren's body and dragged him underwater. Oren struggled, trying to slip free, but to no avail. The monster squeezed Oren like a cherry, forcing the air out of his lungs. Oren felt like his chest was on fire. The pain was unbearable. Oren wanted to scream, but he couldn't. His throat was being crushed. His bones were breaking, shattering under the force of this great sea monster. He felt his skin splitting, his body being ripped apart, his organs stretching and tearing inside of him.

Oren than realized— this was the Hell that the voice was being forced to live through every second of their life, and it was changing all the time, putting the person through one merciless death after another. Oren understood now. The voice was being forced to die in every way that his or her victims had. The voice was being forced to endure the pain of millions, and it would never end as long as they were here. However, they would always be here, enduring never ending torment. Oren was only experiencing an incredibly small part of it. Finally, Oren closed his eyes, letting the cold feeling of death creep over him.

"Hey. Hey, Oren, are you okay?"

Oren's eyes opened lazily. He looked into two green orbs.

"Good. You're alright. I was beginning to worry," Syris said, smiling brightly. "Come on. We have to leave the village now. Orders from Ral."

"Okay," Oren grumbled, pulling himself up.

He looked at his surroundings. He was on a bed at the inn, the sun glaring through cracks in the tightly shut window frames. Oren put his feet on the floor and pushed himself towards the door. His vision blurred and he reeled around, crashing to the floor in a heap. A woman poked her head out of her room and when she saw him, gasped and grabbed his arm to help him stand.

"Are you alright, sir?" she asked, concerned.

Oren nodded lazily and trudged towards the stairs leading to the first floor, his hands against the wall for support. The world was spinning slightly. He felt nauseous and numb, his body making heavy, sluggish motions. Oren descended the stairs clumsily, grappling the banister for support and stumbled out of the inn, into the street. His limbs felt heavy and sloppy, like a stone in water.

"It's time," Ral said, glancing back at him.

Syris sighed unhappily. "Yeah, let's go."

Oren forced his limbs to function, pushing himself across the lane. The sun beat down on him and it almost felt like he was being mocked by some invisible entity. Oren hissed at the bright star and stumbled about. He had never felt so weak in his entire life. It was maddening, being a sloppy piece of jelly, melting like butter for no reason whatsoever. He heard something, small and shrill, and he turned around to see it. There was nothing, save the street, the people, and the men and woman running to collect new material and orcs from the newly hardened walls.

"Interesting, isn't it? How they've managed to make such a livelihood out of such a dangerous habitat?" Ral said, taking note of Oren's pale complexion.

Oren looked at Ral with half-lidded eyes and mumbled a reply. Ral frowned as much as a bear could and nudged Oren forward.

"We need to continue. Time will not wait for the slothful."

Oren nodded and trudged forward heavily. His feet felt like they had iron weights on them. Gravity wasn't helping, either. The momentum of falling was creeping up on him and the ground was blurring, as was everything around him. His ears started to ring, that shrill scream echoing in the air again. He turned around and around. There was nothing out of the ordinary.

"Stupid head. There's no time for your games," he hissed to himself.

Time seemed to slow and almost stop. The world was a foreign concept. Oren was losing all feeling, both physically and emotionally. He felt like a hollowed out shell. Suddenly, his senses snapped to life. The hairs on the back of his neck stood straight up, the air grew cold, and everything seemed to lose its color, save something behind him that was glowing, bright and red. Oren turned around and fell to the ground, unconscious.

Chapter 7

I AM LIFE

–A man with no purpose in life is like a stray dog, roaming to and fro, biting whoever dares to try and take him in. Yet, despite this, he knows he is in need of a purpose, a master. So why, when the truth and solution is evident, do men persist in pride and solitude? Does it not corrupt them? Does it not destroy their minds and serve up their souls to a great evil? Men of pride are like roasted pigs with apples in their mouths, catered on a silver platter. My student is full of pride, but I am not so quick to send him to the slaughter. I have some measure of hope, though it may fail me in the end. I do not want to look at the future and see what may be. There are very few instances where I can change what is to happen, and I'm at more peace not knowing what's to come than knowing and not being able to stop it.

Oren's eyes opened and he sat up, panic rising in him. Yet as he looked around, his fear subsided. The place he was in

103

was a pure white, unlike the black hell he was used to. Oren stood up and walked forward. He heard the ground crunch and plumes of what could only be described as "white fluff" spread around his feet. He looked around, curiosity building up in him. Suddenly, a great force knocked him on his back, and he looked into a shifting silver sky, bewildered.

"Careful," a voice said. It was soft, wispy, and floated through the air like a small breeze. "You'll hurt yourself."

Oren looked down by his feet. Small spikes protruded from the ground. He looked in a wide circle and saw more of them, completely surrounding him.

"This isn't a reality, but it's not a dream, either. You can still be hurt here."

"Where are you?" Oren asked, sitting up and searching the luminous gray and white sky, halos of feeble light drifting through what appeared to be cracks in the air.

"I'm all around you," the voice said, growing louder with every word, as if it were closing in on him. "I am the sky and ground. I feel what you feel, and see what you see with your painfully ignorant, human eyes." The voice paused for a moment. "Or are they?"

"Are they what?" Oren asked, rising to his feet slowly.

"Are your eyes human? Ignorant, yes, there is no doubt that they are, but are they human? Something hides beneath the surface, a lie and a truth, concealed beneath misunderstandings. What is it you see?"

Oren stared into thin air, hoping he might glimpse some shimmer of whatever was speaking to him. A bright, warm, red light flared behind him and he swung around to look. It sat on the floor, perched gracefully on one of the thousands of tiny spikes, a small white flame with a red center, lazily wavering back and forth.

"What is it you see?" the voice said again.

Oren hesitated. "A flame. It's white and red, and so very small. It seems that it will snuff itself out at any moment."

The voice sighed. "You are not yet prepared."

Oren's brows furrowed in confusion. "Prepared for what?"

"Poor boy," the voice mused. "You are so confused. There is trouble in your soul and darkness in your mind. If only you could see. If only. Yet you are blind, almost seeing, but things still blur before you, unclear and uncertain." The voice made no sense to Oren. It seemed to be rambling.

"I don't understand," Oren said, sitting down, his energy drained.

"Let me tell you a story," the voice chimed.

Oren sat straight up and listened intently.

"There was a phoenix that came to roost upon Iscara, our holy mountain that spews fire and ash, and grants rebirth upon the land. It came with a beautiful trail of golden feathers and fur and a ruby on its head so large that it could be seen from far places. It shined so brilliantly in the sun and the mountain's fire. Yet the phoenix, careful as it was for the sake of its plumage, fell into the mountain. It hit the rivers within and burned, turning its beautiful feathers to ash. However, the gem atop its head was not destroyed, and it fell into the rivers, sinking deep down to the depths of the mountain. It grew large with the river's heat, and one day, after such a long time, it hatched.

"The being that rose from it was black and charred, writhing in the mountain's bowels. It was so large that it filled every space in the mountain. It rose from within, long talons *stretching for the sky, thin, and crooked, and hateful, a ruby the size of a house nestled on its head. Yet despite its struggle, it could not escape, and it sank back within the mountain, its corpse, burned and scorched, standing within its depths forever.*

"It is there that the fire took root, that the God of Iscara roosted, his eyes brighter than the furnace into which he stepped. The black, twisted creature became his temple, locked and hidden away except to those who already knew the way in. Deep down, in the crust of the mountain, the Jewel of Iscara sleeps, containing the mountain's wrath.

"Men of greed have long sought this gem, but none could survive the flames of Iscara, and gratefully. To take the ruby on the head of the great phoenix, or destroy it, would be to unleash the mountain's wrath. Be kind to Iscara."

"Why do you know so much about the mountain?" Oren asked. His mind was swimming from the immense amount of seemingly useless information he had been fed.

*"I am the mother of Iscara and her fury. I am **Luveria**."*

The name was strange, and carried a certain amount of grace. The being, apparently a woman, went silent and the flame writhed about in a flurry. The voice began to shout, anger rising in her tone.

"Oh, the foolishness of this age! How many have forgotten the old tongue, the way before? You are all ignorant, and it will drag you to destruction, crafted by your own weak, filthy hands!" she said, a roar rising up from her, shaking the pure white world they were in.

Fires sprang up from the ground, red and white, full of rage and sorrow. Oren stood rigid, for he could run nowhere, and the flames were consuming the ground. The sky bled into an inky orange color, swirling and twisting, bright, blinding light surging through the angry black cracks covering the air. Oren fell to his knees and covered his head, fear welling up inside him. The heat from the fires licked his skin greedily, and he thought for a moment that he must be turning crusty and black beneath its hateful embrace.

Suddenly, the heat faded away and his skin cooled considerably. He lifted his head and looked around. The sky was still an awful shade of orange, light streaming through dark, eerie cracks. The fires had vanished, and in front of him, as it had been before, was the small, feeble flame, red and white swiping the air softly.

"Forgive me," the woman's voice said, quiet and calm. "I had hoped — I had dreamed that perhaps you would be one so favored as to understand the tongue of the ancients. I was mistaken."

"What do you mean? I don't understand," Oren said, rising to his feet.

"The ancient tongue is not lost or dead. It lives, far, far away on **Irasemna**. *You will know of it, for all remember in time what they have lost or forgotten."*

"Your name," Oren began, "is Luveria. Is that — part of the ancient tongue?"

The woman laughed, sweet, melodious tones ringing out all around the orange world that was slowly melting back into white.

"Yes," the woman said.

Oren watched the flame carefully. "What does it mean?" he asked.

The voice of the woman did not answer, but after a while, it roared into existence, clear, strong, and powerful.

"Life," she said. "I am Life."

Oren awoke with a start, or at least, he thought he was waking up. Yet there he stood in the middle of the road, people passing him, everything the same. He didn't understand. He had been gone for what seemed like hours, yet he knew he couldn't have been. What was it he had seen? A vision? A daydream? No, it couldn't have been. Even now, as he looked towards the Mountain of Iscara, the great and fiery volcano, he could see it. Nestled at the top was a small white and red flame that stood out greatly against the orange glow from the volcano's mouth. Oren wondered if anyone else could see it. However, he couldn't ask, as a certain bear grabbed him by the sleeve and was tugging on him, concern etched into the big, brown eyes.

"Are you okay?" Ral asked.

Oren stared at him for a moment, his mouth numb and dry. Finally, after several minutes of licking his lips and flexing his jaw muscles, he found his voice.

"I'm fine."

Ral nodded and began walking towards the exit of the village. Oren called out his name and Ral turned in confusion.

"What is it?" the bear asked.

"Do you know a woman who calls herself *Luveria*?" Oren asked.

Ral's eyes widened. The bear was glued fast to where he was standing and everything in him went numb. "You met *Luveria*?" he said slowly.

"Do you know her?" Oren asked, his mind racing for answers.

Ral stammered slightly. "I'm afraid not," he said. "I've only heard of her in legends."

"What kind of legends?" Oren said, his curiosity growing by the second.

"The old legends, the ones that aren't told anymore. They are lost and forgotten to the ages. Even I can't clearly remember most of them." Ral said, his eyes narrowing with some hidden emotion.

Oren frowned but dropped the subject. It was very obvious to him that this was not something Ral wanted to talk about.

Syris ran down the road, huffing and puffing. He looked annoyed and a bit red.

"What's taking so long?" he fumed. "You keep telling me that we need to leave, so let's go!"

Ral regarded Syris for a moment, but ignored him in the end. The bear turned and began walking, Oren following closely behind. They made their way to the gate at the entrance of the village; the other end of the forest was still covered in cooled magma. Oren tied a rope around the bear's neck as he had done when they first came to the village. It helped people be more open to the thought of a wild animal roaming freely through their streets. Syris jogged to catch up with them and stared at Oren for a while.

"Is something wrong?" he asked.

Oren turned his head slightly. "No," he said. "Everything's fine. I'm just—confused a bit. There are many things I want to know, but no one says a word. I don't understand why everything is such a big secret."

Ral's ears twitched slightly. He picked up on Oren's tone. That last line was directed towards him.

Syris twisted slightly and pulled a bag around his

waist. From within it he pulled a monstrous book. It looked extremely heavy, was red and lined with gold, and had a large, brass lock on it. Syris grabbed a key in his sack and unlocked the front of the book, stuffed the key back into his bag, and open the book's first few thick pages. The page open appeared to be a table of contents.

"W-what is that?" Oren asked, eyes wide. He had never seen such a massive book in his entire life.

"It's a historical index. It tells us about species of animals, plants, genealogy and world evolution, contains a few maps, spells, and has the translation of ancient legends in it," Syris said.

Ral flinched, and Oren's insides were swimming with delight. He might actually get answers, for once. Ral turned his head to watch them, a growl rumbling from his throat. Oren ignored it and grabbed the book from Syris.

"What is it you're looking for?" Syris asked.

Oren flipped through the table of contents greedily. "Legends about mystic beings associated with fire. In particular, a being named Luveria."

Syris smiled. "That sounds familiar. Let me see."

He took the book from Oren and flipped through many pages. His face beamed when he found the desired page, then frowned when he read the text.

"What is it?" Oren asked.

"It says here that there was an ancient scroll that told the story of the beginning of the cosmos, however, the scroll was so tattered and worn that it could not be translated. The only words they could make out were '*Revil, Tereshal,* and *Luveria*'."

Oren's insides froze, yet his legs kept moving. *Luveria*

was there, in a legend about the beginning of the cosmos. She had told him that she was "the mother of Iscara and her fury". She said she was a mother. Oren pondered this, but he was distracted by the fact that there were two other words mentioned and, judging by the text in the book, they had been considered as titles, possibly names. So what was the translation of *Revil* and *Tereshal*? It was a shame that the scroll was so damaged that it could not be read.

"Is there anything else?" Oren asked, staring over Syris' shoulder to get a better look at the text. Syris inched away.

"It just lists some letters in a phrase that they made out. The rest was too damaged to be deciphered," he said.

Oren read the words.

"*A...r Me... a... sin... eia.* That makes no sense whatsoever!" he said, sighing in frustration.

"It's in a dead language. Of course it makes no sense, especially since the whole phrase isn't even visible." Syris said, a blank look on his face.

Ral growled more loudly than last time. "Can we move on?"

Oren and Syris looked at him, then at each other, and nodded silently. Syris locked the book and stuffed it back in his bag. The trio pressed on, leaving the village through the gate.

Syris' heart almost broke in two when he heard the gates clamp shut behind him. He thought of his mother, an old woman, much older than he remembered her being when he was a child. It was amazing, how much people changed over time. Yet Syris felt as if he hadn't changed at all, like he hadn't grown. He felt out of place, a boy in a man's body. Syris didn't belong, not here in his village, not with Oren and Ral, not anywhere. His heart was filling with darkness, the darkness of the void and the loneliness and sorrow of it.

When he slept, he dreamt of that darkness, closing in around him like an iron gauntlet, choking him. He could feel it cutting off his air, his lungs burning from the lack of oxygen, and his vision blurring with spots of color. It was a nightmare that he couldn't escape. Syris' thoughts were disrupted by Oren shoving him forwards.

"Keep moving. We need to keep up with Ral," Oren said.

Syris nodded and kept walking, looking back at the gate every now and then until he couldn't see it anymore. The trees closed in around him and he felt uncomfortable, so constricted and chained down. The tears were threatening to overflow, but Syris held them back, fighting his childish instincts. A soft, warm, furry head nudged his hand. Syris looked into two deep brown eyes.

"Is everything alright?" Ral asked, concern in his voice.

Syris stared at him and as he opened his mouth to speak, the floodgates in his eyes broke and tears ran down his face. His voice caught in his throat and the only sound he could make was small, painful wails of despair. Ral frowned out of sympathy and tried to console Syris. Oren watched from a distance. He felt sorry for him; he understood the pain Syris must be in.

"It's alright, Syris," Ral said soothingly. "It will all be worth it. I promise. You will not be alone, not ever."

Syris dried his eyes with the back of his hands. His bottom lip trembled with pent up emotion.

"I'm fine," he said, though his visage betrayed him. "I'll be fine."

The tears broke from within him again, but he ignored them and continued walking. Syris made it a point to walk ahead of everyone. He didn't want them to see him cry the whole way. The more they walked, the more the thought of time seemed to disappear. Before anyone knew it, night had fallen, and exhaustion was tugging at their eyelids. The crows were silent, flapping their black wings gently and ruffling their soft feathers.

Oren watched them in boredom. Walking through the woods was a pain. He saw the same things over, and over, and over again! Did the scenery ever change? Was there ever going to be a moment of thrill and excitement here? Probably not, for this was a simple forest, covered in ash. During the day, it was hot and smelled of smoke. During the night, it was cool and the scents faded away. The darkness was thick, but the light of the flames boiling within the Mountain of Iscara bounced off the top of the trees. It was dim, but the comfort of being able to see was greatly appreciated. However, there was still one thing that could be desired.

"I'm hungry!" Oren shouted, lagging behind the others slightly. His voice bounced off the close-knit trees and rang in Ral and Syris' ears.

"Do you see anything to eat? If you find some, please,

inform us immediately!" Ral shouted back. "Besides, Syris packed provisions before we left."

"Those are not for now!" Syris seethed. He looked back at Oren. "Why don't you ask the sword where to find food?"

Oren thought about this and grabbed the sword from his back where he had secured it with its chain. Ral said he'd bite off his head if he didn't carry it.

"Blitzkreg — Blitzkrick — Blitz — whatever your name is — do you know where we can find food here?"

The red designs swirled and twisted until a message became clear.

You are Not of Any Concern.

Oren shook the sword violently, yelling in protest to its answer. Syris slowed down and walked by Oren to see what the sword was saying.

"What is that supposed to mean? I'm insulted!" Oren said, glaring at the pure white sheath.

There is One Loyalty.

It is Not to You.

"Well, fine! Be that way. I'm not fond you either," Oren grumbled.

Then Why Do You Speak?

Why Do You Ask?

If You Want Not,

Then Why Does It Last?

"It talks back?" Syris said, eyeing Oren suspiciously.

"Yes," Oren fumed. "It's rude to speak in riddles!"

There is No Thought.

Not of Right or Wrong.

There is Only One Function.

"Oh, really? Tell me, what function is that?" Oren seethed. Syris watched with mild amusement.

To Kill.

No words made it out of anyone's mouth. No one could think of what to say. The response from the sword was so blunt and cruel to them, their minds went blank.

Ral stared at Oren and Syris. "What **exactly** were you expecting? It was made for one purpose and one purpose only."

Oren looked up at Ral with wide eyes that were filled with confusion.

"It's not your friend, Oren. It doesn't have any feelings for **you**, not of regret or happiness, not of sorrow or anger. It does what it's told by its master, nothing more."

The sword shook violently, and Oren dropped to the ground in shock. Slowly, it floated upright and turned, facing Ral. Oren and Syris stepped back, afraid of the sentient, and now mobile, weapon. Line after line of text appeared and disappeared.

You Assume Too Much.

You, the Foolish Son of Lightning and War.

A Weapon With No Feeling Would Obey None.

Not the Creator of Perdiasic or Heaviant,

Nor An Angel of Heaviant,

Nor Even a God That Rules Gods.

Regret is in the Souls of the Dead,

Their Hatred a Flame,

Their Sorrows an Ocean,

Their Happiness a Vivid Memory.

You Who Assume Much, Yet Know Little.

You Will Burn.

The God of Gods Will See to it,

Should You Fail Again.

You Will Not be Forgiven a Second Time.

The air was frozen. Oren could practically see the moisture in the atmosphere solidify. Blitzkrieg was not pleased with Ral and had gone to dramatic lengths to make that known. Syris was staring with an open mouth.

Oren flicked his cheek. "Try not to swallow any bugs."

Syris glared at him, but focused again on the sword. "I've never heard of Perdiasic or Heaviant. What is that?

"Perdiasic is supposedly "Hell" in the ancient language. Heaviant might be —"

In Your Language,

Heaviant Translates to "Heaven".

"There you go," Oren said, patting Syris' arm.

Ral was unmoving and his heart was beating at such a slow pace, it seemed it would stop any moment. His feet felt like iron, stuck fast to the ground. It occurred to him that Oren and Syris were not being fazed by the aura the sword was giving off because it was not directed at them.

To Ral, the air and ground were shaking, power radiating all around him. The bark of trees near the sword began to crack and split. A branch broke and fell down, narrowly missing Oren, who stumbled away in surprise.

"Forgive me," Ral said when he found his ability to speak.

The aura slowly evaporated, slithering back into the sword, likes snakes, ready to strike at any moment if provoked further.

"I should not be so bold," Ral mumbled, lowering his head.

Do Not Forget, Son of Lightning.

She Owns Your Soul,

And if You Should Misstep,

She Will Take it From You.

Piece by Piece,

Till You Shatter.

Ral tried to smile, but his courage was being eaten away by fear. "What, no clever riddles?"

Blunt Words are the Only Effective Speech.

You are Too Prideful.

"I'm insulted. Look, my feelings have been hurt. Can't you tell?" Ral said sarcastically.

He was pushing his luck with the sword, trying to win a fight he knew he had already lost, but Blitzkrieg was right in one regard. Ral was prideful and did not easily submit, least of all to a hunk of tempered steel. However, the sword did not answer this time. It fell to the ground with an echoing thud and the words spiraled back into designs. Oren picked it up cautiously and secured it to his back.

"You shouldn't insult him," Oren whispered to the blade.

It didn't answer with words, but it shook slightly. Oren could feel the aura seeping off of it. Indifference. Blitzkrieg couldn't care less about what anyone thought, especially Ral. What it had said was true. The sword had one loyalty and it was not to any of them.

"I seriously hope we don't meet your owner. I bet she's a royal pain in the neck, and just as indirect when speaking," he said, ruffling his hair.

The sword let out a small wave of emotion and sound. Laughter. Oren didn't think it was possible for a weapon to laugh, but perhaps having a consciousness made all sorts of improbable things possible. If the sword could feel what the souls of the dead had felt, then it could probably simulate an emotion it believed was an appropriate response to a question or statement. It intrigued Oren quite a bit.

Ral interrupted Oren's quiet pondering. "Let's go. We still have a long journey ahead of us. Don't worry; you'll get plenty of chances to talk to it along the way."

Oren and Syris smiled and followed closely behind Ral.

"So," Syris said cheerfully as he walked, "what did it mean when it said you wouldn't be forgiven a second time? Did you piss someone off?"

Ral grunted in annoyance. "It's none of your concern," he said. "Leave me be. I'm trying to concentrate."

"Concentrate on what?" Oren asked, confused. There was nothing around them worth concentrating on.

"I'm focusing on where we're going!" Ral yelled, growing impatient. "The next marker ought to be here, but everything has changed so much I can't tell what's what anymore!"

Oren patted his side softly. Ral's temper was unsettling.

"It's alright," Syris said. "I have maps if we get lost."

"Those maps are over 50,000 years old," Ral growled. "They're useless. The terrain and climate has changed since then, not to mention that most of those maps are of places on other worlds."

Oren lurched to an abrupt halt. "What do you mean 'other worlds'?" he said, eyes lighting up with curiosity.

Ral ignored him and continued walking. Oren pouted, exhaling loudly through his nostrils.

"What did you expect?" Syris said with a coy smile on his face.

DEATH'S RIVER

–If there are any words that can still be spoken with a peaceful mind, I have no understanding of what they are. I am filled with ire, such as I have never known before. It washed over me like a dam breaking open, crushing me inside. I destroyed all that I saw. My student used hateful words against me, and tried to curse me with a spell. I lashed out with power and fury, filling all who watched with fear and awe through its terror and beauty. My dear companion ran out to stop me before I could destroy my student, but the surrounding area suffered greatly. No fire from hell could scorch the ground as black as I did today. My love came to soothe me later. "It will be alright. I promise," he said. I wish I could have faith in those words, but I know the future. I know it, and there is no escaping what is to come.

To be honest, Oren expected people to be more open. He expected honesty and trust considering that he, Ral, and Syris would be traveling together for who knew how long. It seemed highly illogical to always be so evasive about everything. Why was all knowledge Ral had such a secret? Fortunately, Syris had an all-knowing book to give him information, Oren had a living sword strapped to his back, wrapped in flowing, silver silk, and they had obtained a psychic paper – apparently called an Alotom – that could give information on any and every one. Of course, that was only if you were on its records. Judging from the snide remarks of Syris' Alotom, Ral definitely had someone keeping a log of him. Who was it? Who would use so much precious time writing little riddles and poems about the grumpy, fluffy bear? It made Oren's head spin. Everything made his head spin as of late. There was so much he didn't know, so much he had never even imagined or considered. If his father could see him now he'd laugh till he cried.

"Close your mouth," Ral's gruff voice said. "It'd be a shame if you choked on a bug."

It took Oren a moment to realize that his mouth was slightly open. He shut it and licked his now dry lips. Oren watched the bear walk back and forth between trees, small growls of frustration bouncing off the rough bark and floating through the air. Syris walked up beside Oren and chuckled softly.

"This would go by much faster if you'd just take a look at the maps!" Syris called to Ral. Ral responded by kicking a tree which was followed by a jumble of words that no one understood.

"What did he say?" Oren asked, turning his head slightly to face Syris.

"I have no idea. Something about 'foreign foliage' and

'waterlogged paw-pads'," Syris said. A great sigh escaped him as he reached around his waist and took out the large book that was so carefully wrapped in wax-paper.

Oren watched with fascination as Syris flipped through the leather-bound book, colors, shapes, and extremely fancy writing flitting past in blurs. Syris began to slow down the turning of pages, and smiled when he came to his desired text.

It was a series of maps graphing many different areas, stretching across two pages. Syris slid a finger across the page searching for a particular map, and when he found it he grabbed a set of pages and slammed them down. Oren raised an eyebrow in slight confusion. The picture Syris had so dramatically flipped to was an enlarged version of a map on the previous page.

Oren could see the blurry lines of trees. He could also see the faded, swooping lines of rivers and streams that flowed into a large lake. He saw a red mountain looming over a grey-ish colored land, with a land of white behind it. On either side of this grey-ish land were two other provinces. One was colored a lighter shade of black, and the other was a rich brown.

"Is that where we are?" Oren asked with wonder. "Are we in this grey-ish part?"

Syris smiled and nodded. "Yes. This is the ash forest, and over here is the frost forest. The black section is the dead forest, and the brown section is the terra forest." Syris smoothed the page's curled corners and traced a river with his finger. "If this is still accurate, this river comes from around the volcano and," he roamed the page slowly with his eyes, "merges with this second river, which runs down," his eyes left the book and scanned the forest around him, "here. It should pass right by us. Then it flows over into a lake in the frost forest. If we follow the river a ways and then branch off to the south before we reach the border, we should meet this brown land."

Ral swerved around and rushed up to look at the map. He followed the river's path and then gave a great huff. "We'll have to branch off sooner than that. If we go all the way into the brown province, we'll completely overstep our next destination."

Oren and Syris stared at Ral quizzically. "Where are we going, exactly?" they asked in unison.

Ral looked back at them, and sighed. "If you must know, we are not going anywhere, really. Our next stop is—in between shrine villages, the mid-way points where no one lives. It's here." Ral pushed his big moist nose against a part of the page.

Syris and Oren squinted their eyes. A small and oddly-shaped area came into focus. Its color was a mixture of pale brown and deep green.

"What is that?" Syris asked.

Ral gave a low grunt. "That's where we need to go, if I can find the way."

"So we're going to take a nap in a place with no one nearby? My, what a safe and logical suggestion!" Oren sneered.

"I'm beginning to question the validity of this trip we're taking," Syris mused.

Ral looked at the two boys in annoyance. "Is something wrong?"

Oren straightened. "Yes, there is. You won't tell us

what we're supposed to be doing here. What's the point if we don't know? How are we supposed to succeed if we have no idea the importance of our goal?"

Ral stared at him a moment, then sighed deeply. "Fine," he huffed. Ral sat down, and the boys did the same.

"Story time," Syris whispered to Oren.

"You both know of the Goddess of Origin. You both know that she is the creator of the universe, and is frequently called "Mother" by people who believe in her. In truth, she has many titles, some rather rude. You both also know of the God of Rage. Origin and Rage went to war thousands of years ago, supposedly on this planet, in fact. The destruction was immense. Rumor has it that an entire planet was destroyed from our solar system, though that's never been confirmed. The war between these two beings ended in a draw. Origin did not succeed in killing Rage, and likewise, Rage did not succeed in killing Origin. Origin was weakened significantly before their final fight, but she still managed to seal Rage away. However, because of the strain it put on her, Origin's powers divided and left her, and she became a mortal being."

Syris raised an eyebrow. "What does that have to do with us?"

Ral looked up at the sky. "She's still alive, after thousands of years. Origin still walks the earth in her mortal state, kept alive through the power of the other gods and goddesses. She seeks to find her powers again."

"Why does it matter?" Oren asked.

Ral looked at both boys, his face stoic. "The seal on Rage will not hold."

Oren and Syris recoiled slightly. "What do you mean?"

Ral took a deep breath. "The seal Origin put on Rage is imperfect, because she was imperfect at the time of their fight. She was already turning mortal when she battled him, which is why she was unable to kill him. The other gods and goddesses knew this, which is why they've kept her alive. One day, and soon, Rage will break out of his prison to finish what he started. That is where you two come in."

Oren and Syris looked at each other, perplexed.

"The two of you are now messengers for Origin. Our goal, our purpose in this journey, is to find Origin in her mortal state, and aid her in recovering her powers. Once we do, we will fight alongside our goddess in a final confrontation with Rage."

Oren and Syris couldn't process what they were being told. It was outrageous!

"First," Ral began, "we must find the vessel."

"The vessel?" Oren said.

"Yes. The vessel. Origin cannot obtain her powers with her mortal hands. Thusly, a vessel was created, one that could carry the essence of her powers to her, and then merge with Origin. We must find the vessel. Then, we will seek out all the remnants of Origin's powers and return them to her. Along the way, we'll gain more companions."

"Do we need more people?" Syris groaned.

"Yes," Ral said. "Each power of Origin's is linked to an element. Each element must have a human host to coordinate it with the vessel. Thusly, our group of two, not including me, will most likely expand to a group of eight."

Oren shook his head. "Wait. There's nine elements, aren't there? There's fire, ice, water, electricity, wind, earth, light, shadow, and rage. Shouldn't there be nine of us?"

Ral mused for a moment. "Technically, yes. However, there is no host for rage, nor is there a need."

"What do you mean?" Oren asked.

"The reason that the God of Rage was so much stronger than the other gods and goddesses, strong enough to rival Origin, is because he was trained differently."

"What do you mean?" Syris said. The story was getting more complicated by the minute.

"Aros, the God of Fire, was mortal once, as were the other eight apprentices. Aros had a natural penchant for fire magic. Thusly, upon becoming a God, all Origin had to do was train him to better use, understand, and control his abilities on a much larger scale. The same goes for the other apprentices, except the God of Rage. The God of Rage, while mortal like all the others, did not have a connection with any element. In order to train him, Origin had to physically **give** him her power. She separated the power of rage from within herself and merged it with him. Because of this, he was artificially enhanced, made to be stronger than the others. However, the power of rage is twisted and deadly, and it corrupted Origin's apprentice into the horrible being he is now. That is why Origin was weakened, because she had literally, physically given away a piece of herself.

"That is why we will not have a ninth person in our group. There is no rage to obtain for our vessel. It is physically inside of the God of Rage. The only way to get it back is to let him awaken, and then take it from his body."

Oren and Syris were shaking, both in excitement, fear, and disbelief. Ral stood up, watching the two boys quiver.

"Are you alright?" the bear asked.

Syris turned to Oren slowly. "We're gonna die."

Oren looked back at Syris. "We get to fight a **god**."

"We're gonna die!" Syris wailed again.

"We get to meet the Goddess of Origin!" Oren screeched.

Ral backed away, unsure of what to make of these vastly different reactions. "Come on, you two. We need to move."

"You're trying to kill us!" Syris shouted, pointing an accusing finger at the bear.

Ral ignored him and started plodding along slowly, sniffing the ground for any traces of a dried river-bed scent. Once or twice, he rammed his head into a tree. It was slightly frustrating, hearing Oren and Syris' smothered laughter every time he did. You'd think they'd never seen someone hit their head before. You would have thought that perhaps they'd hit their own heads in the past!

Syris watched, his brows furrowed up in a sympathetic way and a slight smile on his face, as Ral paced around the ashy ground. The bear sneezed every now and again when ash flew into his large nostrils. Yet the sneezing seemed to be just what Ral needed. Whether he cleared out his sinuses and was able to smell better, or his sneezing cleared some ash and gave him access to the forest floor, Ral suddenly caught a scent of the long-dried river bed. It was earthy and moist, mixed with decay and mold. Ral's nose crinkled slightly, and then he turned his head round to Syris and Oren.

"I found it," he said. "There's no water on the surface, but an underground vein of water still runs all the way to the lake. However, I'm not sure where its original source is."

Syris looked down at his map. "I can't see the river head, only where it ends. It could be coming from the mountain, or the ocean. I'm not sure."

Oren placed his hands on his hips and marched forward. "The point is we found the river. Now all we have to do is follow it to the border!" Oren stuck a finger out in front of him, pointing in the direction he assumed the river would flow.

Ral chuckled, swaying his body back and forth to free ash from his heavy coat. "Actually," he said slowly, moving Oren's arm with his nose," it's in **that** direction." Oren's face went slightly red. Syris laughed.

Ral put his nose to the ground and began walking, sniffing as he went. Oren and Syris followed closely behind. Syris started waddling, his legs spread apart on either side of what he imagined to be the river's edge. Ral looked back and gave a snort.

"It's wider than that."

Syris spread his legs a little more. Oren saw him cringe in pain as his legs muscles tensed.

"Wider," Ral said, an amused smile on his face.

Syris looked up in shock. "I can't go any farther!"

Oren sighed. "Syris, you could do a full spilt and still not be wide enough to reach either side of the river bank."

Syris frowned, and he shakily put his legs underneath him, standing back up to his full height. Oren turned his head slightly to address Syris.

"Is there anything in your book about the river?" he said.

Syris grunted as he pulled the heavy book from his satchel. Oren waited as Syris searched its pages. He looked at the forest around them, ashen and gray. The leaves were a pale-green with brown around the edges. The bark was black near the ground, and it extended upwards towards the tree tops in ridged, ugly cracks. It looked like a disease, like some evil being was possessing the trees bit by bit. Oren felt the hairs on the back of his neck go upright. He felt like he was being watched, and it unnerved him. Oren jumped slightly when Syris' voice cut the air.

"There is one thing, though it's not very helpful."

"What is it?" Ral said, his nose still pressed to the ground.

"Well," Syris began. He seemed nervous. "It's just a bunch of nonsense, really. It says that the river was a passage for spirits of death, called Shiga. It says they followed the river to all the Shrine villages and picked up lost souls along the way. Then they bring them to—"

Oren waited for the next word. "To what?"

Syris' brows furrowed. He seemed disturbed.

"To what?" Oren said again.

"They bring the souls to two beings, called Floret and Hoarfrost. Floret judges the souls' worth and decides if they reach salvation or are condemned. Hoarfrost then escorts worthy souls to Heaviant and takes unworthy souls to Perdiasic. In some occasions, certain souls are escorted to the Void."

Oren raised an eyebrow. "What's the Void?"

Syris frowned. "It doesn't say."

Ral kept his nose to the ground, but he couldn't help being intrigued by the current subject being investigated. He had only heard mention of the Void once, and that was many years ago. He had never known what the Void was for, or even how things got there. It would seem you had to be dead to get in or be an escort for souls.

"Apparently," Syris began, "Floret and Hoarfrost have the ability to eat souls as well. It says here that they mostly go after the souls of those who contemplate suicide after the death of a loved one. Apparently, suicide is the shedding of innocent blood and is unforgivable. Any soul who commits suicide has no right to enter any kingdom, not the Void, not Heaviant, not even Perdiasic. Eating the souls allows them to be born again."

Oren tilted his head to one side. "Born again?"

"Yes," Syris said. "Apparently, if either Floret or Hoarfrost eat a soul, that soul will be reincarnated as another person, plant, or any other living entity. Through this, all souls have a chance to be worthily judged."

"So," Oren said. He had a childish glint in his eyes, "If I was eaten by one of those weird beings, I could reborn as a fish?"

Ral sighed heavily. "Yes, that's the general idea."

"Has anyone ever seen Floret or Hoarfrost? Have they seen one of those little spirits, the Shiga?"

"There are records of Hoarfrost and Floret being seen in graveyards. They say that they comfort little children during funerals. If it snows while you're visiting the deceased, they say Hoarfrost is nearby. Floret's presence is apparently marked by a shower of blossoms."

Oren looked up at the sky. "Very interesting. I'd like to meet them!"

"What makes you think they'd want to meet you?" Ral said, sneezing.

"Maybe they think his soul looks tasty!" Syris said, grinning.

Oren huffed, waving his hand dismissively. "You're just jealous that my soul is prettier than yours."

"I, for one, want to live a bit longer. Who knows, maybe it's possible to redeem one's soul." Syris said as he turned a page.

"What?" Oren said, walking backwards so he could face Syris. "Does your soul need saving?"

Syris looked up. "It might," he said. "What about your soul? How do we know that you're not headed for certain damnation?"

Oren grinned. "I think I'm alright. I mean, yeah, I was a troublesome child, but that's all water under the bridge by now!"

"Is it?" Ral said, lifting his head slightly. He circled around a tree, following the smell of wet earth. "Hoarfrost and Floret might not see it that way. They may hold you accountable for past mistakes, even if you tried your very best to rectify them. You never know."

Oren frowned and turned back around to follow Ral. "What about you, Mr. Know-It-All?"

Ral's eyes narrowed. "What about me?"

"It has been made very apparent to me, through the words of a magic sword and a mystic paper, that someone, somewhere, has a bone to pick with you."

"Yes. What's your point?"

"You screwed up so badly that even things that aren't alive know about it! You must have pissed off the wrong person. Whatever you did, it was bad. It put you on a watch list that you can't get off. I wonder if Floret or Hoarfrost would have anything to say about that."

"If you find them, go ahead and ask. I personally don't think they exist," Ral muttered.

"You would think that, and you'd be wrong!" a small, young voice chirped.

Ral raised his head quickly and peered ahead of him. "Who are you?" he said.

Out of the trees stepped a small boy. He wore a ragged shirt with patched up pants. His shoes were flats and looked rather feminine on him. The boy's hair was thin and brown. It swayed in front of his face, partially hiding two warm, green eyes. All in all, the boy looked rather unkempt.

"I'm just a runaway slave," the boy said.

Oren scoffed. "Such honesty. Why did you run away?"

"My master is a demon. He is very evil. I was going to turn back, though."

"Why?" Syris said. "You ran from a demon, and now you're going to go back to him?"

"He still has my siblings captive."

"Why didn't you all run away together?"

The boy fidgeted. "Just one person leaving is difficult. If it had been lots of people, it would have been impossible!"

"This demon enslaves children?" Ral said skeptically.

"Yes!" The boy chirped. "Only children!"

"Then where does he get them from? Surely a mother would notice if a demon stole away her children."

"Some say that the children are already dead," the boy whispered. "Others say that they're some kind of doll."

"A doll?" Syris said.

"Yeah. Some say the demon makes dolls and then animates them!" the boy said.

Ral growled. "It would take an awful lot of magic to animate a hoard of dolls to do your bidding."

"Where is this demon?" Oren said.

The boy smiled. "He's in this **big** maze, with these huge traps, and it's really, really, **really** hard to get to him! He's super strong!"

Ral's ears twitched. "He's in a maze?"

"Yep!" the boy said.

"What does this maze look like? What does the entrance look like?"

"Well, its entrance is a huge set of doors that has cool swirls and designs all over them. The walls are covered in ivy, and there's this weird fountain on the other side of the maze."

Ral stared at the ground. He then turned to Oren and Syris. "We're following him," he said.

Oren and Syris looked extremely put out.

"He's a little kid!" Oren said. "You want us to follow **him**?"

"That boy," Ral growled quietly, "just so happens to have escaped from the very place we need to go!"

Oren peered over Ral's large body at the boy. "He said he escaped from a demon."

"Yes," Ral said.

"A demon that possibly enslaves and kills children, and is apparently very, very, **very** strong—"

"Yes, "Ral sighed.

"And you want us to go traipsing into the very place he risked his life to leave? Are you mad?" Oren seethed.

"I might be!" Ral said, his eyes cold. "He knows the way. So are you coming or not?"

Oren frowned. He sat on the ground for a while and thought. Syris sat next to him.

"I wonder what Hoarfrost and Floret would say if they knew you'd left a little boy's siblings to die at the hands of a demon." Syris cooed.

Oren gritted his teeth and got to his feet. "Fine!" he shouted. "We'll follow him and help him out."

Ral stared at Syris for a while, trying to decide if he should be awarded for convincing Oren to come with them. In the end, Ral could only think of all the times Syris had failed to live up to his expectations.

"Come on!" the boy said. "We have a very long way to go!"

Oren followed closely behind Ral. He began to take notice of their surroundings. The leaves were a little bit greener, and there wasn't nearly as much ash. As they continued to walk, the forest they were in was entirely without ash or snow. It was green and beautiful, truly alive.

"There is something you all should know before we get to the maze." The boy said.

Ral and the others eyed him.

"What is it?" Syris asked.

"It's a rhyme. It goes like this—"

The boy began reciting the rhyme over and over. He repeated it verbatim several times. Unfortunately, some people were starting to get a headache.

Chapter 9

THE ANCIENTS

– He's still weak, frail, and utterly unprepared to use this power. Yet, he constantly tries to wield it and fails every time. I subdue his abilities before he loses himself. He's the youngest student I have ever had, and also the most unruly, constantly testing my authority. "Why can't I just move on?" he says. "You're not ready. You can't even begin to comprehend what you're dealing with, what responsibilities you have." He's becoming more frustrated by the minute. I sense confusion in his soul.

Tick, tock, a murderous clock.
Grind, grate, a demon in wait.
Clank, wind, another dead swine.
Click, crash, a metallic clash.
Snip, snap, a child's back.
Father Time's tree is what you'll see.

"Enough!" Oren yelled. He raised a hand.

"Stop it, Oren!" Syris said.

He grabbed Oren's arm, and twisted it behind his back. Oren grabbed Syris' hair and flipped him onto the ground, grunting loudly. Syris kicked Oren's legs out from under him, rolled on top of him, and planted a knee on his chest. Oren reached up, and with a swift turn and jerk, dislocated Syris' shoulder. Syris screeched in pain, falling backwards. Oren then wrapped his arms around Syris' elbow, ready to snap it.

"Stop!"

A flash of fur sent them both rolling in the dust. Oren lifted himself slowly and met Ral's brown eyes.

"What is the matter with you two?" Ral hissed.

"I just want that stupid boy to shut up!" Oren said, pointing past Syris at their new guide.

The boy looked rather alarmed. He wasn't quite sure what he had done wrong. "I told you that I had a rhyme for you. They say repetition is key to learning, so I thought that the more you heard it, the better!"

"I don't need to hear it twenty times. Once was enough! Now it's just a broken record!" Oren seethed. He glared at Syris.

"Maybe you don't," Ral said. "Maybe you don't need to hear it twenty times. Maybe you need to hear it two hundred times, or two thousand times, or two hundred thousand times!"

Oren shrank beneath Ral's malevolent gaze. The boy watched the scene before him with curiosity and confusion.

"Sorry," Oren said, lowering his head. He felt the

sword on his back shake slightly. It was amused. Oren turned his head to leer at it.

"Will you please just convince him to stop chanting that ridiculous rhyme?" Oren muttered.

"Did you think slapping him would make him stop?" Ral said.

"Apparently," Syris muttered.

Oren growled. For a moment, he was tempted to unsheathe Blitzkrieg and go after Syris with it. The only thing that stopped him was the knowledge that he could die if he tried to wield the weapon.

Ral went over to Syris, and without warning, grabbed his shoulder and popped the joint back in place. Syris screamed; the pain seared white hot for a few moments, and then vanished completely. Syris massaged his shoulder, trying to ignore its soreness.

"You should have left it the way it was," Oren hissed. He paused. "How did you do that, anyway? You don't have opposable thumbs."

"Practice makes perfect," Ral said quickly.

"I am very sorry if I have annoyed you at all," the boy whispered.

"Believe it or not, Oren, that rhyme is what's going to keep you alive," Ral growled.

This puzzled Oren. This rhyme would save them? That was complete balderdash. How could a rhyme do that? Of course, Oren – unlike Syris – knew better than to ask Ral that. After all, it was Ral's rule not to. Mind you, no one knew why that rule was made in the first place. Oren sighed. This was starting to become a real pain. He ran the poem through his head over and over.

Tick, tock, a murderous clock.

It's a clock that murders. How? Clocks count time. Is it a clock that kills by counting down on people's lives?

Grind, grate, a demon in wait.

"Grind, grate". Was it the sound of gears turning? There's a demon in wait. Perhaps the demon guards the gears?

Clank, wind, another dead swine.

"Clank, wind". Something is hit producing the clank, but what's the wind? Then there's another dead swine. A pig is killed in the process. Why?

Click, crash, a metallic clash.

"Click, crash". Something locks into place and then something falls? A metallic clash. Something falls down on a metal piece. But what?

Snip, snap, a child's back.

"Snip, snap". Something breaks. Does the child's back break? Why does it break?

Father Time's tree is what you'll see.

Wait. This sounded familiar. Father Time's tree is what you'll see. So Father Time has a tree? Then why are there gears and clocks? Is it a metallic tree? Could it be a tree with a clock built inside of it? It could be a Tree of Time. That was it!

"It's Father Time's legendary Hands of Discord!" Oren sang out.

Three sets of eyes looked at him in wonder.

Ral grinned. "Very good, Oren! You solved the riddle," he said.

"But I thought the Hands of Discord were destroyed ages ago," Syris said. "And how do you know about that?" he sneered at Oren.

Oren glared back. You're not the only student here."

"Well, the Hands were destroyed," the small boy interrupted.

All heads turned to him.

"Go on," Oren urged.

The boy shuffled nervously. "Well, you see, a few years ago, someone found the pieces and put it back together, but—"

"But what?" Syris said, agitated.

"The pieces were originally inside of Father Time himself and due to the lack of an energy source to feed off, the clock wouldn't start, so—"

"So get on with it!" Syris yelled.

The boy flinched at the harshness of his voice.

"So they put it in a tree they had planted in the center of the Maze of Distortion. I don't know anything except for that." the boy said shrilly.

"How do you know this, young one?" Ral asked.

"*Snip snap, a child's back.* Children are taken and forced

to pull cartloads of crushed pig meat to the guardian demon, Tharazar," the boy said.

"What does Tharazar guard?" Oren asked.

"Most likely Father Time's soul. When Father Time was alive, the Hands of Discord were inside of him and fed off him, the gears turning endlessly. It wouldn't surprise me if even after he was blown to pieces that the clock kept a firm grip on some part of him. Without it, the clock would rust and disintegrate," Ral explained.

"Then Tharazar is the demon who enslaves the children? He lives inside the maze?" Oren said, bewildered.

"Yes," Ral said.

"So the demon guards the soul so that the clock won't stop ticking. Why does he even want the stupid thing?" Syris said.

"Perhaps he wants control over time."

"No. That's not the purpose of the clock," the little boy said.

They looked at him again, puzzled.

"The clock killed Father Time, but it also preserved him. Tharazar is using the clock to turn his remaining time backwards and sustain his life. He's dying and doesn't have much of it left. The clock can prolong him," The boy explained.

"Yes. Nevertheless, he's condemning himself to death. It would be easier to seek out the answer for gaining immortality," Ral said.

"How so?" Syris asked.

"When the clock finally stops ticking, time speeds up for however long you slowed it down," the boy said.

"So when the Hands of Discord are gone—" Syris began.

"Then Tharazar will instantly age however many years he turned back, resulting in his immediate death," Oren finished.

"Precisely," Ral said.

"And does Tharazar know this?" Syris asked.

"Most likely, otherwise he wouldn't protect the Hands of Discord so fiercely. He knows without them, he'll die," the boy said.

"Why is Father Time so important, anyway?" Oren asked.

Ral wiggled his nose. "If you must know, he was once a good friend of the Goddess of Origin."

Oren's eyes bugled. "You're serious?"

Ral stared at him, clearly not amused. "Very serious. He was her trusted colleague, and her adviser for wartime implements — her **battle strategist**. Origin is omnipotent in wisdom and intelligence, but she thought it might be fun to have a less omnipotent outsider make those kinds of choices for her. Needless to say, he was excellent at his job, never losing a fight until the day he was killed. That being said, there were other reasons for his hiring."

Oren raised an eyebrow. "Those reasons would be?"

Ral looked up at the sky. "Origin loves her people, all people, as if they were her children. But all children must be punished when they step too far out of line. Origin's punishments were — how to say this — a bit extreme. She was always at her best when inflicting pain on others."

Syris frowned. "A sadist?"

"No!" Ral retorted. "She never took pleasure in what

she did, but if she was going to do anything at all, she was going to be thorough. Sometimes too thorough."

Everyone tried picturing what horrible punishments Origin could dish out. Oren's mind immediately jumped to the Hell he often dreamed of, with the disembodied voice.

"A living Hell," he muttered to himself.

Ral's ears perked up upon hearing this, but he said nothing.

"To be honest," the young boy began, not sure about the atmosphere, "I brought you three here cause I thought maybe you could get rid of Tharazar and the Hands for me. I want to go home, but my brother and sisters are still working for the beast. Please, you have to help!"

The trio looked at each other, then back at the boy. That pleading face was **so** convincing. The three huddled in a small circle.

"What should we do? W-what? Syris, why are you crying?" Oren whispered harshly.

"I'm sorry. I'm a sentimental crier. Don't judge!" Syris sobbed.

"Ugh. You're a hopeless, stupid old man," Oren seethed.

"Quiet, both of you. We need the boy to guide us, and from the looks of it, we have no choice but to help. Besides, it will be good fighting experience for you both," Ral said.

"What? You can't be serious!" Syris and Oren shouted in unison.

"I am. Suck it up or go home, not that you have a home to go to."

"Wait," Oren said, confused. "I thought we already decided on this earlier. We were going with him. Why are we reintroducing this discussion?"

"Because we need to keep our goal fresh in our minds," Ral lied.

Oren grumbled angrily, and Syris picked at a leather strand on his boots.

"Fine! We'll go," Oren said.

"What? Come on. Don't give in that easily." Syris said.

Oren ignored him and turned towards the boy. "It's decided. We'll help you out."

"Really? Thank you so much!" the boy chimed, a grin the size of a mountain appearing on his face.

"I'll tell you all about the Hands of Discord, the Maze of Distortion, Tharazar, and the tree on the way!" the boy said.

"You do that," Syris said. He suddenly screamed.

"What?" Oren said frantically.

"It's a spider!" Syris screeched.

Ral, Oren, and the boy sighed in disbelief.

"It's just a harmless tarantula!" the boy piped.

"Like heck it is!" Syris fumed.

"Keep walking," Ral said, head drooping.

The three began to continue onward.

"Ew. Hey, where're you going? Don't leave me here. Hey, guys! Ew! The spider is touching me! Get it off! " Syris wailed.

Oren began to notice the effects of the sleep Syris had been in. While Syris had matured physically, he was still a little kid emotionally. Syris' shouts were getting fainter and fainter as the trio progressed. It seemed like forever before they heard the ground shaking footsteps behind them.

"Wait!" Syris shouted.

He ran up fast as a gazelle, brushing away twigs and leaves off his clothes.

"What's that sound?" Ral asked.

Syris didn't answer but kept running fast as he could. The thundering grew louder.

"What on earth?" Oren yelled.

"It's pigs!" the boy screeched.

Indeed, there were pigs. There were hundreds of them. They were brown, pink, white, speckled, and black. There were sows and babies, too. Indeed, there were all sorts of pigs, and not just pigs, but ferocious boars with deadly tusks were streaking down the forest path. Oren grabbed the boy and scrambled into a tree. Syris did the same, while Ral did his best to stay out of their way. The squeals filled the dead air while they shot past unbelievably fast. When the dust had settled, Oren inched down the tree trunk.

"What was that?" he gasped.

"Maybe some pigs got away from Tharazar," the boy said.

"Where's Syris?" Ral asked.

"Right here," he said.

Syris was still in his tree, hands gripping a branch.

"Get out of there!" Ral said.

"I would if I could, but—"

"But what?" the boy giggled.

"My finger nails — won't — come out," Syris said, big

crocodile tears bubbling into view. He had held onto the tree for dear life and had gotten his fingers stuck inside the large cracks that ran through the tree's bark.

"No. I think we'll leave you there. You complain too much, anyway," Ral said.

Syris' eyes grew wide and his face turned pale. "W-what? No, please! Don't leave me here!"

Oren clamped his hands over his ears, his teeth clenched together. "Please, make him shut up!" he raged over Syris' whining.

Of course, Syris squirmed around and cried so much, his nails unstuck, and he fell to the pig trampled ground with an echoing thud.

"Nope," Ral said.

"No what?" Oren asked.

Ral glared at him. "You two break the 'No Questions' rule a lot without realizing it."

"I know I'm breaking it. I just don't care," Oren said bluntly.

Syris and Ral were speechless. They walked away in silence.

"Wow. Is that how people his age talk?" the boy said.

"What's your name?" Oren asked the boy, ignoring the slightly degrading comment.

"Huh? Um — it's — well, I don't know my name," he said.

"What? Then what would you like to be called?" Oren said.

"Is Setch okay? It was my dad's name."

Oren suddenly felt sad. Here was a boy who knew his

father's name, but not his own. Oren hadn't ever thought that such a pitiful circumstance could ever exist.

"Yeah. Setch is a perfect name," Oren said, smiling.

The boy ran towards Ral and Syris, shouting out his new name. Oren watched him. He wondered if he remembered anything about his own father. His father's name was – Oren didn't know, but Oren did know that he loved him. Now all Oren wanted was to give this boy, Setch, the love he would probably never get.

"This sucks," Oren grumbled.

What was his dad's eye color, hair color, name, face texture, voice tone, or anything? What did his mom look like in the paintings? They were memories that had been lost and forgotten, never to be seen, never to be reached for again. Oren had only just scratched the surface of the deep mystery behind it all.

"Origin," he said, "if you really are out there, then please, help us to remember. There are so many important things out there, even though they may seem small and insignificant at times. So please, help us."

Oren waited for a whisper, or a gust of wind, or something, but there was nothing. Not even a warm rush through his body. Oren sighed, then rushed towards Setch.

"Lead the way!" he said.

Setch pranced ahead of them, naming everything he saw. He was full of knowledge, that little boy. Oren couldn't believe that one head could hold so much. He could barely remember a four-digit number. Oren carefully followed Setch as they weaved through the forest foliage.

He didn't have any real idea as to where they were headed, but he trusted in the knowledge of his new little friend.

"Oren, you're too slow!" Ral said.

Oren nodded, and sped up to keep time with the ever impatient bear.

"I hope you're ready," Ral said quietly.

Oren stared at him quizzically. "Ready for what?"

Ral lowered his head. "Ready to be disappointed. I hope you're ready to be betrayed, and left feeling like a rotten slab of meat."

Oren said nothing. He didn't understand why Ral was saying these things. "Is something wrong?" he asked.

Ral sighed. "No, nothing is wrong. Not yet, anyway." The bear watched Syris weave through the trees. "I just have this odd little inkling that I'm being deceived."

Oren gave a strangled cough. "Who would be stupid enough to do that?"

"Not you, obviously. It is not a matter of stupidity, but rather a matter of motive. What does this person gain from being dishonest? That is the real question."

"It might help if I knew who you were talking about."

"You don't need to know right now. You need to focus on one thing and one thing only. That thing would be keeping your head firmly mounted upon your neck."

Oren massaged his neck warily. "Is someone planning to take it off?"

Ral's eyes narrowed slightly. "Who can say? Maybe they'll start with your feet instead."

Oren looked fully taken aback. His mouth opened and shut like a fish; he was truly at a loss for words.

Ral bobbed his head. "Forgive me. I am just unsettled."

Oren straightened his back. "You seriously need to relax. This stress can't be good for your old, bear bones."

Ral looked at Oren from the corner of his eye. "I am sensing a joke in that statement."

Oren raised his hands in a sign of submission. "No, no! There's no joke at all! It's very clear to me that you are old, and you are bear. Due to that, it is logically — if childishly — concluded that you have old, bear bones."

Ral huffed. "How would you know if I'm old? Maybe where I come from, I am still considered an infant, completely dependent on the mercies of others."

Oren gave this idea a bit of thought, and then looked at Ral with a strange mock-humor. "Are you?"

"Am I what?" Ral said, bracing himself for the inevitable.

"Are you — a squabbling infant?"

Ral jerked his head up in alarm. "To be an infant is one thing. To be a squabbling infant is another matter entirely, and I assure you that squabbling is not one of my activities!"

Oren gave a light laugh. "Alright, calm down. You don't have to get so riled up!"

Ral sighed as he tried to ignore the perplexed stare from Syris. He had heard part of the conversation, but had only caught small bits of it. The information Syris had compiled from those small bits was very strange.

"Is there something I should be aware of?" Syris asked as he followed closely behind Setch.

Ral gave a toothy grin. "If I told you, I would have to acquaint your facial features with a wall repeatedly in order to make you forget."

Syris' eyes widened considerably. Setch turned his head slightly, his eyes also wide. Oren looked at Ral with mild concern.

"In other words," Ral shook his body like a wet dog, "it's classified."

Oren narrowed his eyes. "You seriously need to chill."

Ral smirked as much as a bear could smirk. "Silence. I'm trying to savor the moment."

Syris whipped around in shock. "What moment? You just threatened to bash my head in!"

Ral looked up at Syris with a mixture of boredom and amusement. "Precisely. I'm savoring your reaction to my reacting to your reaction on a conversation that honestly had nothing to do with you."

Syris pursed his lips. "How very kind of you." There was a hint of anger in his voice.

Ral lowered his head. "You're quite welcome, little grasshopper."

Syris opened his mouth to retort, but his words were drowned out by a deafening, mechanical roar. Ral looked up into the sky, fear stretching his face, his sharp teeth glinting in the sunlight. Setch and Syris covered their ears, and Oren watched Ral in confusion.

"Everyone get back!" Ral shouted. His brown eyes were wide and anxious.

No one questioned Ral or argued with him. Syris grabbed Setch, and they backed into the shadow of the trees. Oren crouched behind some bushes.

"No matter what, you all must stay there till I say otherwise," Ral ordered.

The roar died down after a while, but an eerie

humming replaced it. Oren could not see all of it, but a shadow descended upon Ral. It seemed to completely block out the sun. Ral bowed his head, keeping his eyes level to the ground. It took Oren every ounce of self-control he had to remain silent. Floating above Ral, Oren could see an immense, golden, head-like object. The head appeared to be connected to an even larger body, but Oren couldn't discern it from where he was.

In the center of the head was a large, white, glowing eye. The head itself was angular with sharp protrusions on either side. Oren heard steam hissing, and the sound of cogs and gears turning. There was a distinct clank of an axel dropping. The humming noise grew louder; it was an odd and intriguing sound.

Ral lifted his head warily, but his eyes remained fixed on the ground. "I thought your kind was under orders to stay within —" Ral gave a cautious glance to where Oren was hiding. "You were supposed to stay on the other side, or so I presumed."

The mechanical head drifted closer to Ral. A deep, grinding noise came from within it. Oren thought it almost sounded like a laugh. A pair of pointy, golden appendages drifted into view. One of them had a small spark crackling on its tip. It jabbed Ral in the side. Oren heard Ral growl deeply as a visible current of electricity raced over him. The other appendage had a small coating of refined steel on its tip. This appendage moved quickly across Ral's cheek, cutting him. Ral hissed and backed away in anger. The same grinding noise, presumably a laugh, echoed through the air.

The appendage that had cut Ral had a small drop of

blood on it. It retracted from view, and for a second the machine's eye glowed red.

"Why are you here?" Ral said quietly.

The head twisted on an unseen screw till it was upside-down. Again, the strange laugh echoed.

"Answer me!" Ral demanded, his voice rising.

The head spun back around at a furiously quick pace, and the machine rammed itself into Ral, knocking him over. Oren's entire body tensed, as if it was him who had just been hit.

"*Preve uor mesto, Ralshire, Viis zi Zightra.*" The machine's voice was deep and cold. It rang out as clear as a bell, loud and powerful.

Oren felt a horrible chill run up his spine. He didn't recognize those words. He had never come across them in any textbook. Oren turned his head to Syris, who shrugged upon meeting Oren's gaze. Syris quietly pulled out his large book and began carefully flipping through the index. Oren turned to look at Ral. How would the bear respond to such a creature who spoke a language that had never before been heard?

Ral lowered his head. "*Kortaria. Sem sa skira.*"

Another grinding laugh rang out; it seemed that this creature took pleasure in pushing the poor bear around.

"*Khyo con toris mers beir sons braft tal mira.*" The white eye of the machine brightened as it spoke.

Ral nodded meekly. "*Sok ua proim.*"

The machine's humming softened. A massive gust of wind knocked Oren off his feet. It was accompanied by the winding sound that filled the air, followed by the shrieking of gears. The massive, mechanical creature soared into the sky. A few minutes passed before no one could hear the humming any longer. Oren, Syris, and Setch warily made their way out from the trees.

"What was that thing?" Oren asked breathlessly. His nerves were fraying.

Ral shook his head. "It doesn't concern you."

"Like hell it doesn't!" Syris hissed. "That thing is ancient. I found it in my book. There are no drawings of it, nor is there any name by which to identify it, but they were supposed to be mere myths that were invented over 1.3 million years ago! **1.3 million years!** You expect me to just let this drop? This is historically upsetting!"

"What would you like to know?" Ral shouted. "Would you like me to tell you that those machines were originally designed for war? Would you like to hear how just two of them could wipe out a large portion of an entire army within minutes? Or would you like to know how some of them, not all, have since retired from the war business to patrol highroads and cities, searching for traitors and war criminals so they can grind them up and use their bones for making cinderblocks?" Ral was beyond anger.

Syris backed away, not wanting to provoke the upset bear.

"Why did you tell us to hide? We're not traitors or criminals," Oren asked calmly.

Ral looked at Oren with heavy, tired eyes. "Those things are not kind. They make a mockery of life because they are incredibly hard to kill. It literally takes a god-fire furnace to make them, and very little else has the ability to take them apart. All of that aside — it knew you were there. It didn't mention it, but the machine knew where you were all hiding. I suppose it was a childish effort, making you all conceal yourselves. I simply didn't want you to be subjected to the creature's madness."

Oren looked down as another thought entered his mind. "Why did it take your blood? What the heck is a god-fire furnace?"

Ral sighed. "For cataloging. That's all I can say on that matter. Concerning a god-fire furnace, it's literally what it sounds like: a furnace used for blacksmithing, lit with fire from the mouth of Origin herself. It's an incredibly strong brand of enchantment."

"What does that even —" Syris began.

"That's enough!" Ral's voice raised. "We're falling behind schedule. Setch, please lead the way."

"Wait just a second!" Syris yelled. "I looked up the words that thing said. There's no translation, but according to this," Syris slammed his hands on the cover of his book, "you and that machine were conversing in the language of the ancients!"

Ral glared at Syris. "What language, exactly, would that be?"

Syris' jaw muscles tightened. "It doesn't say. All it states is that the language of the ancients is not of this world."

Ral gave a great huff. "Just because no one remembers how to speak it doesn't mean it was never from here at all."

Oren grew curious. "So that language was native to this world?"

"Not exactly," Ral said. "That language was spoken no matter where you went. It just so happens that it has become lost through the ages here. Elsewhere, that language is still very much alive and has not had any variations in the last 12 millennia."

Setch's eyes grew wide. "That's an awfully long time to speak one language without ever making any changes."

"Other people don't entertain the idea of slang as you might," Ral retorted.

"What does slang have to do with anything?" Oren said, a bit put out.

"It has everything to do with it! Instead of using real words, you use stupid things, like presi! If you want to call someone your brother, just call them brother. It doesn't sound as unintelligent, and it's far more respectful."

Oren smiled. "Alright. Just calm down, presi!"

Ral stared at Oren with such intensity that the air seemed to freeze. Presi was a combination of the words precious and sister. "If you ever call me that again I will put your head between my jaws, and from there on you don't want to know what's going to happen to you."

Oren nodded meekly. "Okay, I get it. Only use proper speech when in your presence."

"Use proper speech at all times!" Ral growled. "I will always be watching. Even when I am dead, I will be watching!"

"How do we arrange that? I'm sure you won't be missed," Syris said flatly.

Ral's eyes went wide for a split second, and then his jaw tightened. Oren looked at Syris disapprovingly; Setch pursed his lips. Silence drifted through the air like an iron weight. It was suffocating and uncomfortable.

"Syris, that was a little too harsh. Apologize to—" Oren began.

"No," Ral interrupted, his head lowered. "He is right. If I were to disappear, I would probably not be missed. I have made an awful mess of things in the past. I have tried to seek redemption for my mistakes and have only plunged further into damnation. I suppose that I would be a burden off of everyone's shoulders. Even — even he would —"

Oren frowned as Ral's face contorted with some pent up anguish. Syris crossed his arms as a sliver of guilt rang in his chest. Setch proceeded to kick Syris in the shin as hard as possible.

Syris gave a small squeak of pain. "What was that for?"

"For being mean!" Setch said. "Say you're sorry."

Syris scoffed at Setch; he refused to be told what to do by a little boy. However, Syris couldn't put up the same front towards Oren.

"Syris, tell Ral you're sorry and that you were being insensitive." Oren leered at Syris, daring him to refuse.

Syris opened his mouth to retort, but thought better of it. He bit the inside of his cheek, mulling over his options. He could bluntly refuse to apologize and offer some argument as to why he had said nothing wrong, or he could apologize to Ral and have the bear exact whatever vengeance he so desired. Either way, someone was going to be dissatisfied. Syris decided to take the road that seemed safer.

"Alright. I'm sorry for what I said." He turned to Oren in mild frustration. "Are you happy now?"

Oren stared blankly at Syris. "No." His voice was rough as sandpaper. "I'm not happy until you lose the attitude."

Syris flinched under Oren's gaze. "I don't have —"

Oren's jaw tightened; Syris shifted uncomfortably. Then, like a dam breaking open, a wave of anger that Syris had never felt before flooded his mind. He started shaking uncontrollably.

"I didn't," Syris' voice wavered, "say anything wrong."

Oren glared at Syris, his purple eyes slowly becoming darker.

"He said it himself. No one will miss him. He admitted to it all on his own. So why — why should I apologize for anything? It was true, wasn't it? Is the truth such an awful thing to say? Is it so wrong to voice what everyone else is already thinking?"

Oren remained silent. He wanted to see where Syris' train of thought would lead to.

"If I had a gaping wound, you would take me to the doctor right? I would want you to tell me I was injured. Ral is — like a gaping wound. Shouldn't he be told? Wouldn't it be better if he knew? So that —"

"To what end?" Oren asked, his voice flat.

Syris stared at him blankly, not fully understanding the question. "What?"

"To what end?" Oren repeated. "To what end does telling him lead to? Does it make you feel better about yourself? Does it make you feel strong to say those kinds of things to someone?"

Syris stood fixed to the ground, his mouth open like a fish. Strangled noises of a forced response came from his throat.

"To what end?" Oren asked, his hands balling into fists.

Syris cringed, his eyes wide with a childish fear that he couldn't understand.

"Oren," Ral's voice was like a bucket of cold water being dumped on everyone's heads. "Thank you for your almost sincere concern, but it is not necessary to say anything further."

Oren bowed his head. He had a feeling that Ral wasn't quite finished with Syris.

"Syris," Ral looked at the red-haired boy, "I thank you for what you perceive to be honesty. In return, allow me to share some information with you."

Syris looked at the ground, his breath quickening and shaking.

"Allow me to inform you of your open wound."

Syris looked up in horror.

"You are a childish, conceited, selfish, arrogant, spoiled, lying brat. You have no regard for anyone save yourself, and you have no respect for anyone or thing. In all honesty, if you were to die, you would not be missed." Syris swallowed the giant lump in his throat. "If you had a gaping wound, I would leave you to bleed."

Silence fell again. Oren stared at Ral in shock. The bear had said many harsh things before, but this reached a whole new level. Oren supposed it was a matter of tick for tack; Syris had been rude to Ral, so now Ral was going to repay him. Nevertheless, it seemed rather cruel. Oren felt the familiar vibrations of laughter against his back, but unlike before, they became stronger, more urgent. It seemed the sword wanted to speak. Oren sighed, and reached around to hold the sword in front of him.

How Blessed Are We to See, On This Day

The Stigma of Pain Clearly Portrayed.

Yet, You Forget, as Others Do,

That Death Comes Swiftly, Even for You.

The Words You Once Condemned Now Spill

From Your Mouth, Like Acid Rivers.

Yet You Dare?

You Dare Stand Before Another,

And Pass Blame?

When You, Yourself, Have Committed

The Greatest Sin.

Ral shook his head.

The Greatest Sin of Them All.

You Will Bleed Retribution

For the Sinners of This World.

Oren's grip tightened on the sheath; his hands were shaking and sweating. He didn't like how the sword talked. He didn't like how it felt when it dug its sheath into his back while he slept. He always got up to check, and it hadn't moved, but Oren could feel its desires nonetheless.

"Well," Setch said, picking at his ragged shirt, "I think we should get going."

Oren nodded in agreement. "Yeah, probably. You know the way, right?"

Setch smiled, jumping in affirmation. "Of course! I'll lead if — everyone's ready to go." Setch took a quick glance at Ral and Syris.

Oren made his way over to Ral and tapped him on his side. Ral twitched, but made no movement other than that. Syris had his head bowed. He exuded an aura of solitude and defeat.

"Are we ready to move on?" Oren asked quietly.

Ral nodded, glared at the sword Oren held, and he moved past Syris without a single word. Syris felt like a lead weight. He forced his feet to slide across the ground, stumbling as he went. Ral heard the sluggish shuffling behind him and slowly became more and more irritated. Syris eventually tripped, and Ral snapped.

"Pick up your feet!" Ral shouted. Syris jumped backwards, shaking like a leaf. "You're almost twenty, yet you act like a child. I understand perfectly — you didn't experience life as others did, but that doesn't grant you any special privilege. You always wanted so badly to be an adult. You wanted to do the things that adults did, but you didn't want the responsibilities and consequences that came with those things. You wanted to pet the lion without having to worry about the claws. That's not how it works. That is never how it has worked!"

"Ral, take it easy," Oren said, trying to diffuse the situation.

"Don't tell me what to do, human!" Ral's eyes flashed hazel, his teeth elongating for a second. The furious bear wheeled back on Syris, his eyes burning like hot coals. "Enough of your whining! Enough of your self-pity! Do you think you're the only one who has felt loss in this world? There were wars throughout the ages! Mothers lost their daughters, fathers lost their sons, and children younger than Setch lost their entire family, and everything they held dear to them!"

Syris shrank back. "I — I didn't say that —"

"Silence!" Ral roared. His fur was standing on end, and the bear seemed to have gotten a bit larger.

Oren watched Ral in confusion. It seemed to Oren that Ral was undergoing some change, but whatever was happening was barely noticeable.

"I do not need any more of your pathetic excuses! What I need is for you to grow up!"

Oren put an arm around Setch. Syris stood rigid, his heart racing. Ral's eyes, now hazel, were boring into him like white-hot irons. The bear's teeth were like daggers.

Ral took a deep breath and held it. His eyes gradually melted back into a deep brown, and his teeth shrunk back. The fur on Ral's back flattened into place. Syris wrung his hands together, willing himself to calm down.

"Pick up your feet," Ral ordered, his voice level and soft. "Straighten your back, broaden your shoulders, and lift up your head."

Syris did as he was told. He was still shaking, but somehow he felt stronger than he had before.

"Now," Ral lifted his head up, staring at some unknown presence in the sky, "walk forward, never looking back. Keep yourself on the straight and narrow path. If you never falter, you will never fail."

Syris nodded, a fire starting to burn through him. Oren smiled, and Setch puffed his cheeks out in impatience.

"Can we go now?" Setch asked, tapping his feet on the ground.

Ral turned to face Setch. "Yes, we can go now. Please lead the way."

Setch smiled enthusiastically as he bounced away with the spring of a kangaroo. Oren and the others followed after him, their spirits slowly lifting. They kept to the road for quite a while. Setch veered off to the right into the forest, pushing past thorns and branches. Ral followed with piqued curiosity.

"It should be," Setch cleared away fallen leafs and vines, "somewhere around here."

Oren looked at the ground. "What is?"

Setch leered at the soil. "The trail! There's a trail I followed to get here. It's old and made from stone. It forks off in two directions from the maze, but I don't know where the second path leads."

Syris tilted his head to the side. "Maybe it's further in the forest?"

"Perhaps," Ral said, scanning the area. "However, if it is further in, it will become even more difficult to find it."

Oren pursed his lips. "Hm." He strode forward at a brisk pace, covering much ground with long strides.

"Hey! Where are you going?" Setch called after him.

"I'll look over here," Oren called back, twisting around to look at Setch. "Maybe if we just walk we'll run into it!" Oren twisted back around, and Setch shouted something at him.

Oren felt the painful, cold impact of his face against stone. He stumbled back, falling to the ground. Oren massaged his nose and looked up to see what he had hit. A crumbling, moss-covered column was in front of him. It wasn't very large; years of erosion seemed to have taken its toll.

Oren stood up and paced around the column. "I think I found it!" he called to the others.

Ral was the first to meet Oren, followed by Setch, who was followed by Syris, who was covered in bits of foliage. Oren did his best not to laugh as Syris began plucking leaves and twigs from his person.

Setch bowed low to the ground, examining its surface. It took a while, but he found a large corner of a stone. Setch followed the bits of stone that had fallen from it till he saw a whole slab. The whole slab was followed by another, which was followed by three. Setch smiled broadly as the stones became a solid trail.

"It seems we found it," Ral said, shaking leaves from his fur. "Thank you, Oren, for your blunders."

"Oren grunted, rubbing his nose. "You're quite welcome. I do hope to be of more use to you in the future."

Syris grinned meekly. "I'm sure you will be."

"Onward!" Setch shouted. There was a noticeable enthusiasm in his voice.

Ral, Oren, and Syris smiled at the boy. They followed

closely behind Setch as he bounded down the trail. Wildflowers grew on either side of it in arrays of purple and gold. It smelled of honey and sugar; Oren heard his stomach growl.

The path was straight, then eventually bended to the right in a graceful arch. The stone took on a smoother texture, like marble. Setch began hopping from one slab to the next, avoiding fresh puddles of crystal water. The wildflowers began to wilt and were replaced with briars and shriveled vines. Ral wrinkled his nose as the smell of honey was replaced with that of mold. A sneeze from Syris made Oren flinch.

"You okay?" Oren asked, producing a tissue from a pocket in his pants that no one knew he had.

"Yes, I'm fine." Syris looked ahead and then smiled. "You should duck."

Oren tilted his head to the side in confusion. "What?"

"Duck," Syris repeated.

"I don't understa —" Oren felt something sticky and thick cover his face. He screamed and flailed, trying to get what he now realized was a large cobweb off of him. A small black circle moved through Oren's vision, and he screamed even more. "Get it off!"

After much chaos, Oren removed the web from his person and frantically searched himself for any black, eight-legged creatures that might want to exact revenge.

"Are you okay?" Syris patronized.

Oren was spitting and slobbering. "It gut in muh mout!" Syris could barely make out what Oren was saying.

"Just be glad you're not a grizzly," Syris said while pointing to a particular bear.

Ral was grinding his teeth together in aggravation. His plush, black fur was covered in patches of wispy, white tendrils. Every now and then he would rub against a tree to try and rid himself of the webs. It wasn't until after Ral's furious scratching that he would realize that the tree had yet another cobweb on it.

Oren sighed and raked a hand through his black and red hair. "I guess it can't be helped."

Syris shrugged. "We could always dump water on him."

"You want to do it?"

"As if! I say you do it."

"We could flip a coin."

"God knows one of us would rig it."

"Than do you know how to play cards?"

"You mean gambling?"

"No, just cards. There's no money involved."

"It's still a bet. We're betting on dumping a bucket of freezing or searing water on an already angry bear."

Oren tapped his forehead. "True." A few moments of silence passed. "We could both do it."

Syris stepped over a pond. "We could have Setch do it."

Oren chuckled at the thought of Setch dousing Ral. He was positive that it would not go over well. "Maybe not. Let's just leave Ral be."

"A wise decision," the bear's gruff voice chilled Oren and Syris to the bone.

"You heard us, huh?" Oren asked. He wrung his hands together in discomfort.

"Every word. You whisper with bull horns." Ral said.

Syris squinted at the bear. "We weren't whispering in the first place."

Ral smiled. "Exactly."

Setch laughed. "Such cheeky little kids! You really should pay attention to what you're doing, though. These "puddles" are quite deep."

Oren waved his hand dismissively. "How much farther?"

"Not much," Setch replied. "We just have to go a bit deeper in."

"People probably don't find this maze on accident," Syris mused.

"Sometimes they do. Mostly, you have to know where it is in advance if you want to find it. Traveling merchants sometimes come across it, as well as rogues. They never enter, though."

"With good reason," Ral said.

Setch grinned. "I guess so. Come on!" He started jogging down the trail. "We're almost there."

Chapter 10

DISTORTIONS AND LIES

– The city, so luxurious and beautiful, is tainted to its core. It has been washed away, but blood has darkened the walls and eroded paintings of majesty. I saw the stains of war upon the hearts of my people, horrible and unspeakable things etched into their retinas. They only smile to hide their anguish from their descendants. A man selling gears and springs to Cenriotens took back his goods in fear when he saw a spot of red rust, mistaking it for blood. He laughed when he realized his mistake and sent the gears back for polishing, but his voice cracked under sorrow and regret. If only those scars would heal.

Setch had taken them through bushes and trees, past small streams that fed concourses of flowers, and finally to a large hedge where a massive double door of brown, red, and blue chipped paint stood, blocking their path. The smell of rusted metal filled the air as the large iron doors grinded open. Slowly the axels turned, easing the gap wider and wider. The hot, stale air flooded through the opening, greeting the fresher air outside, talking with it, and at times fighting with it. The doors came to a screeching stop as they brushed up against the vegetation inside the maze. Everyone stood silently. Whispers filled the air, muttering, rambling, pausing to think about long regrets.

"Welcome to the Maze of Distortion! People come from all around to get taste of this place's deadly humor!" Setch sang.

"Don't sound so happy about it. Do you know how much I hate the anticipation of certain death?" Syris mused.

"It really is well named. The paths are always changing, and not in the ways you would think," Setch chirped.

"In what ways do they change?" Oren asked.

"Well, a couple of ways. The walls could rotate ninety degrees to create a floor and ceiling, the ground could tilt to one side. Oh! In some areas, the gravity shifts so that instead of walking on the floor, you walk on the walls or the ceiling!"

"But there is no ceiling," Syris said.

"That is where you meet certain death," Ral stated.

"Above the Maze is a shield from high in the sky to deep in the ground, giving complete coverage on all sides. The only way in or out is through the gates on either side of the maze. If you hit it, it'll destroy you. Simple as that!" Setch said.

"Then how do we avoid that in places where the gravity changes?" Syris said.

"By testing it out with other objects. Throw a rock or leaf in, and see what happens to it. Sometimes the gravity rotates in a circle. You'll get thrown all over the place. In other areas, the ground falls away when you step on it. Also, I should warn you, the plants may try to grab you. If so, stand still. They know if you move, and can sense fear."

"Any other warnings for the day?" Syris muttered.

Setch turned around and stared at them sternly. "Watch out for shadows. They can play tricks on you. You'll see things that aren't there. The only safe places in this maze are places where there is direct sunlight. Anything else is almost always a trap. Okay?"

"U-understood," Syris said, trembling.

"It's not that bad!" Oren said.

Everyone's mouths hung open. Not that bad? It was a suicide mission.

"Do you understand the concept of dying? We could perish in here, and **no one** would know! Have you no fear?" Syris yelled.

"Don't hurt him, Syris," Ral said. "He's brave!"

"It would seem that bravery begets stupidity," Syris sighed.

"Yeah, right. I guess that makes you the most cowardly," Oren joked.

"I guess that makes me the smartest!" Syris fumed.

"Syris, embrace your inner wimp," Ral said.

"I am not a wimp!" Syris yelled. His face was beet red.

Oren patted his shoulder gently. "Take a chill pill," he said.

"Bite me," Syris grumbled.

The Maze of Distortion was a death trap for any

unlucky visitor. Would they really survive? Something else was bugging Oren as well. For now, he shoved it to the back of his mind. However, it kept nagging him, chewing at his brain, like a disease without a cure. Oren was becoming slightly frustrated with his subconscious, driving subjects of suspicion into his head despite the want to be rid of them. Oren was tempted to ram his forehead into a wall, if only to be rid of it.

"Something wrong?" Ral asked, feeling the aura of anger ebbing off Oren.

Oren glanced at Ral. "No, nothing at all. I just — I can't shake this feeling that something here is not as it seems."

"You have sharp instincts," Ral said, almost impressed.

"So, something is fishy?" Oren said, raising an eyebrow.

Ral chuckled softly. "Perhaps, perhaps not. Maybe you're just a bit on edge, heading into — literally — unknown territory."

Oren scrunched up his nose at Ral. "I'm not scared."

"I didn't say you were," Ral said, a smile tugging at the edge of his bear lips.

"You said it in more sophisticated terms," Oren accused.

"Yes, well, it's true. Now, I suggest we move. We're wasting time standing here doing nothing," Ral said.

"We're talking, so technically we're doing something," Oren said.

Ral gave Oren a half glare, shoving him towards the maze. When Oren had moved forward into the entrance, Ral lowered his head in silence, trying to understand the will of the higher powers that would want the boys to trek through a killer maze with no experience.

"Sending them into this — what are you thinking, Mistress?" Ral whispered. He waited, wondering if he would receive some kind of premonition. Nothing came, and Ral felt absolutely pathetic. "Don't question her majesty!" he said, chastising himself.

"Ugh. Go away!" Oren hissed.

Ral looked up. Oren was swatting viciously at a fly that had decided to annoy him by flitting around his head. Ral shook his head, several reasons why they were going to die passing through his mind. Nevertheless, Ral shoved Oren and the others into the maze, putting aside his doubts and fears, trusting in some celestial glory to protect them.

Walking ensued, the wet vegetation rubbing their clothing and tickling their arms. Syris watched the ground and stopped. A poor little baby bird was on the ground, quietly squawking, asking for help. Syris narrowed his eyes, a sudden familiar urge from when he was a child boiling up in his stomach. Syris raised his foot and listened as a small crunching noise sounded beneath his shoe, after which he wiped off some feathers from his sole.

"Which way?' Syris asked, looking up from the ground, flinching slightly when Ral's judging gaze bore into him like knives. Even though no one else had witnessed Syris' act, Ral had. The bear was tempted to stick him in a State again, but it wasn't the time.

The path split in four different directions.

"The one less distorted," Oren said shakily. The maze was starting to get to him.

"*Please, Origin, don't kill me*," Syris thought frantically. Oren chuckled.

"What?" Syris said.

"Origin is not going to kill you. I wouldn't worry anyway. There's no definitive proof she even exists," he said, patting Syris on the back.

Ral walked up to the stunned and breathless Syris. "Now you know how I feel," he said, laughing a little.

Syris turned to him. "Since when did —"

"I don't know! Who do I look like, his mother?' Ral hissed.

Syris shrugged. "You look like a girl."

Oren burst into laughter.

Ral's eyes flared with a malevolent fire. He charged at Syris with a wild fury, and Syris ran like a mad-man to avoid him, screaming as he went. Setch watched with wide, shocked eyes at the scene before him. Ral spat out threat after threat. Eventually, his words became nothing more than angry roars and slobbery snarls. Oren continued laughing.

"Come on, you can fight petty battles later," he said, wiping tears from his eyes.

"Save me!" Syris screeched. He latched onto Oren's arm, shielding himself from Ral's rage.

"Give him to me!" Ral snarled.

"Take him," Oren said as he shoved Syris into Ral's nose. "He's all yours!"

"Oren, you traitor!" Syris yelled over Ral's roars.

"How does surrendering the guilty make me a traitor?"

"Be quiet!" Setch hollered.

The fighting, laughing, and screaming all stopped. Setch was glaring into the abyss ahead of them.

"Walk quietly," he said.

No one knew what was happening, but they followed Setch's lead.

"What's going on?" Oren whispered.

"That," Setch said, pointing.

Ral clamped a paw over Syris' mouth to keep him quiet. Oren breathed deeply. There were children, lots of them, hundreds of them. They were pulling cartloads of pigs.

"Should we follow them?" Oren asked.

"Maybe, but at a distance," Setch replied.

"No problem," Oren said, shuffling forward.

He stopped at a turn and peered down the path. He watched a few seconds more. Then it came, a dark shroud that surrounded the children and carts. When the darkness cleared, the carts were gone. Slumped against the walls and floor were the children's bodies. They appeared lifeless and cold. Oren's gag reflex punched his insides.

"Not that way," Oren said. "The children die over there."

"That's cruel," Syris growled.

"Follow me!" Setch whispered. They stood and walked swiftly after Setch.

Oren felt something cold and rough latch onto his ankle. He yelled and turned around. Ral looked back at Oren, and was at a loss for words. The thing that had grabbed Oren was made from wood. It looked like a real, human child. However, now that they were up close to one, the ball joints at the elbows, shoulders, wrists, neck, and everywhere else were clearly visible.

"It's a doll," Oren said softly.

He looked down the hall at the other bodies slumped against the walls. Slowly, with the sound of splintering wood, they all rose to their feet. Some flexed their fingers and swung their limbs in circles, while others just stood in place. They all turned in unison, and began walking down the corridor opposite of Oren.

"Don't go," said a voice.

Oren looked down at his feet in surprise.

"Don't go," the doll said. Its voice was like sandpaper. "It's not—" the doll's head twisted with a loud pop. Its jaw settled back into place with a soft click, "Safe. It's not — safe."

Ral watched the doll at Oren's feet. It was slightly disturbing, seeing something that was supposed to be inanimate talk and move.

"He's — a liar!" the doll said, its voice rising in pitch.

Oren furrowed his brow. "What?"

The doll pointed past Oren. "He's — a liar! He's not — safe! He's not — safe! He's — demon — not —"

The doll's jaw made popping sounds. It seemed like it was having something akin to a seizure. Suddenly, the doll stood on its feet. It grabbed Oren's shoulders and pressed its rough forehead to his cheek.

"Run."

The same darkness shot out of the passageway, grabbed the doll, and slammed it against the floor. Oren and the others watched in horror as the doll began to break and splinter. The doll started screaming, its sandpaper voice like nails down a chalkboard. Oren covered his ears, but he couldn't pull his eyes away. The darkness slammed the doll into the ground over and over. Finally, it held the doll, now a broken and scarred mass, in the air and let it drop. The darkness then vanished, like smoke.

The doll was completely destroyed. Oren slowly dropped to his knees, sifting through stray splinters. A small gear fell to the ground. Ral walked up to it and sniffed.

"This doll wasn't animated with magic. It was clever crafting. It was wired to perform one function, and only one function. Yet, along the way it somehow grew a conscience. It became aware of the dangers here. It tried to warn us, but —"

"Something didn't want it to speak," Oren said.

Ral looked at him with pity. "Precisely."

Oren grabbed a large, glass marble. It was an eye as blue and vibrant as the sky.

Setch shifted nervously. "We should go."

Oren nodded, stood to his feet, and turned to follow the boy. Suddenly, something struck him. The doll had pointed past Oren. It had pointed behind him, trying to label something as evil. The person behind Oren was –

"You should leave it," Ral said, making Oren's train of thought crash. "Leave the eye."

Oren looked at his hand that was clutching the eye. His grip was so tight that his knuckles had lost their color. He slowly loosened his grip, and the eye dropped. It hit the ground, and shattered. Setch frowned and began to walk away. Oren quickly followed behind him.

The group went around several more corners, choosing

between many different paths. Finally, Setch stopped and smiled.

"We finally made it!" he said.

"Whoa! We can't go in there!" Syris said.

"We don't have a choice," Setch yawned.

The first distortion had arrived. The passage walls would press together, and then pull apart. In the ivy walls were large dents.

"To survive, we must make it through without getting crushed. When it begins to shrink, step inside the wall imprints. Those are safe areas," Setch explained.

"What happens if we don't?" Syris asked.

"You get smashed flat as paper," Ral said bluntly.

"We'll have to time this. Keep a good grip on everything you own," Oren said, his nerves coiling.

They all watched as the walls pressed together and then slowly peeled apart. Oren could hear the sound of old cogs and wheels fighting against each other as they worked to make the walls move.

"Now!" Setch said. However, just as he told them to go, he quickly recanted. "Wait, wait! Stop!"

"What now?" Syris said, nearly falling over.

Ral's low growl made its way from his throat.

"What's your problem?" Oren asked, eyeing him.

"*That* is my problem," Ral hissed.

Oren looked out into the corridor. The only strange thing he saw was what seemed to be a tree. It was a creepy tree with glowing green eyes, two tails, and spear like arms. It stood on six, pointy legs that bent and twisted in strange ways. The tree-like creature had many large, rectangular openings in its body. Oren could see the corridor through them.

"What is that?" Oren said, pointing at it while keeping his hand near his chest.

"That," Syris began, "is a **Yarifit**."

"Yarifit?" Oren parroted.

"Yes. Yarifits are made from the toughest wood to be found. The leaves on their heads and arms can slice through almost anything. They eat meat, plants, and are in constant need of sunlight. They usually only appear in places with high vegetation," Ral said.

"Wait, they eat? How? Look at him. He has no insides!" Oren said.

"They stuff food in their mouth and absorb it into their body. After that, they spit out the dried remains," Syris said.

"Sounds delightful," Oren muttered, a shiver running up his spine.

Oren had always thought that the Slathe were the creepiest monsters to be found. This tree branch, for lack of a better comparison, had proved Oren wrong.

The Yarifit stretched some of its legs, its whip like tails sweeping along the ground. It opened its mouth and let out a sound that was akin to an underwater gurgle.

"I wouldn't mind the Yarifit being here if it weren't for the fact," Ral's voice dropped almost a whole octave, "that they only appear in packs."

"So there are more of these creepy twig monsters?" Oren said.

"Yes," Setch said.

As the walls started to slide back together, the Yarifit

used its sharp legs to grapple up the ivy wall, perching itself on the top.

"On my mark," Setch said.

The monster let out another gurgle and the walls spread apart. Setch dashed forward, the others following. The walls began to slide together again.

"Find an opening!" Setch hollered.

Oren slid into one easily, holding his cape and sword close to him. Syris tripped and crawled hastily into small hole. Ral managed to press his body together so he could squeeze inside an opening. Setch crouched into a sitting position while the walls of ivy quickly spread over his head. As the walls pressed together, the Yarifit jumped from its place, sending a sharp arm in Oren's direction. Oren ducked, and the Yarifit's extended arm lodged in the wall behind him. Oren stood, drew his sword, and tried to cut through the arm, only to have his blade stopped without putting a single scratch on the monster. The Yarifit growled at Oren and advanced, constantly trying to free its arm. Oren held up his sword, blocking the Yarifit's attack. The monster pushed itself inside the imprint as the walls finally closed all the way. Oren struggled with the monster, trying to keep its gaping jaws away from him.

The Yarifit's breath smelled like mold, rotted wood, and some kind of fungi. Oren greatly disliked how close together they were.

"Hey. I just met you, so sorry to tell you this," Oren said as the walls slid apart, "but we're still on a last name basis!"

Oren pushed the Yarifit back and drove his sword through its eyes, slicing its head in half. Oren watched as the Yarifit fell to the ground, turning into millions of splinters.

"Go!" Ral said, catching Oren's attention.

Everyone ran, faster and faster. Again, the process of squishing inside imprints was repeated. Another Yarifit charged from the foliage, going after Setch.

"I don't think so!" Syris hollered.

Syris drew a pair of short swords and threw them like daggers at the Yarifit's seemingly empty eye sockets. They hit their mark and the Yarifit crashed around the corridor, blind and lost, eventually dislodging the short swords, which fell to the ground. The walls closed, and the Yarifit was crushed, its fading calls rustling through the ivy.

"*Once more,*" Oren thought.

The walls pulled themselves apart, revealing scraps of paper strewn across the ground.

"I thought you said we got squished flat as paper, not ended up as it!" Oren shouted, looking at Setch.

"Allow me to correct myself: **you become paper**!" Ral hollered.

No signal was given. Feet automatically moved, one in front of the other. Oren grabbed Syris' short swords amid the paper. Setch skidded out of the chamber, Ral and Oren coming to a halt beside him. They all gasped in relief.

"Wait. Where's Syris?" Oren shouted.

Syris had fallen, tripping over the tail of a Yarifit that had jumped into the passage, and was crawling towards them.

"Get up! Run!' Setch yelled.

However, the walls were already closing in on him.

"**Syris**!" Oren screamed.

As the walls pressed together, the Yarifit jumped onto the top of the wall to avoid being crushed. Once again, the walls stretched apart. Everyone held their breath. Ral's muscles tensed as he glared at the Yarifit. There was Syris, curled up on the floor.

"Syris, get up!' Oren yelled.

Syris lifted his gaze and scrambled to his feet. He ran hastily and hurled, full speed into Oren, knocking them both to the ground. The Yarifit jumped down from where it crouched and sent one of its tails out to impale one of the possible prey that stood before it. Ral moved forward and caught the Yarifit's tail in his jaws, splintering through the wood. The Yarifit let out a glass shattering screech. Ral used the tail to pull the Yarifit towards him. The now furious bear slammed the Yarifit into the ground and used his teeth to rip through the monster's neck. Wood splinters began to decorate the ground. Syris started jumping around, forever happy that he was alive.

"But you fell!" Oren gasped.

"There are gaps underneath the walls as well," Syris said.

Ral swatted Syris over the head.

"Next time, watch where you step!" he snarled, spitting wood out of his mouth.

"Yes sir!" Syris said.

"Good job. Keep up the pace," Setch said.

Syris' exclamations of being alive were interrupted by the sound of water. Everyone turned to see more Yarifits perched atop the walls. There were six of them total.

When the walls pulled apart, one of the Yarifit swooped down and collected the splinters of its deceased kin in its mouth. It made a chewing motion, and Ral watched in anger as the creature absorbed the splinters into its body.

"Cannibals," Ral hissed.

The Yarifits all hunched over, making soft bubbling noises. Ral tensed as he made to charge. However, the creatures reared back, screeching and wailing. The clouds in the sky moved over the sun, casting shadows around Ral and the others. The Yarifits hissed at them and slid away, disappearing within the more sunny parts of the maze.

"Well," Oren began, "that was rather anti-climactic."

"Can we go now?" Setch said.

"Yes, and I suggest we walk quickly," Ral said.

The group continued on their journey. Everyone watched the shadows of the maze, and peered around corners. Ral kept his gaze to the tops of the walls, scoping out places where monsters could be hiding. In a place like this, there was no telling what kind of creatures could have made their home. There was no telling where they might be lurking.

"Wait," Setch said.

Everyone stopped and looked forward. They had arrived at the second distortion. Oren's eyes widened considerably at what lay before him.

"You failed to mention this," Syris sneered.

The floor itself was deadly. Spikes shot up in small groups, threatening to impale anything over them.

"Just watch the pattern," Oren said.

"There isn't one," Setch retorted.

"The turns of which they rise is different every time. There is no distinct sequence," Ral explained.

"And how do we get through this?' Syris asked, his anger boiling high.

"I suppose we'll find out," Oren said, yawning.

"Good luck with that!" Setch laughed.

"Thanks. I'll need it."

"What?"

Oren had raced out into the storm of shining steel. Spikes grinded to the surface. As Oren went to sidestep them, he was thrown against a wall. A low, deep growl filled the air. Oren looked up, wincing at the new headache he had.

"What — Syris, what is this thing?" Oren yelled, his eyes widening, fear etched on his face.

Syris studied the new creature before answering. "It's a Menira," he said.

"Could I have a quick summary of them, please?" Oren said, slowly standing, his hand on his sword.

"They like to inhabit areas with high amounts of metallic substances!"

"Well, then this place is just perfect!" Oren hissed.

"They only eat iron, steel, or copper, and will eat the spikes off of their own bodies. Conveniently, if they eat their own spikes, the spikes will quickly grow back. Their blade legs can cut through any metal unless it is forged with magic. The blades on their arms can only be used in short bursts because of their lack of balance when standing upright. Don't let your sword get caught in its mouth or you'll have no weapon. Watch out for its tail and don't let it succeed in ramming you with its head.

Also, don't try dodging underneath it. They are extremely flexible and can impale with the blade on their chin if you try to slide beneath it!" Syris finished.

"Okay," Oren said warily. "So pretty much, don't do anything. Just hope you die quick."

The Menira had a sharp metal plate over its face. Two large canines jutted from its mouth at the front, and a blade grew out from its chin. Sharp spikes decorated its body. On its arms were axe shaped blades. It legs had no feet. Instead, the Menira had large growths of steel that scraped against the ground, constantly refining their edges. Its tail was slamming the ground, sending cracks along the surface. The Menira's tail had a glistening blade on it as well. The beast, when on all fours, stood at Oren's chest.

Oren watched the Menira's movements, and also watched where he stepped. As the spikes receded Oren ran from the Menira. The monster followed him, its legs sending out showers of sparks. The spikes reappeared, forcing Oren to jump over them, and halt abruptly to avoid being stabbed. Oren ran quickly. He flipped over another pair and landed gingerly on his feet. A sharp pain entered him. The steel had scratched the side of his arm.

"Not far to go," he said to himself.

The spikes retracted, sheering his flesh again. Oren flinched, but continued onward. The alloy storm kept flashing to the surface, shredding skin off Oren as he went along, the Menira clawing its way along the walls, trying to catch up to Oren. Nearing the end of the chamber, Oren tripped. His body hit the ground. Below his ear, Oren heard the swift turning of cogs.

Oren rolled to his left. The Menira pounced and stopped inches from Oren's skin. Blood started to drip from the Menira's mouth. Oren saw his sliced up reflection in the cold, now bloody steel. It was only a couple of centimeters from his body, and the Menira's head was mounted upon it.

"Careful, you fool!" Setch hollered from the other end.

"Yeah, whatever!" Oren said, struggling to his feet.

He braced himself, the gears turned underneath him, the spikes embraced the air, and Oren entered the final dash. Another Menira clawed its way into existence from the shadows of the maze, knocking Oren off his feet. It stopped to eat the spikes off the body of the dead Menira, and then turned back to face Oren. The Menira rushed after Oren and swung its tail at the ground. Oren rolled to the side and stood up, backing away. The Menira moved forward, and for a split second, stood on its hind legs, slicing at the air with the blades on its arms. Oren narrowly missed the razor edges. The Menira fell back on all fours and advanced on Oren. As the Menira's jaws opened, Oren slid behind a row of spikes. The Menira closed its jaws on a spike and tried to crush it, but failed. Oren's eyes grew wide.

"Ha!" Oren shouted to the Menira, "They're branded with magic. You can't bite through them!"

The Menira responded to this with a loud roar and Oren scrambled away. As Oren neared the end of the chamber, he took out his sword and swung it at the Menira, hitting the monster in the head. The metallic monster stumbled around for a few seconds, allowing Oren to reach the end of the corridor. The Menira regained itself and pounced, claws extended. Oren held his sword up in defense, but the only thing to hit him was a spray of blood. Oren looked up and saw the Menira's body suspended on a row of spikes, blood slowly pooling onto the floor.

"And he lives!" Syris shouted in joy.

"Get over here!" Oren yelled.

Oren picked up the dead monster's body. He hacked away at the floor, revealing the gears that worked the distortion and plunged the monster into the mechanism below him, halting the process of the spikes. He watched as the Menira was crushed, squished, and ripped apart between the gears. Syris and the others rushed up to Oren.

"Good job, bud!" Syris said, flipping Oren's hair.

"A marvelous performance," Ral said, lowering his head in respect, only to nearly vomit when he saw what remained of the poor steel monster.

"Marvelous, but stupid," Setch muttered.

"But it worked, right?" Oren said, patting Setch's' shoulders.

Setch thought for a moment. "I suppose so. But still really stupid."

Oren smiled. "Thanks!"

"Let's move. We still have one distortion to get through," Setch sighed.

"You know how many there are?" Syris asked.

"There are hundreds. But you can only go through three in a sequence before reaching the center. That's the rule," Setch explained.

"Oh. Then let's go, and Oren can be our little hero again!" Syris said.

"Don't make me hurt you," Oren threatened.

Syris raised his hands protectively.

"Easy, Oren," Ral said, "or you'll have to go to the time-out corner."

Oren shrugged and started down the ivy passage. Setch jogged up to his side.

"What do you reckon the last distortion will be?" Oren asked.

"I don't know. Like I said, there are hundreds of them. The sequence is never the same, no matter where you go. We could return to this same path tomorrow and the distortion would be completely different. That's how it is here," Setch explained.

"Sounds complicated," Syris mused.

"*But how do you know so much about it,*" Oren thought.

Ral and Syris eventually caught up to them. The ivy was beginning to turn brown, brittle, and dry. The leaves and vines began to shrivel.

"It's all dead-ish," Syris said.

"But why?" Oren said.

"The clock draws energy from around itself. That includes plant life," Ral said.

"What about people life?" Syris asked.

"Or animal life?" Oren chimed, looking at Ral from the corner of his eye.

"Probably not, since we don't seem to be getting hurt from it," Setch said.

Ral was in deep thought. How were they supposed to destroy the clock? How would they kill Tharazar? All they had were two untrained, carefree idiots with swords, and a little boy who couldn't fight or do anything else except navigate a maze. It was hopeless, absolutely hopeless. There was no way to fight back, unless—no, that was such a crazy idea. Ral couldn't afford to give himself away just yet. His Mistress needed him to stay like this until all was well again.

"We're here," Setch said.

Ral looked up. The third, and final, distortion left no room for fear. Sure, the prospect was terrifying, but it struck everyone with so much awe that they couldn't bring themselves to feel much of anything else.

"What is this?" Oren said.

It was another corridor, nothing unusual, except for the dark, massive, spinning sphere in the center.

"It looks like a Karma," Syris said.

"Yeah, but I thought those things were myths!" Oren said.

"Apparently not," Setch muttered.

Ral stared at the dark, turning sphere. "Any action or being producing magical or physical energy is captured inside the sphere, held there until it reaches a critical level, and then released back towards the original user."

"So, if we attack that thing —" Syris began.

"Then it will send our own offensive attempt flying right back at us?" Oren finished.

"Yes," Ral said.

"Then how are we supposed to get past it?" Syris asked in annoyance.

"Well if we don't attack, shouldn't we be okay?' Oren said.

"Theoretically, yes," Ral began, frowning, "but Karmas suck up any energy, no matter what kind, no matter where it comes from, good or bad. It will use everything it can against us."

Oren raised his gaze towards the heavens. "What if we were to deflect the energy back at the evil mass of blackness?"

"The destructive force would only increase," Ral said.

"Then what do we do?' Syris said.

Ral gazed into the dark sphere. "There is nothing we can do. Though, I have heard of Karma being forced to feed off of themselves, collapsing, and ceasing to exist."

"And did it say **how** we make it do that?" Syris asked, his brows raising.

"No," Ral replied curtly.

Oren paced back and forth. Setch watched him closely.

"What if we rid the Karma of all energy except its own? It wouldn't have a choice in that matter," Oren said.

"But how do remove all the "food" around it?" Syris said.

"Destroy the energy. Remove the dead ivy on the walls and get rid of anything that can emit a force of some kind."

"Like us?"

"Yes," Setch said.

"Then let's start!" Oren said, puffing his chest out.

"Wait, what happened to touching things and turning to ash?" Syris said.

"Dead stuff doesn't count," Setch replied.

Oren grabbed a giant string of ivy and yanked it from the walls. Brick, metal, and clay were revealed beneath the vegetation. Syris and Setch worked on ripping ivy from the walls closer to the sphere of dark matter. The ivy was piled a ways from the entrance to the chamber.

"What's it doing?" Syris asked quietly, his eyes flying up to the magic sphere hovering in the air.

The Karma was pulsing, flashing vibrant purple and white.

Ral stiffened. "Get down!" he yelled.

Oren grabbed Setch and smothered him against the ground. Ral and Syris pushed themselves to the wall. The Karma let out a long, groaning echo. Suddenly, streams of electricity and fire shot out in all directions, vaporizing anything they touched. The wind sliced through the walls and broke through the floor. It howled like an angry tempest, screaming in the ears of Setch, Syris, Oren, and Ral. It ripped their clothing and reduced the pile of ivy leaves to nothing but dust in the wind. Then, it was quiet. Silence ensued, and all was at peace. Ral raised his brown eyes. He snarled and growled angrily. The Karma was still there, and was more threatening than ever.

"What happened?" Syris said.

"It's angry that we stripped its food sources away," Ral said.

"Then why isn't it gone?" Oren said, brushing dirt and rocks off himself.

"Because there is still "food" to eat away at. The wind acted as a backup system. It used the destructive force that broke through the walls to power itself."

Ral looked around, his eyes scanning meticulously for one thing. "Look there," he said.

Through the floor, or what was left of it, the turning gears could be seen.

"It is feeding off of the machine beneath us."

"How are we supposed to stop the mechanisms?" Syris groaned in anguish.

"I think I can help with that," Setch said.

"You?' Oren said, surprise overtaking him.

"Yes. I can jam the top gears. It should cause a full outage to the entire system beneath this chamber."

Ral mulled this over. "Go."

Setch nodded and grabbed a metal floor plate that had been ripped up from the ground in the searing attack.

"Good luck," Oren said.

Setch smiled. "Thanks. I'm going to need it."

Setch inched toward the Karma. The winds picked up and began pulling him inward. Setch laid flat against the floor, crawling slowly toward the gears. The black, magic made hole groaned and sent out a quick electric burst. It narrowly missed Setch. He looked up and saw that the gears were only a few inches away.

"Just a little farther — just a little farther," he whispered to himself.

The wind became stronger. It tugged at Setch. He began to slide forward, and the edge was just in reach.

"Come on, keep going," Setch gasped.

Setch's hands were ripped off the ground and he was sent over the edge of the floor. The grinding and churning of rust covered axels was deafening. It was just within reach, the one wedge that would stop everything beneath this chamber. The Karma groaned loudly. There must have been two hundred feet or more of gears, axels, and all sorts of mechanisms beneath Setch. He marveled at the clockwork, at how massive, immense, and extensive it was in design.

"Setch, hurry!" Oren yelled.

The wind lashed out around him, sending rocks and all manner of objects everywhere. The Karma was enraged. It groaned and fire swirled around it in an ominous halo.

"Setch, now!" Ral shouted.

"Okay!"

Setch turned and shoved the floor plate into the axel. The gears shrieked uncontrollably, fighting against the floor piece. The axel churned, and then cracked, halting all other gears beneath the floor. Several hundred feet of metal, iron, silver, gold, and steel groaned under the pressure before stopping their rhythmic counting. Setch lifted himself over the edge and pulled himself back towards the others, fighting the pull of both the wind and the Karma — the sphere longed for the boy's energy as a last, desperate attempt to save itself.

"Setch, take my hand!" Oren hollered over the howling winds.

Setch grabbed Oren's fingertips, straining against the pull of the Karma and its rage. Oren swept him up in a fatherly embrace.

"Retreat!" Ral shouted over the wind.

They all fled back to the entrance of the chamber. The dark mass let out a long, bellowing roar. It flashed frantically. Long streams of water, ice, and fire spun out in giant spirals of anger from the Karma's center, destroying everything. The floor, the walls, the gears beneath it, and even the air set itself afire. The Karma let out a final roar of defeat and hatred before its swirls shifted directions and it grew smaller and smaller, until the destructive force burst apart in a rain of fire and acid. The thundering, punishing winds calmed, and the empty roar of the Karma ceased. Ral lifted his head.

"It's over," he said.

The chamber was gone. All that remained was sand and dust. The walls, the ivy, the gears beneath the floor, all things that were once there, were now gone, never to be seen again. The Karma had destroyed both them and itself.

"It really ate itself. It really worked," Oren breathed.

"I'm alive!" Syris shouted in joy.

"Calm down!" Ral said.

"We owe it all to our dear little friend, Setch!" Oren said proudly.

"Thanks. It was no trouble," Setch replied, a little flustered.

"Do you think we'll ever meet up with a Karma again?" Syris asked.

"I certainly hope not. That one nearly blew us to pieces," Oren replied meekly.

"The third distortion is over. Let's continue," Setch said.

"After I eat. I need some energy of my own. It's surprising what a little workout will do to you," Oren laughed.

Ral chuckled. "I think we all need some refreshments. Let's eat."

"Hear, hear!" Syris said.

"I'm starved!" Setch said happily.

"Thank you, Syris, for packing food before we left

your village!" Oren said, his eyes brimming with grateful tears. "Though, I'm not sure how you managed to make it without anyone noticing, including us."

"The skill of stealth is rare among commoners. Don't feel bad if you don't have it," Syris turned his nose up for effect.

Oren laughed and slapped Syris on his back. They feasted on small sandwiches, and drank water in place of wine. It tasted good after such a treacherous journey. However, Ral knew it was not to last.

When the meal was over, they all stood and braced themselves for the end of the maze. Oren was shaking with anticipation, wondering what would await them. Syris shook with fear, hoping that the demon wouldn't be there to guard the clock. Ral kept his head down, watching for any deceptions or foes. As they all moved forward, they took several turns, stopped a few times to catch their breath, and took short sips of water. Finally, after getting lost once or twice, the group emerged into an open space.

The area was large, and filled with trees. The trees didn't look wooden; rather, they were metal and steel. They had screws and rivets holding their branches on, and the leaves looked sharp enough to cut someone. The sky above the trees was gray and smoky. In front of all the trees was a massive steel chair, and on the chair rested a huge, iron mace.

"Here we are," Setch said.

"They must really exist. Father Time's —" Syris' eyes were bulging out of their sockets.

"Hands of Discord," Oren finished.

"Yeah, but I don't see them."

"Where is the Thar guy?" Oren asked suspiciously.

Setch walked forward and traced a finger along the large spiked mace. "What do you mean?"

Ral took a few steps back, pulling Oren and Syris with him.

Setch laughed hideously. "He's right here!"

Setch turned around to face them, a wicked grin on his face. His body shifted awkwardly, convulsing and expanding.

His laugh became deep and garbled.

"It's nice to finally meet you," said the deformed Setch.

The skin split open to reveal a brown head with two sets of horns. His teeth were all sharp points. His oversized hands had long sharp claws on them, as did the feet. A tail slithered into view.

"Setch?" Oren choked.

Syris pulled him back a few paces. Ral snarled and growled, a deep hatred concealed in the back of his throat.

"No, my dear friend," the creature said. It stood upright, towering over everyone; fluids ran down the creature, remnants of its meat disguise of a child.

Oren's knees shook in anger.

"I am Tharazar."

JUDGMENT OF TIME

– A man visited me and my student today. I knew him, though his appearance has changed greatly over the past few centuries. His robes of golden silk were ripped and frayed. His human visage, flesh and muscle, was completely gone. He was literally a walking skeleton, one eye still in its white socket. He swayed to and fro, a boney hand stretched forward. His soul was shattered and Discord was slowing counting down. He was about to die, fully and infinitely. I suppose he saw something in time that shook him to the core, so greatly that he broke. He left one warning, slurred and empty. "Purge the evil within this sanctuary." His skeleton fell to the ground and his bones broke into pieces. I took his robes and had them mended, but Discord left, latched onto a remnant of its master. This evil has already dug its way in. Only death will rid us of it.

"It was you all this time?" Oren said.

His legs felt like jelly, and his heart was as loud as a drum and twice as fast. Why hadn't he seen it before? Setch knew so much about the maze, the obstacles; perhaps he had known too much. Setch knew so much about Tharazar as well. Plain as it had been, no one had realized. If they did, they didn't show it.

"I thought so," Ral said, his voice low and cold.

Oren looked at him, confusion set on his face like a mask. "You knew? Then why didn't you say anything?"

Ral stared at Oren, his large brown eyes silently answering his question.

"You're cruel!" Oren snapped.

"Maybe so, but it was for your benefit," Ral said.

Benefit? How could Ral say that? Why did he allow Oren believe Setch was good, and small, and frail?

"You care too much. You must learn to control your emotions, to trust no one. At times, you cannot even trust yourself," Ral said. His voice was the equivalent of a hot branding iron being shoved down Oren's windpipe.

Oren ground his teeth together. Ral was such a jerk! How dare he speak to him like that – Ral was nothing but a lowly animal! Yet, that lowly animal was correct.

"I have grown quite bored of your squabbling," the demon growled.

Ral snarled, his teeth flashing in the fading rays of sun. The demon smiled, a deep gurgling laugh erupting from its throat. Syris slid up to Ral's ear, whispering so Oren wouldn't hear.

"We can't outrun this one. How do we win? Oren won't stand a chance, considering —"

"Destroy the Hands," Ral replied.

"Easier said than done," Syris grumbled.

"Indeed! And you will perish before you can get half that far!" Tharazar roared.

Ral glared at him, rage visible within his dark pupils. A vile, toothy grin stretched across his face. "We'll see about that."

The demon smiled, black, sharp teeth filling the gap between his crusty, purple lips.

"You should get your boy," Tharazar said.

Syris flinched, his eyes widening.

"Oren, get up!" Ral yelled.

Oren didn't move. He was paralyzed, frozen on his knees. The demon's massive hand rose and swiftly descended.

"Oren!" Syris screamed.

The sound of flesh being torn filled the musky air. A screech of pain vibrated off the surroundings. Tharazar reared back, resentment and agony throbbing through his silver blood.

"Curse you! Curse you, boy! I'll kill you!" Tharazar bellowed.

He held his clawed hand, a large slice running from one end to the other. Oren, frozen as he was, had unsheathed his sword, defending himself. His terror and fury fueled his strength. Oren stood, mouth clamped shut, his hand fiercely gripping the handle of his weapon.

"I curse you, too. I curse you with death, and shall send you to hell!" Oren's eyes lit up with rage; the purple had brightened to an almost crimson color.

Oren advanced, charging at Tharazar, his footsteps sounding like thunder against steel plates in the ground.

"You've got a big mouth, boy," Tharazar hissed.

Fire spread through Oren's body as he fell to the floor. Blood steadily dripped from his head and leg. The outer maze wasn't the only place with hidden mechanisms, such as the sharp, silver spikes that shot up from the ground. Adrenaline shot through Oren's nervous system like lava spewing from a volcano. He started to push off from the floor.

"Stay still!" Ral shouted.

He hadn't noticed it before, but there, just grazing Oren's cheek was the cold touch of a steel spike. One fast movement, one flinch, and Oren would be skewered, but still he smiled.

Tharazar growled, taking two steps towards him. "What are you smirking at, boy?"

"You have your tricks, I have mine."

Oren lifted his arm slowly, and using as much wrist strength as possible, threw his sword towards Tharazar's feet. Tharazar roared. He wheeled around trying to step away from Oren's blade as it skidded across the ground. Steel spikes followed the sliding sword, and buried their tips and bodies into Tharazar's feet. The demon fell backward in pain.

"You will burn for this!" he shouted, hissing, blood and foam flowing over the cracked, blackened soles and his feet.

Ral rushed forward, pulling Oren off the floor, the deadly, shining, silver spikes missing his body by centimeters.

"Syris, hold him here," Ral said.

"Ral, don't!" Syris yelled.

Being the leader, Ral ignored him. "Find the Hands and get rid of them!" he growled.

Syris nodded, and dragged Oren towards the trees. Ral drove his claws into the floor. His eyes closed, his lips forming inaudible words. The air started to whistle, the wind whipped widely, and the ground was racked with tremors. Syris struggled to stay upright with Oren leaning on him, and he thought for certain the ground would give out underneath him.

Ral summoned every ounce of strength in his body. A crest flashed on his forehead. It was an upside-down lightning bolt with two triangles on either side pointing out diagonally. There was a triangle underneath his eyes as well. The crest glowed a fierce shade of gold. Gold symbols lit up on his arms and legs as well. The final word that left Ral's lips was more powerful than anything Syris or Oren had ever encountered.

"Vashire!"

Syris and Oren couldn't see what happened next; it blinded them, and left purple spots in their vision. Surges of electricity rained from the heavens, incinerating anything they hit. The metallic leaves on the Trees of Time vaporized in a shower of sparks. Thunder deafened everyone's ears, lightning blinding them, each bolt engulfing some part of Tharazar's massive body in magical flames, but unlike the lifeless, fake trees, Tharazar was able to prevent himself from being immediately turned to ash. Ral stood his ground, roaring the word "strike" over and over again, slowly chipping away at the magic barrier Tharazar was using to protect himself.

Syris dragged Oren up the fire lit slope towards Father Time's tree. The steel was hot. Flashes continued to light the sky, the spidery zigzags of airborne fire stretching over the clouds like fingers. Syris laid Oren on his back. It was still extremely difficult to see.

"How do we find the clock?" Oren screamed over the thunder.

Syris shut his mouth and opened his ears. There, almost inaudible over Tharazar's wails of pain, was a soft, rhythmic ticking.

"You can hear it. Follow the sound!" Syris shouted.

It was easier said than done. The ticking seemed to be resonating from everywhere. Pinpointing the source was seemingly impossible. Oren slid his face against the tree, listening intently for a sound louder than all others, besides Tharazar. Currently, he was the loudest thing around them. Syris mimicked Oren, searching for the source. Both of them met at the back side of the tree.

We're never going to find it!" Oren said, twisting his neck to smooth the stiff muscles.

"We have to," Syris said, "Ral is —"

A hand rushed up to seal his lips. There it was – a sound louder than all others. Oren lifted his eyes, staring at the top of the tree.

"It's up there," he said, panic starting to seep in.

Syris gazed up as well. At the top of the tree, barely visible, was a large set of hands screwed onto a thin, golden circle, but the circle had no numbers on it. The whole thing was encompassed inside a golden casing with a keyhole in the front. The hands flitted from point to point, but turned counter clockwise; it was visibly prolonging Tharazar's life. A small blue swirl, something like a mist and a liquid mixed together, was at the joint of the two hands.

"I thought the Hands were supposed to be inside of the tree, not hovering above it," Syris said.

"Stop complaining!" Oren snapped.

Now the only problem was scaling hundreds of feet up a giant, metal – and not to mention noisy – bush. It seemed relatively easy. The metal tree had notches and ledges all over its surface; they would provide a climbable surface. Not for long, unfortunately. A streak of lightning cascaded down, shredding through the tree's center. The tree creaked and groaned, shifting uneasily, and then it began to plummet downwards in two large halves.

"Move!" Syris yelled, yanking Oren in-between the falling pieces. Dirt flew up into the air as the two halves crushed the earth.

"Nice going, Ral!" Oren screeched.

Ral hissed, ignoring Oren, focused solely on turning Tharazar into ash. Syris stood distressed and deep in thought. They had no fifty foot ladders, no massive slingshot, no arrows, and no wings. There were so many problems, but there were practically no solutions. Ral was beginning to look weak and frail; Syris knew he wouldn't be able to keep up the assault for much longer. Since the clock still existed, Tharazar would still be alive, despite the massive beating he was currently taking. Syris ran the dilemma through his head, pausing here and there to see where a solution might be lurking, unseen and waiting.

"Syris!" Oren slammed into him full force, knocking him off his feet and onto the ground.

Light blinded them for a few seconds, and when the colors adjusted themselves, Syris saw a large scorch mark where he had previously been standing.

"We need to get to that clock," Oren said, out of breath.

"What we need is a miracle!" Syris yelled in frustration.

"I can do miracles."

Syris and Oren jumped at the unfamiliar feminine voice. Again, there she was, the strange cloaked woman who had offered advice and given away artifacts.

"Are you following me?" Oren said, instantly recognizing her black apparel.

"No. I'm here because you "need" me!" she tilted her head at an odd angle.

Syris leaned towards Oren. "You know her?"

"Not at all, but she seems to know me."

"Don't lie! We've met before! In the woods by the Shrine of Aros!" she said.

"Oh," Oren grunted. His crossed his arms in front of his chest.

The woman flinched. "Oh? That's all you have to say? After I went to all the trouble of giving you that key? How rude."

"What's your name?" Syris asked.

She looked at Syris, and he saw her lips curve into a smile. "You can call me — *Gudra*."

Syris raised an eyebrow at the strange name.

"What is the key for?" Oren snapped.

Gudra chuckled. "If you think that Tharazar and the

tree your friend destroyed were the only things guarding the clock, you're dead wrong."

"What do you mean?" Syris said, leaning towards her.

"The Hands of Discord are kept in special element resistant casing. No power can destroy it except for the power that made it."

"There's seems to be an awful lot of this 'indestructible' business going around," Syris muttered. Just about every strange thing they had come across was either invincible, with a few exceptions, or extremely difficult to get rid of.

"You still haven't mentioned why you gave me the key," Oren said. He was growing impatient.

"Well, I may have snuck in here while Tharazar was asleep —" Gudra began.

"Okay," Syris said in boredom.

"And I may have noticed the casing on the clock —" she continued.

"Okay," Oren said. He rubbed his temple in annoyance.

"And I may have, just a little bit, with full knowledge of the danger, but only wanting to assist you, and knowing you'd never succeed if I didn't —" Gudra continued rambling.

"**Get on with it!**" the two boys yelled.

"I may have snatched the key away for you! Stop shouting like a bunch of Agihs!" she screeched back.

The three of them glared at each other until Oren broke the silence. "What's an Agihs?"

"You don't need to know," Gudra snapped.

"So," Syris began, "The reason you gave Oren this ridiculously big, blue key was for the casing on the clock?"

"Yep! I can raise you to the clock's height, but the rest is up to you," she said.

"Then what are we waiting for?" Syris said, his voice barely audible above the roaring of thunder.

"Fine with me," she said. Her voice exuded a slick, velvet tone; Oren guessed that she had quite the smile on her face.

Gudra pressed her hand to the floor. It shook ever so slightly. Then it pulsed, throbbed, and turned a light shade of green. The green turned to a glow that brightened and intensified. It expanded and covered the roots of the trees, shifting from a light to a dark green as the glow dimmed and brightened. Small luminescent orbs came up from the ground and floated through the air.

Sound seemed to dissolve into pure silence. The thunder could not be heard; the lightning could not be seen. All was still within this moment. The floating lights formed a small circle in the air, and then, within the blink of an eye, flew up into the clouds. Around Gudra's fingers that had buried their tips in the soil, small vines stretched and wrapped around her hand, coiling and swirling delicately. With force and grace, she tightened her grip on the vines and wrenched them out of the ground. The vines swiftly became larger, and wrapped themselves around Syris' and Oren's waists, twisting skyward. They formed a circular platform and rested the boys upon it, steadying them until they regained balance. The platform of plants continued to rise. Down below, Gudra's voice pierced the thunder's roars, sound returning to the world.

"Try not to fall off, and watch out for the lightning!

If it hits the vines, it's a long drop and a sudden stop for you both!"

"What? You never told us that!" Syris shouted.

She ignored them both, turned on her heel, and sped away. A wave of childish, though sadistic, humor washed over her. A deep, cynical laugh bubbled inside of her.

Oren watched her until her figure disappeared. He then turned to face his final obstacle. There they were, inches away from it, but still so far from ridding themselves of it. The clock ticked noisily, slowly counting backwards. Oren held up the key, examining it, wondering if what the woman had said was true.

"Oren," Syris said, "let's finish this."

Oren nodded, and searched for the key hole he had seen from the ground. Finding it, Oren held the key up, bracing himself for a possible shock – the clock could have more than a casing on it.

Syris gripped his arm. "Do it."

Oren shifted all his weight forward, thrusting the key into the hole. Syris then gripped the handle and attempted to turn it. It wouldn't budge. A shattering roar filled the air.

"I'll rip you apart!" Tharazar was charging towards their platform of vines. "Weak, pathetic humans!"

"Hit the floor!" Ral yelled.

Oren and Syris laid flat against the plants, peeking over the edge to watch Tharazar and Ral. Something was building; Oren could taste power in the air.

"Look at me, you puss-bathing pig!" Ral shouted.

Tharazar stopped in his tracks, and glared at Ral with

fury. "How dare you," he growled. Tharazar lifted a hand towards the vines.

"I wouldn't do that if I were you," Ral said calmly.

Tharazar laughed. "Oh?" He crouched down and charged at the bear.

Ral stood his ground with zeal. Tharazar was quickly advancing on him.

"Ral, run!" Oren screeched.

Ral smiled, and new words escaped his lips. "**Keeper of Greed, Bind Him!**"

Massive, golden chains ripped through the ground and wrapped themselves around Tharazar. They dug into the demon's legs, arms, torso, and neck.

Tharazar screamed and flailed, outraged at the sudden assault. "You wretched beast! Just what are you?"

Ral grinned at Tharazar as the chains picked the demon up and slammed him into the ground, tightening their hold.

"Answer me, swine!" Tharazar was beyond anger.

Ral glared at the demon. "**Keeper of Wrath, Punish Him.**"

Electricity ran through the chains, and shocked Tharazar to his bones. Lightning rained from the sky and surged through the metal restraints, sending streaks of fire through the air and over the demon's body.

Oren screwed his eyes shut; it was an awesome yet frightful display of power. He had never known the bear could do this. It chilled him to the bone.

"Oren," Syris' voice was low and rough. "We have to smash the clock."

Oren nodded. He and Syris picked themselves up and

each put a hand on the blue key. They tried to turn it with all their might, but it wouldn't budge.

"Come on!" Oren seethed. "We didn't come this far only to be stopped by some rusted piece of junk!"

A chill blew through Oren and Syris.

"Junk, is it?"

The key swiftly turned, and Syris fell to the ground after losing his grip. Oren awkwardly tried to put his feet underneath him.

"What was that?" Syris asked, his skin paling.

"I don't know," Oren replied.

The key sank into the casing a little bit. It clicked once, and then once more. The key began spinning on its own, and then clicked a third time. It started disintegrating and vanished inside the clock. Gears turned and grinded loudly, some straining due to extensive rust; others were whirling effortlessly. The casing split in half and tumbled down until it hit the ground with a loud clank. Tharazar turned his head.

"No!" he screeched. He pulled against Ral's chains, stumbling to his feet. Tharazar reached out a hand and grabbed the vines.

Ral's fury peaked, and the chains constricted Tharazar till his skin broke. **"Keeper of Pride, Dethrone Him!"**

Ral's chains lifted Tharazar into the air and slammed him into the metal spikes sticking out of the ground. More chains ripped through the earth and impaled Tharazar through one side and out the other, piercing organs. A chain split through his side and exited out his right eye before coiling around his head – a gruesome sight.

Tharazar writhed in agony. Silver blood flowed from his body. "I'll rip your heart out, filthy beast!"

"Oren!" Ral bellowed. "It is now or never!"

Oren shouted in agreement and drew his sword. He raised it, and held it level to the clock. Tharazar began crawling towards them with unholy determination.

"Oren, do it now!" Syris yelled above the thunder.

Oren's arms flexed, and he plunged the steel through the clock until he could push it no farther. Tharazar screamed out in anguish. The clock went from bright silver to a brown. It ceased ticking and cracked in several places. Then, it burst into pieces. A shower of lightning wracked the vines. Oren and Syris came tumbling through the air.

"Keepers, Release! Salvage!" Ral yelled.

The chains binding Tharazar quickly unwound themselves, and shot to Oren and Syris. They caught the two boys in a firm, static embrace. Ral approached them, concern bleeding through his eyes. He caught the boys in a furry hug. A wild howl echoed through the air.

Tharazar grabbed his head and wheeled, slamming against the trees, his claws scrapping his head. He fell to his knees, stretched a hand towards the sky, and fell to the ground. His remains turned black, and then the dead monster turned into black smoke and ash, twisting skyward, floating away on the wind. Gudra laughed behind them.

"Great job!" she said.

Ral glared at her, but smiled as if he knew her.

"You," Oren breathed. He rushed up and grabbed her cloak. "What are you trying to pull?" he yelled.

Gudra swatted his hands away, and she yelled at him, anger evident in her voice. "What am I trying to pull? What about you? You have no idea what your purpose really is, do you? You're so childish. Grow up! I haven't done anything! I'm just trying to help you. Is that really so terrible?"

"You keep showing up wherever we are. Are you following us?" Oren hissed.

"More like you're following me. That is Ral's job. If you want to blame it on someone, blame it on your stupid bear."

She turned around and began to walk away. "I don't need to prove or explain anything to you. Just do what you're told and you'll get through your life fine."

"Who exactly do you think you —?"

"**Enough**! I don't want to hear it. Just shut up and follow Ral's orders. Otherwise, you'll end up just like Tharazar."

"Is that a threat?" Oren said.

She laughed. "No," she bent over and glared at him, "it's a **death sentence**."

Oren felt his insides freeze with fear. Gudra laughed and ran from sight.

"See you soon!' she called out.

DESERT OF THE DEAD

– I was given a present today from my dearest companion, made from the silk robe belonging to our skeletal ally. He had it re-dyed to match my tastes. It was still a robe, but instead of gold, it was black, with shimmering red trimming along all the edges and a hood that would effectively cover most of my face. There was a small flap of fabric with an elastic string that could cover my mouth if I found it necessary. He told me, "I have a feeling you'll be going on a journey." He was correct. There was sorrow in his eyes, and my heart almost broke when I saw it. He suddenly smiled, bright and hopeful. "You'll return swiftly, though." I let my mask slip momentarily, sadness clearly portrayed. His smile faded and I felt his heart and soul stiffen. "You're coming home, right?" I didn't answer, and his arms wrapped all the tighter around me.

Oren watched Gudra's billowing cloak until it disappeared amid the trees and ivy hedges. He felt angry, enflamed at her words. She had an uncanny way of striking at someone's nerves in just the right manner. It was her words and voice that made a man's courage and strength shrivel up like leaves in mid-fall. Oh, how Oren was beginning to hate that woman. The lightness of her step, the grace in every movement, the coyness in her words, the power in her stride, and that truly annoying fact that no matter how frustrating her actions were, or how hurtful her words, you couldn't stay angry with her for more than three seconds. If all women were like her, Oren never wanted to get married.

Of course, there was also something pleasant and inviting in her manner, warmth that seemed to hug you and reel you in close until it smothered you. It was a light that pierced even the darkest night. She seemed to dance on air, as if her feet never touched the ground when she walked, or ran, or jumped, not even when she landed on the ground after flipping off a platform. Oren wondered if all women flipped when they jumped off the tops of things, or if maybe she was more masculine than he originally thought. Oren couldn't help but smile at the thought of her. She was truly annoying, but so refreshing at the same time.

"How much longer do you intend to stare into space?" Ral said.

Oren jumped at his voice. He eyed Ral and laughed so hard he felt his insides were going to burst. Ral simply grunted at the childish behavior.

"What happened — to your fur?" Oren said through tightly clenched teeth, trying to smother another outburst.

"Too much electricity, I think," Syris said, concealing a smile.

"I hope you're enjoying this humorous moment while it lasts," Ral said.

Ral's fur had become so filled with static from the lightning that it now stood straight up, making a giant puff of black. He was more of a large, circular blob with little feet poking out the bottom. It reminded Oren of his cat when he had thrown it into the air to see if it would really land on all fours. The cat landed in deep snow and when it emerged, it was so frightened it had become an icy, white ball. Oren was scolded by his father and told never to throw the cat again.

So, instead of throwing the cat, he threw the dead mice. It would have been alright if one mouse hadn't landed in Mertha's blouse. She screamed so loudly every man came running. That was the beginning of the fierce battle between the two of them. Oren had been four and Mertha was somewhere near the age of thirty. She had come from a wealthy family, but no man was interested in a snobby, high minded woman who thought she was better than all others because her coats were made from wolf fur instead of rabbit or bear. Oren turned and frowned at Ral. At that moment, Oren could have been wearing Ral's long lost cousin. He didn't want to think of the fit Ral would throw if Oren's fine coat was indeed the bear's family member.

"Please, Origin, make him ignorant!" Oren prayed silently.

Syris looked down the path the woman had run down. "Maybe we should follow?" he said.

Oren frowned at him in dismay. Despite not being able to stay angry at Gudra, he didn't want to see her again.

"For heaven's glory, why?" Oren snarled.

"Well, she seems to know where she's going, and she said she'd see us soon," Syris said, inching away. It was obvious that Oren was resentful of her.

"And if she is going the wrong way, then what?" Oren said.

Ral ignored them and started down the path. Syris, eager to escape Oren's burning gaze, quickly followed. Oren sighed, disappointed that once again he would have to tolerate her. He shifted his weight, and walked quickly to regain his ground with the others.

The way out of the maze was far easier and shorter than the way in. There were no distortions, fewer split paths, and Gudra had left trail markers for them to follow. Syris smiled at Oren, who was scanning the ground.

"Just say it and end your agony," Ral said.

Oren shook his head. Syris continued to stare at him. Finally Oren gave in.

"Alright, she knows where she's going and it was wise to follow her! Are you happy, Syris?" Oren seethed.

"Quite!" Syris said, whistling a tune.

Oren watched the childish ginger, and smacked him over the head. Syris looked at Oren in bewilderment.

"Wipe that smile off your arrogant face," Oren hissed.

Oren walked ahead, and Syris stood still. Syris felt his sleeve being tugged as he was pulled along by the bear.

Some right turns, left turns, and a curious roundabout brought them into an oval room with a wooden ceiling; flowers lined the walls. Two benches made from wood rested on either side of a marble fountain spewing the purest water Oren had ever seen, but half of the fountain was dry and barren, as if water hadn't touched it in one thousand years. A butterfly flitted in front of Oren's eyes, and drifted towards a purple petal. Other butterflies began to follow, and soon every flower had a small insect on it.

Their wings were gold, blue, green, pink, and white, like light reflected through a prism window. They filled their small stomachs, and floated into the air in unison. They spiraled round the room, and it seemed as if they were dancing. All the colors drifted higher and higher until they disappeared among the clouds, until their silent songs were lost on the wind.

Oren sat down on a bench, wanting to rest, to gather his thoughts. Syris snuck over and carefully swiped Oren's filed claw from his bag, desperately wanting to get rid of his ridiculous beard and moustache. Syris shaved using the water in the fountain. He noticed that as he cleaned his grime covered face in the water, the water never seemed to get dirty. It was a curiosity, to say the least, but Syris paid it no mind, and turned around to look at Oren, a smile on the energetic, red haired man's face.

"So, what do you think?" Syris said, beaming.

Oren looked at him for a split second and returned to his thoughts. "You look the same," he muttered.

Syris' eyebrow twitched in annoyance, the large grin still present on his face.

"I think I look young," Syris huffed.

"You are young," Oren mused.

"I'm older than you!"

Oren glanced up at Syris. "You have the maturity of a five year old," he said, a grim smile slithering across his face.

Syris stamped his foot and marched away, Oren's eyes digging into his back. Ral crossed the room and waited quietly at the other end. Oren and Syris followed. As they left the chamber, Syris turned to look back. One butterfly remained. It was red with black spots. It fluttered up towards the fountain and vanished within the small ripples. The light seemed to fade now that all the winged dancers were gone.

They walked into a stone room, its ceiling a thin slab of marble. Another massive double door with flecks of paint on it stood at the end. The door grinded open, sand brushing along the cracked surface of the floor. Ral was first to step into the harsh light of day. Sand shifted around his feet, and the wind howled noisily. Oren and Syris shielded their eyes from the desert sun.

"How did we go from a maze with grass and butterflies to sand and heat?" Syris said, kicking a small dune.

"That's the way it is here on this world," an all too familiar voice chimed.

Oren groaned with despair, and turned to see Gudra sitting gingerly on a weathered rock. She stood, and flapped her cloak to get the loose sand out.

"Every region of this world is centered on a Shrine village. In the middle of this blasted desert is the famed Shrine of Usher. Quiz time, Syris: who is the Shrine of

Usher dedicated to? Please tell Oren, seeing as he is the only one within one million miles who knows nothing of the Gods or Goddesses," Gudra said loudly.

"For your information, I —" Oren protested.

She raised a hand to Oren, commanding him to remain silent. Syris shouted over the wind.

"Dedicated in what is believed to be over 8 thousand years, the Shrine of Usher is the one of the oldest shrines ever made. Statues of Usher, the God of Earth, were uncovered twelve thousand years ago suggesting that something else may have stood in the village's place before hand."

"What — like a temple for the God of Earth?" Oren said.

"What do you know about temples?" Ral asked.

"Nothing, really. There was rumor that a temple laid beneath the Lake of Tears in the Shrine of Silice. It was never proven."

"The ice is too thick and the water too cold. Of course it was never proven. What did I expect? Here I was hoping that some faith may have remained for —" Gudra stopped. Ral had kicked her in the leg. Her rambling had been noticed.

"You were saying?" Oren said.

Her gaze flitted over to Ral, who shook his head.

"Nothing. However, did you notice the way the climate changed when you were half-way between your Shrine village — and his?" she said, pointing at Syris.

"It became hotter, more humid," Oren said.

"Exactly! It is the same here. That maze is the mid-way point between shrines. The mid-way point between the Shrine of Silice and the Shrine of Aros is a pond that is half frozen and half thawed. A forest resides on both sides, one side covered in snow and the other side covered in ash. If you remember, that is the same pond and very small clearing near where you and I first met."

"Half of the fountain was dry," Oren said.

"That half represented the desert beyond," Ral said.

"I remember that pond. You gave me the key there. Syris was resurrected there, and my father said once that I had been born by its waters. I was told that my mother drank from it to calm her down."

"She — drank from —" Gudra stuttered. Suddenly, she burst into laughter.

"So, it is you? You are the child? How interesting," she said. "Well, Ral, now it should make sense why he can hear you when you're silent. You're a child of both the flame and freeze. This day keeps getting better and better!"

"And the sun is setting. We should go," Ral said.

Oren stood perplexed by the sudden interaction and use of words. Gudra turned towards the distance, and tried to break into a run across the sand, but before she could move two inches, Oren grabbed her by the upper arm. She snarled, teeth like fangs flashing. She grabbed Oren's wrist and twisted, bringing him to his knees before she shoved him face first into the sand.

"Don't touch me," she hissed.

Gudra let go of Oren's wrist and sped away, allowing Oren to raise his head swiftly as he coughed out the sand he had been forced to swallow. As Gudra ran, she turned around.

"Ral, there is no need for unscheduled meetings. Take them around the shrine, by the Runes of Silence!" Her figure vanished with the wind and sand.

"Syris, history lesson on Runes of Silence," Oren snapped, picking at grains of sand on his tongue.

Syris smiled and followed Ral as the bear trudged forward, his feet sinking every now and then.

"The Runes of Silence — not much is written on them. All that remains of them, according to rumor, is a large, stone archway. They were named the Runes of Silence because apparently, there is no sound when you're near them. No one has been able to document anything on the archway, though. They say that people run away screaming about voices. Apparently, near the arch, there was an inscription that said the archway was called the Gate of Trials. Don't ask why, I don't know."

"Why does she want us to pass through that area, Ral?" Oren turned his head towards the bear.

Ral remained silent. It seemed there was something he was not allowed to say. Oren was determined to find out what, if anything. The Runes belonged to the Shrine of Usher.

"Syris, what does Usher govern over, besides earth and sand?"

"Well, it is written that he was ordered by Origin to test the apprentices before they could become a god or goddess. Despite belief, it is said that Usher was the first apprentice that Origin accepted, not Aros, though not proven. The Gods and Goddesses were supposed to pass through an ancient door known as the Gate of Trials, located at something called the Vesion."

Oren smiled. "You needed a book to find that out?"

Syris clutched his book defensively, cradling it like a precious child. He turned his back to Oren slightly, deflecting the imaginary verbal blows against his literary pride and joy.

"I didn't know that the gate in the Runes of Silence was linked with Usher." Syris retorted.

"How could you not? This is his region," Oren huffed.

"That doesn't mean he knows everything about it," Ral said.

Oren stared at the bear's back. "Are you going to answer my question?" he said.

Ral smiled. "If you're trying to give your words that subtle edge that makes that hot-headed girl so threatening and scary, you're failing miserably."

Oren grunted in defiance. Syris chuckled at Ral's answer. Oren's words would never have the sharp, sword-like edge that Gudra's words did. She was clever as a witch, and as sinister as a demon, or demoness, in this case. Yet, it seemed that behind that cold, hard exterior, she was fragile on the inside. Fragile as she seemed, she put up one heck of a charade, acting tough and strong. Was it her strength, or was it her weakness?

So many things about her were unclear. So many questions remained unanswered. Oren would ask Ral, but he seemed negligent to answer anything concerning Gudra. In fact, he seemed somewhat afraid of her, though he was capable of ordering her to remain silent. Oren decided to pressure Ral with questions anyway.

"So," he began, "what do you know about that woman?"

Ral glanced back at him. "Why do you assume I know anything?"

Oren narrowed his eyes. "She talks to you as if you're an old friend. Also, you order her around quite a bit."

Ral laughed. "You think I could order her around? She'd rip my heart out if I tried!"

Oren smiled. "So, you do know her?"

Ral ceased walking and turned to face Oren. "Yes, I know her. Why does it concern you? Why should it matter?"

"Who is she? What is she?"

Ral smiled. "What do you mean 'what is she'? What do you suspect her of being? She seems human to me. Do you think different?"

Oren grinded his teeth together, frustrated by Ral's ability to slither away from answering questions directly. "Stop messing with me!"

"I'm not. You are making this bigger than it actually is."

"Just answer me! You keep wiggling away from the truth, like a worm!"

Ral chuckled. "Wiggle, wiggle, wiggle, stop! Wiggle, wiggle, wiggle, stop!"

Oren's eyes widened. "Sometimes, I keep forgetting you're not human."

"Who said I'm not human?"

Oren took a step back. Was Ral suggesting that he wasn't actually a bear? That wasn't possible. Ral may have the extraordinary ability to use human speech and possess the smarts of a human, along with being fairly wise, but he was a bear in every physical aspect. Oren had seen his paws first hand and they didn't appear to have any hidden opposable thumbs.

"What is it you're saying?"

"I don't recall saying anything," Ral said.

"Syris, does that oversized encyclopedia of yours have anything on shape shifters?"

Syris looked up at Oren in surprise. "Shape shifters? Let me take a look."

Syris flipped the pages until he found what appeared to be an index. He scanned the page, following his finger into the S section. Syris then grabbed at the book and flipped through it. He smiled, suggesting that he had found what he was looking for.

"Shape shifters: a being in possession of the ability to alter his or her form into any other being of any type. The form of shifting is chosen by the being at the respective age of twelve when the body is prepared to undergo the first transformation ceremony. These ceremonies are painful, but physical change after that is painless and can occur in an instant. In some cases, a shape shifter may decide to live out the remainder of his or her days as the chosen alternative form, which results in a permanent change that cannot be undone. The only known way of detecting a shape shifter is by the color of their blood, which is silver."

"Like Tharazar," Oren said. "Syris, what kind of monster is the one that Tharazar chose to be?" Oren asked.

Syris flipped through the pages, brown and fading edges creasing easily underneath his fingertips.

"The species that Tharazar copied is known as the

Ugly Demon. They usually live alone, feasting on pigs, goats, sheep, and an occasional human. They usually have large iron maces with them, though it's only for decoration. They never actually use it. The Ugly Demons have been nicknamed the Chicken Foot Ox. It's a fitting name, all things considered."

Oren looked at Ral and smiled creepily, lightly touching the hilt of his sword.

"You keep that thing away from me, or else," Ral snarled.

"Or else what?" Oren sneered.

Ral took two giant steps forward so that he towered over Oren, his shadow stretching across the ground.

"Or else," he snarled, "you'll find out if you try."

"Then just answer me straight. Are you a shape shifter?"

Ral's muscles eased from their tension and he backed away.

"No," he said, "I am not. I never have been anything but a bear. Now, I would appreciate if you would follow me. We still have a fairly long way to go until we reach our destination. The sands will shift soon, and we want to be on solid ground when they do."

"Syris, what does he mean the sands will shift?"

Syris flipped through his book again, to the geography section of the desert.

"When the sands of the desert "shift", that means that the entire landscape changes. In the morning the desert will appear flat and even. By midday, dunes will have formed almost everywhere.

At night, just before the sun sets, the ground shifts

and the sand ceases to exist, revealing rocky ground and deep, endless chasms. Many people have been known to fall prey to these bottomless pits, for the sands conceal them perfectly until they are stepped upon. On rare but fatal occasions, the rocky ground will fall away. Many believe that eventually the chasms will spread so far that no ground will be left, but this is mere speculation."

"And now you know why I would like to be at the Gate of Trials before sunset," Ral hissed.

Oren glared at him with distrust. "You could have mentioned that beforehand."

Ral looked at him. "Would you have acted any differently towards me?"

Oren flinched. Even though simple, Ral's words were still harsh. Also, Ral was right; Oren probably would still have had the same attitude with him. It made sense now, why Ral was so quiet. He was focused on leaving the sands behind. The Desert of the Dead was well named. If it was true that sands gave way to endless pits of darkness, swallowing everything that they claimed, then Oren, as well as Ral, did not want to be here when the sands disappeared.

Oren looked at the sky. Twilight was close. The blue sky was beginning to fade away into deeper shades. "How much farther is this Gate?"

Syris flipped through his book again.

"According to this, we should first pass by a sign."

"We already did," Ral said.

"What did the sign say?" Oren asked.

"Turn back," Ral mused.

Oren raised an eyebrow. He hadn't seen any signs, but

then again, Oren hadn't really been paying any attention. "Should we listen to it?"

"No," Ral replied curtly.

Syris hid a small smile in his shoulder. Ral was obviously tired, and therefore grumpy. Seeing his childish display was proving to be slightly amusing, and it distracted Syris from thinking of home, of possibly dying, and of all the unknown factors in front of him. He followed closely behind Oren, who stayed a foot or two away from Ral.

Syris swore he could feel it: the pulsing of the earth. He could feel it beneath his shoes, vibrating into the soles of his feet, up his legs and ribs, and into his head. He wanted to stoop down, press his ear to the sand, and listen for the heartbeat he knew had to exist. He looked up to the sky, and saw the vibrant shades of blue begin to melt into a creamy, thick orange. The orange was met with a candy pink, and a light, brilliant lilac. Syris wondered what this moment looked like from the stars. If a being was staring down at their little planet, what did this gorgeous array of colors look like to them?

Syris jumped, his breath hitched; he could not have imagined it, that painful, hot throbbing beneath his feet. It had to be real – it was too vivid not to be. Forgetting all about Ral and Oren, he dropped to the ground, pressing his hands and face against the sand. He waited in anxious anticipation, waited perfectly quiet and still. Suddenly, his cheek felt as if it had been slapped with a wet, wooden spoon. He recoiled, and then instantly pressed his face back down. It was not the heat of the sand that scorched him, but rather a pulsing coming from down below. He could feel it: the planet's heartbeat. It was soft, steady, a low humming, almost like the purring of a cat. Yet every so often, it would surge to life, beating against its rocky body like cannon fire.

Syris felt it in his hands, and despite the pain, he kept his palms flat against the ground, taking in the interesting sensation of the way the ground seemed to wriggle and slide beneath his fingers. The more he felt, the more unsettled he became. It occurred to him that the planet was far too beautiful, too peaceful, for this throbbing heart to belong to it. This heartbeat he felt was angry, violent; it couldn't belong to this world.

Syris pressed his face firmly against the sand, ignoring the fact that it was curling into his ear. He listened intently, waiting. Something flashed in his vision, a scene he had never encountered before – a vision of his home burned to a crisp, of the whole world itself cracking apart and caving in on its hollowed out shell – a monster ripping through the earth, dragging everything it touched into the pits of Hell – flesh being strewn across the ground, and creatures Syris knew didn't exist feasted on it.

A scream ripped through Syris, and he fell back. Oren and Ral turned to him with a start, each ready to pounce on the unseen threat. Syris' face was twisted in fear, confusion, and some other emotion that couldn't be recognized by anyone present.

"What's wrong?" Ral asked harshly.

Syris stuttered, his voice lost. "Y-you didn't hear it?"

Ral's brow furrowed. "Hear what?"

Syris looked around, bewildered. "The screaming. From down there."

Ral flinched, but remained composed. "Screaming?"

Syris nodded weakly.

"Did you hear anything else?" Ral asked quietly.

Syris looked at the ground. "A heartbeat. And I saw – something."

Ral moved closer to Syris, sitting down in front of him.

"What did you see?" the bear asked softly.

Syris looked up into his huge, brown eyes, eyes that were soft and strong at the same time. He opened his mouth, and tears bubbled in his eyes.

"Syris?" Oren said. He moved closer, and squatted down just behind Ral.

"I saw it," Syris breathed. "The end of the world."

Ral recoiled, his eyes widening. "What do you mean?"

"I saw the ground break apart and fall. I saw all the cities and villages burn. I saw the sea turn to blood, and people being skinned alive. There was a monster, a huge, demonic creature — it came out of the ground, and destroyed everything."

Ral watched Syris carefully. "What color was it?"

Syris tilted his head to one side. "What?"

"What color was this creature that was in the ground?"

Syris lowered his head, trying to recall that small detail among the flashes of pictures going through his mind. "Red, I think? It must have been red. A dark red, maybe even purple."

Ral took a deep breath and held it. His lips twitched, his fur stood on end. All of a sudden, he could feel it, the heartbeat Syris talked about. He could feel it drumming beneath his paw pads, soft and steady, then violently and hot. Ral looked down at the sand, rage slowly stretching across his face, his gums pulling back to reveal the sharp, white canines that lined his jaw. Oren watched Ral intently, slowly inching away as if the bear would explode right there.

Ral slammed a paw into the ground, his fur growing darker, and his eyes flaring. "**Quiet, you pig.**"

Syris looked at Ral, completely bewildered, but he noticed that the beating beneath him became dull. It practically disappeared, but Syris knew that despite no longer feeling it, it was still there. Ral had forced it into remission, but it would surely return in its own time.

Oren stood up, wiping the sand from his pants. "Will someone please explain what's going on?"

Ral shook his head. "Don't worry about it. It's not something you need to deal with."

Oren raised an eyebrow. "Alright, I guess."

Syris stood up shakily, using Ral as a crutch. Ral slowly turned, and the trio began walking again. Oren watched them from behind, analyzing every movement.

Syris leaned into Ral. "What was that?"

"What was what?" Ral said, glancing at the red-haired boy.

"That thing in the ground. What was screaming down there?"

Ral looked straight ahead. "Nothing you can help."

"But **what?**" Syris pressed.

Ral sighed deeply and looked at him. "A demon. The worst kind. That kind that wants to consume everything in its path."

Syris scanned the texts. "We're not too far off. In fact, we should be able to see it once we reach the top of this sand dune."

Oren lifted his hand to his brow. The sun was almost gone but still bright and blinding.

"Is that it?" Oren asked, pointing towards a looped shaped.

Oren's finger traveled across the sands and past several dunes. In the distance was a tall archway. Fallen columns sat in the sands, and a few more sat atop the stone circle where the archway rested. Part of the top of the archway was missing, and an old, rusty chain was looped around one side, with an immense lock lying on the ground next to the end of it. The lock still had small flakes of blue and gold on it, showing that the archway may have been the door to a much bigger complex at some point. Even at a distance, the archway was large enough so that these details could be seen.

Ral shifted his weight and carefully trudged down the sand dune, making sure he didn't fall or slip.

"Hurry up," he grunted.

Oren and Syris took heavy steps down the dune, each foot sinking deeper into the sand. Syris had some trouble keeping his balance on the unsteady area and fell more than once. The dunes were steep no matter which side you went up or down. Oren drove his hands into the sand to help him climb the dunes, for his strength was starting to get low. When descending, Syris had finally decided to slide down on his back, though his shirt was full with sand when he was done.

As Syris flapped his shirt, trying to get the sand out, a withered piece of plant fell out as well. Syris stopped what he was doing and looked down at it. Suddenly, a fresh, green vine shot out from within the withered thing and wrapped around his leg. Syris screamed in alarm, catching the attention of Ral and Oren. The vine became thicker and roots started to grow into the dry sand.

"What is this thing?" Syris screeched as his book and short swords dropped from his person. The plant grew incredibly fast, both in size and length. It picked Syris up into the air, where he swung upside-down.

Oren picked up the book from the sand and began flipping through it.

"It's called a Shezur! Their seed pods are grown off plants called Dream Mist. However, they can only thrive in dry, hot climates. In that respect, they are rarely ever seen. They were nicknamed the Man Eater," Oren read, squinting his eyes at the text.

"Well, that's absolutely wonderful! Now, Oren, look in the big book of all-knowing, perfectly helpful information, and tell me — **how do I kill it**?" Syris hollered.

Oren searched the text furiously.

"Hm, doesn't say — how odd."

Syris' eyes nearly popped from their sockets.

"O-odd? I don't care if it's odd! Help me, fool!" he yelled.

"Help yourself!" Oren said, closing the book and throwing Syris' short swords towards him. Syris caught them, unsheathed one, and sliced the vine holding him, dropping to the sand. Syris pushed himself up and away, stumbling around on the thick sand. The severed vine writhed around, smashing into the ground.

"Please, can we worry about this thing later? Apparently, they're not mobile." Oren said.

Ral nodded and they all ran from the plant until they were sure it wouldn't be able to reach them with its surprisingly long roots.

The arch still seemed to be miles and miles away, as if while they tried to get closer, the arch inched away, although more of the arch could clearly be seen.

The Gate of Trials had iron claw-like grips holding it to the floor. The grips were built around the base of the arch and seem to drill into the ground.

"Whoever made this wasn't confident it wouldn't fall over."

Ral huffed.

"You misunderstand the point of those iron bases," he said.

Syris narrowed his eyes. "Then explain."

Ral chuckled. "In time, my friend."

Oren's back was hot and damp. He turned around to let the desert wind hit his face. It was somewhat refreshing, considering that even the wind was hot and dry. Oren opened his eyes and looked out over the sky. It was black directly above him, but as he stared closer to the horizon, it became pink, red, and a light shade of orange. It was a very peaceful sight, a sight which smacked Oren with harsh realization. He spun around to face Ral who had stopped momentarily.

"Time is not something we have right now!"

Ral glanced in his direction.

"I am already aware of this," he said.

It hadn't occurred to Oren to ask why Ral had stopped with such precious time wasting away.

About a foot in front of Ral's sharp bear claws, the sand had trickled away like an hourglass, revealing part of a large, deep chasm. Sand continued to slowly but surely pour away, unveiling more and more and the jagged hole in the earth's surface. Syris looked around to see how far they were from safe, solid ground.

"Wasn't there a dune behind us?" Syris mused quietly.

Oren looked in the direction that Syris had stated and became confused. Syris was right. Oren could clearly remember a dune being there, casting a shadow down on them, but now, it had vanished into thin air – or into deep ground. Suddenly, Oren was lifted into the air. Oren squirmed like a snake, kicking his legs and scrapping his hands through sky.

"Stop moving!"

Oren ceased movement and looked below him. Two furry paws were latched around his waist with two furry feet on the ground. A big, moist nose was blowing hot air on the back of his legs. Oren flinched involuntarily.

"Wow!" Syris said, delight burning in his green eyes. "Lift me up, too, Ral!" he said, stretching his hands above his head in the same way that Ral was holding Oren up.

Ral, being a bear with human-like attributes, had good balance. He had stood up on two feet to give Oren a clear view of their surroundings.

"Are you on drugs?" Oren yelled. "Put me down!"

"What do you see?" Ral snorted.

Oren stopped his shouting long enough to scan the area.

"Oh."

The sand that had once made up the desert was rapidly disappearing. Large cracks and fissures could be seen spanning out all over the place. Oren then hit the ground with a loud thud.

"What was that for?" he said, rubbing his back.

"Don't move," Ral hissed.

"Why not?" Oren said, glaring up at him.

Ral leered at Oren.

"You're sitting on top of the largest chasm on the entire planet, known as Riddle's End."

Oren turned pale and looked down. It was true. The sand was starting to show the opening of a large drop that went right beneath Oren's feet. Riddle's End was a chasm that was at least four miles long and stretched thirty feet wide, a deadly and well hidden trap.

"Won't sitting here be worse?" Oren said.

"The more you move, the faster the sand disappears."

"They should rename this desert," Oren hissed.

Ral chuckled. "I agree."

Syris sighed.

"We were so close," he mused.

Ral looked behind him. It was true; they were only about twenty feet from the arch, twenty feet that could probably be covered with one quick sprint, but, in Oren's current predicament, that dash might not be possible. Ral narrowed his eyes.

"Where are you when I need you?" he growled.

"Ral, what is that?"

It seemed like nothing more than a small hill of sand. However, it was growing in size, slowly becoming larger and larger, and was moving towards Oren. The bump then disappeared. The ground began to vibrate, shaking violently and then becoming still again.

All Oren could see was sand, like it was raining dirt, but Oren knew that sand didn't fall out of the sky. This sand seemed to be alive. It was moving and had eight legs and brown, glowing markings all over it. Oren couldn't remember when the sand had becoming hairy and white, almost grey, but not quite. Once again, sand covered everything and he could hear Ral shouting.

"Feser!"

Who was Feser? Did he mean this blob of moving sand? It took Oren a while to realize that he was no longer moving but laying on rock. A large, broken iron chain was just within reach. Oren forced himself into a sitting position. Large furry paws grabbed at Oren's waist, setting him on his feet.

"Do you hurt anywhere?" Ral asked. Syris was running around with a crazed but happy look on his face.

"I'm — fine. What's wrong with Syris?" Oren said, raising an eyebrow.

"He's having a heavenly experience of realizing he is one of the few people to come this close to the Gate of Trials, though he's overreacting."

Oren peered up at Ral's big, brown eyes.

"Who is Feser?"

"No one important."

Oren followed at Ral's big bear feet as he walked away.

"Is he an animal, like you?" Oren asked.

Ral looked at Oren before answering. "In time, my friend. Now, if you'll excuse me, I need to go stop Syris from destroying an ancient monument in the name of history, discovery, and so forth."

Oren laughed a little. Ral was right; Syris was getting a little too carried away, dusting the rubble to see the stonework clearly and chipping away at stones to see if there were any gems hidden within. Oren remembered something else about the sand. Not only were there eight legs, but there had been sticky, silk-like threads, and a pair of fangs with liquid dripping off the ends. Oren immediately thought of a spider, but there was no way that a spider could become big enough for someone to ride on one.

"Well, well, you made it at last!" a voice chimed.

"I see you made it, too," Oren hissed.

Gudra paused before answering.

"I don't think you like me very much," she pouted.

"You could have helped us," Oren said.

Gudra laughed.

"Earth to Oren! I did help you! Just ask Ral. You'd be dead without me."

"If you helped us here, then tell me who Feser is."

"No can do."

"Why not?"

Oren couldn't see her eyes, but he could feel them staring at him, almost digging into his very soul.

"In time, my friend," she said.

Oren would have yelled at her, but she was so serious it almost made him go numb.

She was sitting on top of the arch, kicking her legs back and forth. On her fifth kick, she fell backwards and flipped through the air, landing on her feet so lightly that she didn't even disturb the sand beneath her.

"I think I shall stay with you for a little while," she said, looking out over the desert. "Why did you leave that plant alive?"

Oren was a little surprised that she knew about that plant monster, but then again, she had been sitting on an arch which gave a very clear view of the terrain.

"Why does it matter?" Oren asked.

"Because," she said, extending her hand in front of her. A small red orb of light started to grow at the center of her palm. "You shouldn't have left it there."

The red orb grew and shot off so fast it couldn't be seen, towards the Shezur. No one could see the impact, but they saw the effect. The ground shook and fire spewed into the air. An explosion sent sand, rock, and pieces of the Shezur flying into the sky. The flames writhed around and sent shadows cascading down into the growing chasms. The earth rumbled and broke, falling away into the endless black pits. Gudra had just blown a crater into the earth, swallowing what little land had originally been there, resulting in the Riddle's End's expansion by at least another thirty feet. Oren and Syris gawked at her in amazement.

"H-how did you do that?" Syris said, completely fascinated with her sudden ability to detonate objects at will.

Gudra laughed. "That's not all I can do. However, those secrets are for later," she said, concealing a smile beneath the dark fabric of her cloak.

She motioned for them to follow her.

"So, where do you want us to go now?" Syris said.

"One more step and you're there," she said.

Gudra walked over to a stone door at the end of the large circular platform, past the arch.

"Don't talk to the voices," she said quietly.

Ral grabbed Oren and Syris with his paws and moved them forward. It was true, what people had said about the arch. Voices could be heard around them. Oren kicked some sand up, but he didn't even hear his boot scrape across the ground.

"It really is silent here," he said to himself.

"Hence the name, the Runes of Silence, home to the Gate of Trials," Syris said proudly.

He had done his homework, Oren was well aware of that.

"Unless you built it, stop bragging," Gudra said.

She pressed her hand against the stone surface and mumbled something softly. A crest appeared on the door and it cracked in two.

"Let me guess: the Throne of Usher?" Oren said, eyeing the jagged, symmetrical pattern.

Gudra turned to him and smiled, but she said nothing to him. This surprised Oren. It was something she hadn't done before, and was completely out of character.

The stone slid apart, grinding into sand as it scraped along the ground. Gudra walked into the bright opening and disappeared. Oren hesitated as Ral shoved him closer to the opening.

"Don't be a chicken," Syris said, pushing his shoulder.

Oren looked at Syris and coughed. Syris was, as they

said, the pot calling the kettle black. He put on a brave face, but anyone could see that he was shaking all down his spine, like an unstable pillar ready to topple over at any second. Oren smiled and hit him on the back.

"I'm fine," he said, "but you look like you're about to cry!"

Syris flinched and hit Oren's arm. "I am not crying! I just got some sand in my eye!"

Oren looked around him.

"Speaking of sand," he said, "it's all gone."

Syris gazed out over the desert. It was true, all the sand had vanished. It had fallen beneath the earth, and great chasms with jagged openings had taken its place. Ral looked at the sky. It was beginning to turn a dark blue with small flecks of red and light pink near the sliver of sunlight that remained. Oren looked towards the new source of light. They had gotten closer to the door, but the entrance still seemed so far away, as if it was a path with no end. Ral continued to push him and Syris along the weathered stone. The wind picked up a few pebbles and pelted them against the large arch, which was shrinking as the trio progressed towards the stone door. The wind was strong, but still, in the Runes of Silence, nothing made a sound. It was a perfect silence that not even a war could disrupt. Oren began to wonder if Usher was silent as well, if he was solitary and reclined like these ruins.

"Oren, go," Ral said.

Oren looked up into the light filled opening. It seemed even brighter than before. He looked back at the arch and the evening sky. Stars were beginning to appear like specks of white paint on a black canvas. A hand grabbed his wrist. Gudra's head poked through and she smiled again, a sweet smile of comfort and kindness. She tugged on Oren and pulled him through. The light seemed to last forever and there was warmth with it. A fresh, cool breeze rustled Oren's hair. Oren's eyes opened and he held his breath at the sight. Syris stepped through and nearly lost his balance. Ral followed after Syris and chuckled at their faces. Their reactions were perfect, one of kind. Gudra danced and spun in front of them, her cloak billowing out behind her in the wind's forceful breeze. She twirled towards Oren and laughed when she saw his face. She grabbed his wrist and spun him in a large circle before releasing him and watching him roll on the green grass and land in a small bed of pink and white flowers.

"Yes, Oren, places like this do exist!

Chapter 13

THE VALLEY OF WIND

- My student kept falling behind, stumbling on the sand and earth. I urged him to keep pace. Night was falling and he has no tolerance for the cold. I, on the other hand, love the winter chill. I could lie on the ice and sleep if I really wanted to. When we made it to the Vesion, he marveled at the size of the doors, and even more at the architecture inside. I pushed him into the first room, and the test began. Now he could not leave, and none could enter. I heard Usher above us, his voice unsure as he gave instructions to my student. They were all watching, even my dearest love. I could feel his soul shaking with uncertainty. If there was anything I could do to ease his worries, I would do it. I would lay down my life to give him peace. I may very well end up having to.

Questions were running through Oren's mind like little mice running on small metal wheels. It was a beautiful sight. The sky was blue and stretched on forever, as if it had no end. The grass was green and lush, full of life, and it smelled wonderful. The wind was strong and everything swayed and danced in its wake. Oren lifted himself into a sitting position. Gudra laughed and skipped over to him. She ran her fingers through his hair, picking all the pink and white flower petals out. She bent down and grabbed a handful of flowers, sniffing them. She smiled and put them in front of Oren's nose. He glanced up at her before smelling them. The fragrance was sweet.

Oren gazed out over the valley. It was green and spotted with large circles of white and pink, yellow and red, and purple and blue here and there. Off to the right and left, in front of Oren were two mountain peaks covered with snow. Oren turned around and saw another mountain peak, stretching into the sky beyond the clouds, so high he couldn't see the top. Oren looked all around, seeing only sky, and he realized that this expansion of land was not on ground level, that it was tens of thousands of feet in the air. Oren knew this because the plant that the woman had just made him sniff was a rare plant, called Pare, which could only be found in places of extremely high elevation, and there was only one place that wasn't ground level here on First World. In this sacred place, a lush valley was nestled on a mountain with three peaks, far above the ground.

"That plant," Oren said, looking at Gudra. "It only grows above ten thousand feet. Where are we, exactly?"

"You are on a mountain. You're not on the top, but you're not anywhere near the bottom, either. You're in between. This mountain has three different peaks.

Wedged in between these peaks, far above the ground, is a plateau — a valley of sorts," she said.

"We're on a mountain?" Oren said, amazed.

He had paid enough attention in school when he was younger to know that there was only one, single mountain in all of First World that didn't reside near any ocean and didn't erupt every few years. It rested in the middle of the land and rose so high people said it stretched into the clouds, even into space. Were they really standing on the same mountain that the stories said was the holy ground of Saate, the Goddess of Wind? Oren looked back at the door that had closed behind them. A new crest was on its surface. Oren guessed it was the Gales of Saate. It was an elegant design, but simple – far more simple than some of the other crests; there were less individual shapes involved.

On this side of the stone door, vines of ivy grew around it. The door still had some paint left on it. Flecks of light green were on the crest and gold could be seen as well. The crest flashed once and disappeared until someone would call on the door to open. Oren again looked out over the valley. Even at this height, Oren couldn't see the top of the third peak. He wondered if this was the fabled mountain peak that stretched into the cosmos, the Heaven's Bridge. It seemed that it could touch the surface of the moon.

"Impressive, isn't it?" a young voice chimed.

Oren looked up at Gudra and her billowing cloak.

"This is the highest valley in First World, resting between the three peaks of the Summit of Spring. It was so named because here, in the land of Saate, it is always spring. Snow never falls, and rain is always abundant. The door is the only way to get from the desert to this valley. The mountain cannot be climbed," she said.

"But where is the desert?" Oren asked.

She looked down at him, and then pointed down below the clouds. Through the puffs of white, Oren could see a vast extension of land, but no desert.

"I don't see it," he said.

The woman sighed. "That's exactly the point. There are two continents on this world. Only two, and they are separated by the ocean."

"Shouldn't we have hit a mid-way point, then?" Oren asked.

"The maze was the mid-way point between the desert and this mountain, although it is out of place for a mid-way point," the woman said.

"Then what lands rest on this continent?" Syris asked, walking up behind them.

"On your continent, there are the Shrines of Aros, Silice, Usher, and Kryptos. This continent has the Shrines of Saate, Vashire, Lunatra, and Osaea. Technically, the Ocean of Two Worlds is under Osaea's control, but they say she spilt the ownership with Silice. That is why half of the year, the entire ocean freezes," Ral said.

"The Ocean of Two Worlds?" Oren said.

"Yes, the ocean that covers this planet. They say that the ocean has no bottom and that it leads straight to Hell. Of course, that's only speculation and stories made up to entertain little children," Gudra said.

Ral looked at her with disapproval. Oren continued to look at the clouds. The land below seemed so small.

He could even see the salty sea. Oren turned his gaze towards the heavens. It was true, this mountain stretched beyond the clouds, maybe even farther to places no one could see or go.

"I wonder why the continents are separate," Oren said to himself.

The woman smiled. "Think about it," she said, "If there was a war between two celestial beings, what do you think would happen to the human population?"

Oren looked at her, curious.

"Do you mean to say that this continent fought under one being during the war while the other continent pledged allegiance to another being? Then they were separated onto different lands to avoid further conflict?" Syris said.

"No, but the followers of Tora wanted a mountain stronghold, so the gods flooded to eastern edge of the world. Now there is no need for it, seeing as all the followers of the evil God are dead. It was done for protection, and we, being mere mortals in the presence of such power, have no room to argue about it. It is what it is," Ral said, looking up at the blue and pink sky.

"The three of us may be mortal, but I don't know about you," Gudra said, laughing to herself. "And you've got it all backwards. The continental split had nothing to do with followers or the war. It happened at the conclusion of the war."

"Well, clearly we went to different schools. Also, do you mean to put yourself among the ranks of the weak, my dear?" Ral said with a sly smile on his black face.

The woman reached up, took Ral's ears between her

thumb and index fingers, pinched them, and began to pull in different directions.

"What did you say?" she yelled.

Oren and Syris watched them, trying desperately to suppress smiles and stifle their laughter.

"Ow! Please, my friend, stop pulling!" Ral said, jerking his head around to try and get his ears away from her.

She continued to pull and yank his ears until she decided to grab his lips and pull them around, showing his big teeth. Ral's next few words came out muffled.

"Plese, my frond, stop plling!"

"Not until you take it back!" she shrieked.

"Tak what ack?" Ral said.

"What you said about me being weak!" she said, twisting his big lips in circles.

"How can I hen I cat spek?" Ral said, forcing part of the words to form.

Gudra stopped pulling and thought about what he had tried to say. She gave his lips one last yank, stretching them as far as they would go, and then released his lips, watching them slingshot back into their proper position. Ral sat back on his haunches and massaged his mouth with his soft paw pads.

"Was that truly necessary?" Ral asked, tears threatening to form in his big bear eyes.

"Yes," Gudra snapped.

She was about to say more but stopped at a loud uproar behind her. Oren and Syris had doubled over in laughter, rolling about in the flowers. She marched over to them and grabbed their ears, forcing them to stand. The two boys winced in pain.

"What are you laughing about?" she growled.

Oren and Syris looked at each other hesitantly.

"N-nothing," Oren said shakily.

"Yeah, nothing at all," Syris said, smiling as innocently as possible.

Gudra stared at them for a little while longer, her facial features hidden behind her cloak as always. She then released their ears and turned to face Ral.

"One more word out of you," she said, pointing at him with a stiff finger, "and you won't have any ears left!"

It was true; she could be very frightening when she wanted to be. Oren leaned over to Syris.

"Remind me never to cross her," he whispered.

Syris nodded slightly, rubbing his earlobe.

"Alright!" she yelled, causing everyone to jump, "Let's go! We have places to be, and people to see, and no time to waste! If you don't want to be knee deep in mud when it rains, then hurry up!"

No one questioned her, and ran quickly to catch up with her swiftly moving figure.

The wind was still strong as ever. Oren looked at the sky. It was becoming bright and blue. It had been night in the desert, so why was it dawn here?

"Why is it morning here when the desert is dark?" Syris said, stealing the words right out of Oren's mouth.

"This continent is on the other side of the planet. The sun is rising into the sky here while it has set over there. Don't you know anything?" Gudra scolded.

Oren laughed at this. Syris, who seemed to know everything, had just been told that he knew nothing.

"Oren," she said, "you have no room to laugh, seeing as how you were wondering the same thing!"

Ral chuckled as Oren's face went pale.

"I never said I didn't know," he protested.

"Stupid boy, it's all in the eyes! The eyes are the window to the soul," she said, pulling on Oren's lower lid.

Oren backed away from her, rubbing his eye, trying to see if she had done any damage. He found the word "stupid" slightly offensive.

"Alright, stop being so slow and let's go!" she hollered.

Oren smiled. You had to love her enthusiasm, even if she was a little bossy.

The grass bent underneath their feet and popped back up once they had walked past. The flowers swayed freely, some of their blossoms just beginning to open, some closed tight against the wind, and others opened completely, allowing their sweet scents to be swirled in the cool gales. Oren looked down at the ground. He watched the greenery twist, forming shadows, making patterns and, at times, faces. There were no faces he knew. Oren looked up at the sky.

The clouds drifted past quickly. There was one cloud that caught Oren's attention. It seemed to be a person with wings; however, the wings were on their head, not their back. Oren blinked, and the cloud was gone. Someone shoved him from behind.

"You're too slow," Gudra said, circling in front of him.

Oren looked at her silently.

"You are very," she pressed her thumb to her upper lip, "interesting."

Oren was surprised at this comment.

"I'm — interesting?"

"Yes," she said, smiling. "Very!"

"What happened to hurrying up?" Ral yelled.

Gudra turned to face him. "That's cheap coming from a slow poke like you!" she said.

"At least I have the time to be slow," Ral shot back.

"At least I have opposable thumbs!" the woman countered.

Ral silenced himself at this.

"Is there a reason you're still arguing?" Syris asked.

The woman snarled. "Be quiet, soulless child!"

Syris closed his mouth, eyes wide.

"Soulless child?" Ral said.

"Yes. It is a universally accepted fact that redheads have no soul. That, and there's the issue of his heritage," Gudra replied, her hands on her hips.

Syris looked at her with extreme confusion, not understanding what heritage had to do with anything. Gudra looked at Oren, then grabbed his wrist and pulled him along. Her grip was strong, and after a few seconds it became too strong. Oren winced under the slight pain it caused him. The woman continued to drag him, even after she had reached Ral and Syris. Finally, Oren wrenched his wrist from her iron grasp. She stopped and looked at him. Oren couldn't see if she was confused by his sudden action.

"Uh — sorry," she said, "for being too rough, but you know, it is your fault. If you were quicker, then I wouldn't have a need to drag you around."

"Ugh — arrogant as always, refusing to take responsibility," Ral said, shaking his head.

"Quiet. At least I understand the definition of the word 'responsibility'!" she snapped. "You, on the other hand, refuse to take it. Even then, you were constantly blaming others. Your arrogance and cowardice nearly led to the downfall of an entire civilization!"

"I was young and weak! What did you expect of me?" Ral shot back.

"You disobeyed me! You ran away from what you had caused and cost many people their lives in the process. You are nothing more than a disgrace to your kind. You — you are lucky that I let you keep what you had then, because if you screw up again, I will rip it all away! Your father is twice the man you are. Even when he was young, he took care of his problems and never, not once, did he disobey me. That was what kept him safe. That was what kept us all safe. I have never been wrong, but you, you are so — so — selfish!" the woman roared.

Ral lowered his head before responding.

"At least — at least I still have people, unlike you," he said.

The woman's temper flared high and bright and the whole world seemed to grow cold.

"Take. That. Back," she hissed.

"No," Ral said, defiance burning in his eyes.

That was the straw that broke the camel's back, and the woman wrapped her right hand around Ral's large throat and squeezed. Ral tried to move away, but the woman's grip tightened greatly. Oren's and Syris' mouths dropped open as they watched. The woman lifted Ral's feet off the ground and held him in the air as if the bear were nothing more than a ragdoll, light and fragile.

"I won't repeat myself," the woman said. Her voice had become deeper, cutting the air like a knife.

Ral choked out a response. "I-I'm — sorry!"

Gudra said nothing, but her hand let go of Ral and the bear dropped swiftly to the floor.

A few moments of Ral coughing passed. "I suppose that will do," she said.

She turned from Ral and walked away, continuing on her journey. Suddenly, she stopped and turned back around.

"You're too slow!" Gudra shouted to the boys.

"You're too loud!" Ral hollered at her.

"So are you!" she shouted back.

Syris took a few heavy steps forward and straightened his back. *"Both of you, shut up!"* he yelled.

Oren and Ral looked at him with stunned silence. Gudra growled, walked up to him, and shoved a pale finger at his face. Her nails were pointed, like claws, but not lethally long. Still, they looked sharp enough to rip the skin off of your face, and they were painted black.

"It is a very foolish thing to do, to yell at me," she said, waving her finger back and forth. "The only reason that bag of fleas gets away with it is because I owe him!"

Oren raised his head. "What do you mean you 'owe' him?"

Gudra looked at Oren, her eyes and nose still, and always, concealed beneath the dark fabric of her cloak. "None of your business!"

She then turned and marched ahead of the others, not seeming to care if they followed or not. Oren wondered why she seemed to get angry at every little thing. In truth, she had an appearance like an adult, but was quite childish. Oren sighed deeply.

"Let's go!"

Her voice was loud and Oren was tempted to put his hands over his ears. Ral nudged Oren forward with his nose.

"Keep moving, or she'll really lose it," he said, stealing a glance at the tall cloaked figure.

Oren and the others began to follow the graceful moving figure of the woman who had taken it into her own power to become leader of their group.

"So, where exactly are we going?" Syris said.

Gudra stopped.

"I am not going anywhere. The three of you should continue in this direction. Ral knows what you're looking for. Just leave it to him. I — have different business to attend to, so I am afraid I have to leave you here," she said, turning to face them.

She looked at Ral and smiled. Ral nodded in reply, and with that the woman bolted in another direction. Ral stepped in front of the group.

"Let's go," he said.

"Why did she have to leave?" Oren said, almost sad.

"Why? Do you miss her already?" Ral said, smirking.

Oren stamped his foot. "Not in the least!"

Oren knew that what he had just said was a lie, but he would never admit that she was starting to grow on him. He was just surprised at her sudden departure. She didn't even pick a fight before she left, or allow anyone time to argue.

"I'll ask again. Where are we going?" Syris said.

Ral ignored him and continued walking. Oren quickly followed him, and Syris ran ahead so he could sit and rest as he waited for them.

"She has her reasons, all of which are valid and important," Ral said, eyeing Oren.

Oren looked up at Ral.

"Do some of her reasons involve us?" he asked.

Ral smiled. "You'd have to ask her about that."

Oren looked at the ground as they walked, staring at the passing flowers. It seemed like the time went by in an instant. Oren's mind had wandered about in his subconscious. Before he knew it, he had bumped into Syris.

"Watch it!" Syris said.

"Why are we stopping?" Oren asked, bewildered.

Ral walked forward and pressed a stone slab with his foot. It sank into the ground, and the mountain began to rumble. Oren looked at the ground in front of him and saw a large circular stone door split in two and rumble open. It descended into what appeared to be the inside of the mountain.

"How on earth — there is no way in all of creation this is possible!" Oren yelled.

"Surprising, I know, but the mountain is indeed hollow. Now follow me," Ral said, dragging the dazed Oren along.

Glowing white and green stairs appeared, and Ral carefully scaled down them with Oren behind him and Syris following Oren, happy as ever that he would be privileged to see such an amazing sight. The descent was a very long one. After walking down several flights of stairs, Ral, Oren, and Syris stepped onto a large circular platform. This platform was white, and as it began to move, green patterns lit up on its surface. It dropped rapidly and then slowed down a great deal before stopping completely, hovering slightly above the ground. The trio stepped off, and Syris grasped Oren for support. He couldn't believe what he was seeing. Light poured in through the top of the mountain. The walls were jagged and dark, colors of gray, black, and charcoal blending into one another. It also seemed that a large structure had once stood here. All that was left were ruins and shadows.

"Your questions answered, the truths revealed. This is the place I was supposed to bring you to. Now follow me, please. We have little time, and I would prefer not to waste it," Ral said.

Oren walked, and as he did, spun in a circle so that he could take in everything around him. The mountain's inside was immense.

"I've just noticed but, the inside is not to outside scale. Why is that?" Syris asked.

"There is a floor beneath us, but beneath this floor is another hollow space which expands to ground level," Ral explained.

"So if the floor were to fall away, then we would be a lot further down?" Oren asked.

"Yes, and you wouldn't be able to see the light from the lowest level. It would be total darkness, and freezing cold," Ral said.

Oren looked ahead and saw a vast structure. "What is that?" he said.

Ral smiled at him. "My friends, welcome to the Temple of Ruins. This is where we will find our vessel."

WOMAN WITHIN THE HOUSE OF RAGE

- Somehow, I am not surprised. He failed. My student failed the first test before even one minute had passed. His soul froze in fear and his mind stiffened. All rational thoughts left him and he ran about in frantic patterns, hitting every wall, looking for an exit. I can't really blame him for feeling fear, but I have never had any student do so poorly. Each of them made it pass the first trial. Only one made it through all the tests in one go. I do not imagine there will be anyone like him ever again. We returned home and my dearest companion greeted me with unabashed joy, swinging me around in the air effortlessly. It made my stomach roll. What would I ever do without him? I folded my robe up and placed it in a special box, vowing to keep it there and never let it tarnish. Instead, I went out into the market and bought an old one. It was still black, covered my face, and had a flap of fabric to cover my

mouth and nose if I found it necessary. Somehow, I feel better when no one can see who I really am.

"So, what is the Temple of Ruins?" Syris asked.

"The Temple of Ruins was originally the Temple of Tora, the God of Rage. After his betrayal to Origin, his temple was destroyed. No one comes here anymore."

"Then, why are we here?"

"This is where we will perform the Awakening."

Oren was confused. He had never heard, in all his life, of anything called the "Awakening".

"Awakening of what?" Syris asked.

Ral chuckled. "Of the vessel, of course. That is the whole reason we've come here, to obtain the vessel that will be used to hold Origin's powers until she has claimed them all."

Columns of stone and marble rose high into the air, disappearing into the darkness around them, the darkness of the mountain's insides. Walls stood in random places, and the entrance to the temple was half-way gone. The crest of Tora could still be seen. It was dark, but somehow it didn't seem threatening even though it belonged to the God of Rage, Origin's sworn enemy.

Even so, Oren could feel an evil radiating from within the entrance of the ancient temple. The entrance archway loomed high over them, years of erosion visible on the worn out surfaces. The light from the opening that had led them here slowly faded as they were embraced by the cold darkness within the ruined temple, and was altogether snuffed out when the opening atop the mountain closed with an echoing thud, shaking the mountain's insides.

"I can't see anything," Syris said.

"Give me a second," Ral said.

He struck a wall with his claws, sparks dancing, and fire swirled around the room as a trench filled with oil lit up. The trenches extended up the walls and onto the ceiling. Small droplets of fire fell from the ceiling, turning into smoke when they hit the floor. The room was circular and small, but had a relatively high ceiling, with a large round door on the other side. Columns held the ceiling up, and a snake carving decorated the floor. Ral walked slowly across the rough, dusty floor.

"This is where Tora's followers would gather to pray to him." Oren traced the carving as Ral spoke. "The high priest would stand on the eye of the serpent, and call up to Tora in song. The followers would sit on the serpent's body and tail. The councilors would kneel on the serpent's fangs, and the holy priestess would rest on the serpent's tongue. After Tora's betrayal, Origin's followers destroyed the temple, drove out his followers, and sent them to wander in the desert where they eventually perished," Ral said.

Pictures were etched onto the walls, the faint glossy colors of red, blue, green, yellow, and white still visible in some places.

"These tell the story of how Origin and Tora became friends. Origin was weak for she had been in a battle with another god. Tora, although of humble descent, carried her to the nearest village, and stayed with her till she was healed. Origin was moved by his loyalty and offered him a place in her celestial home. He accepted, and they grew close to one another. Origin gave him knowledge, and he developed a system so that people could live more peacefully." Ral laughed, almost as if he couldn't stand what he was saying. "If only that were true."

Oren frowned. "Is it not? Is this history false as well?"

Ral smiled mockingly, and continued speaking as if Oren had never said anything. "The tragedy of this story isn't carved into these surfaces. Tora became greedy for power. He strived to be stronger than Origin. He fought with her, and eventually he was able to deceive many of her followers. A massacre ensued. Millions of Excelsias were killed. The main village where they lived was burned to the ground. Origin became enraged and poured out an evil vengeance upon them, destroying them, burning them, wrenching the earth open to swallow them whole, drowning them in their own blood, and many more horrid, painful things. She obliterated them, and then engaged Tora in a final struggle." Sadness portrayed itself in Ral's face.

"Where she lost her powers," Oren said.

Ral looked back at him in dismay. "Yes. She fought for her people, for her world, and all those that she loved."

"And she lost," Syris said.

"No," Oren began, "she didn't lose. It was a draw. Tora was sealed, and she lost her powers. Neither lost nor won. There is still a battle to be fought."

Oren traced the pictures lit by the small flames on the floor and the fire falling slowly from the ceiling. It was then that he came to a great realization.

"All of these trials we've been through, they are only the beginning of what's going to happen. Even now, without her powers, she is calling all her forces together to strike the final blow, and the three of us are in the middle of it. We will be her fighters."

Ral watched Oren with indifference. "Yes, you are in the middle of it. Many others are part of this, all of whom have some role to play in this. Some are valuable and irreplaceable, while others are simply pawns, pieces in a chess game that can be discarded easily, as they hold no significance unless they manage to reach the other side of the board."

"What does she want?" Oren said, almost to himself. "What does she want with us? Are we important? Or are we one of those pawns that don't matter?"

Ral laughed. "You'll have to ask her. She is the only one who knows for sure."

"Where is she?" Syris asked.

"I can't tell you that. I haven't the faintest idea." Ral stood in front of the circular door. "You two, open it."

Oren glared at him. "What's behind it?"

"You'll see once you open it. I don't have opposable thumbs."

Oren chuckled. "You're right, you don't have opposable thumbs." He tried his best to mimic Gudra's voice, who had previously railed on Ral for being – well – Ral.

Oren and Syris grabbed one side and pulled with all their might. The door shook, friction rumbling in its frame, and slowly began to roll. It scraped against the stone floor and walls, turning until it hit another wall, and a metal slab shut over where it had gone. Behind this door was a steel wall, symbols etched into it. They were in peak condition. There was no rust or chipping, which lead the group to believe that the stone door had air locked it against the elements, preserving it. Syris went forward to see if he could move the wall by pushing it, but was yanked back by Ral.

All at once, the floor lifted beneath them and the metal wall in front of them began to turn, symbols flying by in blurs. Oren looked behind him and saw that the entrance was gone, now covered by the same wall they had just seen in front of him. He turned back around and saw that the metal wall was also gone and had been replaced by an open archway, allowing them to move forward.

"What just happened?" Syris asked warily. Ral smirked as much as a bear could.

"The floor of this room sits on a screw-like pole. Inside the walls of this room is a separate wall with no ceiling that revolves around that screw when the floor lifts off the ground. By effect, it opens closed doors, and closes open ones. So, basically —"

"The room just rotated beneath our feet because some architect had the crazy idea of revolving rooms." Oren said, slightly impressed.

Ral stared at him for a moment before he spoke. "As I was saying," he said, clearing his throat loudly, "Basically, the room turned 180 degrees so that the path in front of us could open while the path behind us closed. Origin thought it would be fun to incorporate it into the temple schematics at random, and let the builders figure it out on their own."

Oren lifted an eyebrow. "I'm going to assume that didn't end well."

Ral frowned slightly. "Needless to say, the builders

were working on this temple for twenty-three more years than they expected."

Syris blinked slowly, trying to process the information. "So," he said in a slow drawl, "Origin was a bit of a trickster?"

Ral laughed loudly, his belly shaking. "I suppose you could say that." He shook his furry head and began walking. "Let's move on."

The next and final room was immense.

"My God of Fire," Syris said.

The room was fifty feet across and forty feet high. The walls were gold, and the floor had blue trimmed tiles made from silver. The ceiling was covered in elaborate paintings that seemed so real it was almost as if living creatures had flown into the paint and gotten stuck there, becoming a permanent decoration. Torches lined the walls and lit the fabulous detail on everything. Near the back wall was the largest blue crystal Oren and Syris had ever seen. It stood perfectly still, held at the top and bottom by large, golden claws. The crystal's middle stretched at least fifteen feet across, meeting in sharp points at the top and bottom and the edges of all the faces. It must have been thirty feet high, just ten feet smaller than the room itself. What was even more impressive about this crystal, large and beautiful as it was, was the woman held inside it.

Chains were connected to her arms and legs, which stretched and twisted until they clasped onto the inner walls of the crystal. She was held upright, perfectly still. Her visage was not visible, as what appeared to be a helmet covered her face. It bulged at the back slightly, and Syris assumed that perhaps her hair was in there.

A knee-length, yet somewhat tattered white dress with short sleeves covered her body. It wasn't much, but it was enough to make her appear decent.

"She — seems pretty?" Syris said, his eyes wide.

"Right now, that's an understatement. A pity she's concealed so well," Ral snapped, obviously displeased with Syris' poor choice of adjectives. Syris jumped slightly and willed himself to become invisible, but to no avail.

"She seems beautiful," Oren whispered, enchanted by her appearance in its mysterious glory. Never in his life had he seen someone so unique, yet so seemingly simple.

Ral smiled, pleased with Oren's description. "That's much better." He sent a fierce glare at Syris, who was trying his very best to be a wall flower.

"Who is she?" Oren asked, never taking his eyes off her.

"She is our vessel. I can't tell you who exactly she is, though. That's her job, but I can tell you how to get her out of that crystal," Ral said, a hint of sinister playfulness flashing through his big brown eyes.

The bear turned and walked toward one of the many torches on the walls. He grabbed it with his mouth and began to tug against it, trying to release it from its current domain. It took a while, but eventually the metal clasp holding the torch in place bent open, allowing Ral to free the torch from its confines. The bear returned to his original spot and gave his head a quick jerk, sending the torch flying through the air and straight at the crystal, piercing the face directly in front of him. The crystal shimmered with an ominous blue light that grew and then faded. It shook, groaned, and began to turn slowly at first, but then it sped up greatly. However, the woman inside did not turn, nor did her chains. They seemed to be connected to a separate wall inside the crystal that was not affected by outside influence. The fire from the torch formed a dangerous ring around the crystal as it spun tremendously fast. Eventually, the wind snuffed the torch out, leaving a ring of smoke instead. The bottom and top of the crystal grinded against the golden claws, sparks flying up and out.

"It's rotating at a ridiculous rate, so much that your eyes can't really process it, and if you look closely enough, you'll see that it's actually slicing the wall behind it. Touch it, and you'll lose an arm. Keep this in mind: that crystal is the only thing holding the roof up. When it goes, we're either out of here or we go along with it."

"And how do we break it open?" Oren asked, perplexed. He knew the crystal was rotating and there was a ring of smoke surrounding it. The torch was leaving charcoal marks on the wall behind the crystal as it slammed against it. Yet, every now and then, the crystal seemed to glitch and he would see slight blurs of the torch being on a different side.

Suddenly, Oren's feet slid from underneath him, and he was being dragged towards the crystal. Ral grabbed him and held him back. The rapid spinning of the crystal had created a vortex, sucking in air and compressing it. Everyone ducked as the torch flew across the room and smashed into a wall.

"Centrifugal force," Ral huffed. "That's going to be a problem."

"I don't like the idea of the roof falling on our heads," Syris muttered, wanting to leave.

"No choice. The room behind us spun back around and sealed the exit. It won't reopen until we grab her. Then, and only then, can we run," Ral said. However, as simple as he was making it sound, he was worried about whether or not the room would be able to revolve fast enough for them to escape.

"That's stupid," Syris grumbled, glaring at the metal wall behind him.

"It is what it is!" Oren yelled, "Let's get this done."

Ral smiled, enjoying his sudden display of bravery. "Yes sir."

"Again, how do we open it?" Syris said, annoyed with the fact that no one seemed to care about their own well-being. He was also worrying if that meant that he was selfish.

"It's fragile. Break it," Ral said, "Go ahead and try to surprise me."

Oren unsheathed his sword, raised it above his head, and even though he would have been beaten at home for treating a blade so poorly, threw it at the crystal. It planted itself firmly in the gem, just above where the torch had been, and became a blur of color as it revolved with the crystal. The structure began to crack until the fissures had covered the middle and upper part of the large, rotating gem.

"It's not enough." Oren growled, wishing he had another sword.

"Syris, it's your turn," Ral said.

Syris took out the two short swords he had bought back at the Shrine of Aros. He threw them with all his might, only to have them hit the crystal and ricochet back at him. When they connected with the surface, one of the swords broke into several pieces; Syris leapt out of the path of the shrapnel. The sword still intact stuck fast in the wall behind where his head had originally been.

"I almost lost my face!" Syris screamed in anger, panic rising in him.

"Calm down. Honestly, it's a giant rotating jewel. It's not meant to be easy," Ral said, sighing. "Besides, it's just your face. It's not that bad."

Syris stared at Ral with disbelief. It's just his face? Ridiculous! It was his only face, the only face he'd get in the whole world. He'd die without his face.

"Swords shouldn't bounce off things!" Syris said, fuming.

Ral looked at Syris. "Three sides of that crystal are shielded by magic that mimics a Karma. They return an attack to the user. The one side that does not have a shield is the side where Oren's sword, and formerly the torch, resides. You need to try to hit that face of the gem."

It was easier said than done, no doubt. However, Syris wasn't a quitter, and he didn't like the idea of some lifeless piece of melted, tempered, colored sand getting the better of him. Syris went to his short sword and yanked it out of the wall, wiping gold flakes off it. He then walked back to where he had been standing, raised the short sword, and waited, watching the crystal closely. Oren's sword flashed by, a blur of blue and silver. Syris threw the short sword. When Oren's sword flew by again, Syris' weapon ripped through the crystal below the torch's former position. The cracks connected with Oren's and extended up. They touched the bottom of the crystal and stopped, the very top still untouched.

"Why isn't it breaking?" Syris yelled angrily. He really wanted to leave.

"It's still not enough," Oren growled. "Ral, it is your turn. Do what you did to Tharazar."

"I'm not so sure-"

"Just do it!" Oren yelled, angered and impatient.

Ral stared at Oren's eyes. "As you wish. In the future, don't shout at me. You've no business giving me orders."

Oren stared at Ral, a bit stunned at his choice of words.

Ral's crest reappeared, and lightning blinded Oren and Syris. The symbols lit up brightly, flashing with fury.

"*Vashire!*" Ral roared, his voice like a hundred claps of thunder, echoing through the building, shaking it to its core.

Electric bolts erupted from the ceiling and streaked along the floor, creating pillars of lightning until they connected with the crystal. They struck right through the middle in a magnificent surge. The gem lit up like a beacon, shaking and groaning, and then it burst into pieces. Blue shards flew out in all directions, and the ceiling began to shake violently. The woman fell to ground, her chains breaking apart with the inner walls of the crystal, Oren's sword and Syris' short sword falling with her. She hit the floor with a loud thud, and Oren heard a sharp, metallic crack. Ral raced into the falling rubble and snatched her up. Oren ran alongside Ral, grabbed his sword, put it in his sheath, and picked up Syris' short sword. They ran from the room with haste, watching the metal wall as it spun around to let them through. The second everyone passed through the opening, the wall began to turn back around to grant them another exit.

The ceiling fell in and covered the doorway after they had passed through it. The woman hung limply on Ral's back. The floor split open, swallowing the serpent in the center. Ral rushed towards the entrance, trying to avoid the ceiling crashing down all around them. Just as the archway was about to fully open up in the wall, a large, falling rock hit the ceiling and knocked the metal wall off its screw. The metal walls stopped, only granting a fourth of the width of the exit. Ral stared at it worriedly. Oren, Syris, and the woman would fit through, but he wasn't so sure about himself, being a big, fat bear.

Oren squeezed through and pulled Syris after him. He then pressed his hands against the walls and pushed with all his might, willing them to move. Ral and Oren heard them slide a few centimeters, and then stop again. Oren gave another great heave, heard the wall slide a bit farther, and then it stopped. He tried again to make the wall move, but this time it wouldn't budge at all. Oren looked at Ral with fear.

"Ral," he said, his voice catching. "I —"

"It's okay," Ral said. "I'll just wait for a miracle."

All at once, a stone wall to their left exploded, knocking the metal walls back on their screw, and the exit opened up fully. Ral stared at the archway silently, thinking about how much he loved coincidences, then raced out from the temple to avoid falling debris.

The trio raced from the ruins, the large archway shaking wildly. It collapsed, breaking into large chunks of rock and brick. Dust flew into the air, shrouding them. After a few minutes, the musky cloud cleared, and all that remained of the ruins was a large pile of rubble.

"Well," Oren coughed, "that was — fun."

"I'll say," Syris coughed, dirt coming out of his mouth in thick brown puffs.

"Ral, you okay? How's the girl?" Oren asked.

"She's fine. A little dirty, but other than that — everything's fine." Ral set her on the ground, and immediately noticed that the right side of the helmet covering her eye had broken off, presumably from the fall. Her skin was pale and lifeless. "It's time for the Awakening."

Oren looked at Ral. The symbols reappeared as he chanted something. Lightning came down and struck her. Her body jolted up and then lay still again. She jolted again, and a spell circle glowed beneath her. After a while, it pulsed three times and faded.

"Get up," Ral said, closing his eyes in anguish. "Please."

She lay still as stone. Oren touched her face: cold as ice. Suddenly, her hand jerked up and latched onto Oren's wrist with an iron grip, pulling his hand away. Oren tried to free himself, but she tightened her hold on him till it began to hurt, until it started to feel like fire. Syris backed away, and Ral inched forward. Slowly, as if moving for the first time after a thousand year sleep, she opened her beautiful, calm eye. It was an eye of red, which could call a thousand men to fight, or lull a restless child to sleep. It was an eye of power; Oren saw then, something he had not ever known before. This was the eye of a demon: a slit pupil, cold and bloody, and it demanded war.

"Our vessel awakes." Ral whispered. "Now the real journey begins." He looked into the woman's face with earnest. "Will you take us to Origin?"

But Joy left, and the One was alone
And the One wept
From the rivers of her tears, the stars were born
The stars bowed before the Queen of Joy
Unto her, as an offering, their fire became Life

About the Author

Anna Clark, originally born in North Carolina, now lives in Florida. She loves rainy days, spending time with her animals, and greatly enjoys playing video games. Anna is thrilled to write, no matter the story or audience.

Printed in the United States
By Bookmasters